Fred finally pointed down the  to a long legged brunette coming towa the street.

"Good choice, little brother, let's take her."

The two men stepped back into the alley. No sense in having her cross the street to avoid them. They let the woman go by. As she passed, George grabbed her arms and pulled her to him. Fred threw the bag over her head and together they dragged her toward the van.

A shapeless form stepped out of the shadows of the alley and blocked their way. They did not see it until it was too late.

"Release her," the form commanded. The brothers could now see that it was a man dresses in a dark grey robe, a monk's habit. A deep cowl hid his head and face and long sleeves covered his hands.

No priest was going to ruin their fun. George was ready to use his sap when the figure brought one arm up. The sleeve dropped back – a .45 appeared. George stopped quickly.

"Release her," the command came again. Fred loosed his hold on the woman's arms. She pulled off the bag and ran from the alley. It was she who would give the police their first description of the city's new defender.

"Okay, she's gone," said George. "And now what, we wait for the cops? Simple assault, no time." George looked back in the direction his victim had fled. "That's if she shows for court."

"You're right," said the man in the monk's garb. He pulled the trigger of the .45.

The blast tore a hole in George's chest, knocking him to the ground. Fred turned to run, but a second shot took him in the leg. He fell face forward. Before he could move, the warm metal of the gun barrel pressed against the back of his neck.

"Tell them," a cold voice whispered, "The Grey Monk is here."

THE GREY MONK

SOULS ON FIRE

JOHN L. FRENCH

PADWOLF PUBLISHING

PADWOLF PUBLISHING INC.
WWW.PADWOLF.COM

THE GREY MONK: SOULS ON FIRE © 2008, 2015 John L. French

Cover Art Ver Curtis
Cover design Roy Mauritsen

ISBN 13 digit 978-1-890096-59-5

Publishing history
Crusade- published as "The Grey Monk's Crusade," The Grey Monk's Crusade, Double Danger Tales 39, August 2000, Fading Shadows Publications
- ThrillerUK 12, October 2002

Den of Thieves- published as part of "The Grey Monk," Double Danger Tales 35, January 2000, Fading Shadows Publications
- ThrillerUK 7, July 2001

The Grey Monk's JusticeDouble Danger Tales 44, May 2001, Fading Shadows Publications

In the Beginning - published as part of "The Grey Monk," Double Danger Tales 35, January 2000, Fading Shadows Publications

- ThrillerUK 7, July 2001

The Only JusticeDouble Danger Tales 57, December 2002, Fading Shadows Publications

Seeds of EvilDouble Danger Tales 55, October 2002, Fading Shadows Publications

Souls on FireDouble Danger Tales 43, April 2001, Fading Shadows Publications

Things Left UndoneDouble Danger Tales 54, September 2002, Fading Shadows Publications

I Will Repayoriginal to this book

If Thy Hand Offend original to this book

The Living Goddess original to this book

To Elaine,
Who brings joy to my life and makes everything worthwhile

"Vengeance is Mine; I will repay," says the Lord – Romans 12, 20

You shall give life for life, eye for eye, tooth for tooth, hand for hand, foot for foot, burning for burning, wound for wound, stripe for stripe — Exodus 21, 23-25

CONTENTS

IN THE BEGINNING

Two men lingered in the mouth of an alley off Calvert St. Passing a bottle back and forth, they watched people go by, waiting for the right one. Some of those who passed were students who had stayed late at the university. Despite the chill in the air, they were wearing only jeans and shirts. Others, a little better dressed in off-the-rack suits, seemed to be on their way home from work. Those that passed wearing finer clothes probably had early dinner reservations and tickets for the theater or symphony. None of them were the one the men were waiting for – an attractive woman alone, one too pre-occupied with her own business to take the precautions needed to walk alone in the city.

"Remember, George," said the younger of the two, "this time I get to pick."

"I hope you pick better than the last time, Fred," his brother complained. "That one didn't last more than two days."

The brothers had done this before. The first time was a bungling affair, their victim yelling and fighting all the way to their van. It was only luck – good for them, bad for her – that no one heard her screams. The second time was a little smoother, but still not perfect. By now, though, after their fifth time, they had it planned out and were working it smoothly.

The alley they had chosen opened on to a parking lot. At this time of day, it was empty. The people who parked there for work had already left; the ones who lived nearby weren't home yet. Fred had a bag ready to throw over their victim's head, and George had a sap in case she struggled. Covered by the early darkness of November, they'd pick a good one, snatch her and take her to their van. Then they'd drive back to their house. An attached garage insured that no one would see them take her from the van into their home. Once safe inside, they would do what they liked until they tired of her, then kill her. From her ID, they'd find out where she lived, and dump her body close to her home. This would keep attention from being drawn to their hunting ground.

After a longer wait than they had planned, Fred finally pointed down the street. "That one," he said, pointing to a long legged brunette coming toward them. There was no one else on the street.

"Good choice, little brother, let's take her."

The two men stepped back into the alley. No sense in having her cross the street to avoid them. They let the woman go by. As she passed,

George grabbed her arms and pulled her to him. Fred threw the bag over her head and together they dragged her toward the van.

A shapeless form stepped out of the shadows of the alley and blocked their way. They did not see it until it was too late.

"Release her," the form commanded. The brothers could now see that it was a man dresses in a dark grey robe, a monk's habit. A deep cowl hid his head and face and long sleeves covered his hands.

No priest was going to ruin their fun. George was ready to use his sap when the figure brought one arm up. The sleeve dropped back – a .45 appeared. George stopped quickly.

"Release her," the command came again. Fred loosed his hold on the woman's arms. She pulled off the bag and ran from the alley. It was she who would give the police their first description of the city's new defender.

"Okay, she's gone," said George. "And now what, we wait for the cops? Simple assault, no time." George looked back in the direction his victim had fled. "That's if she shows for court."

"You're right," said the man in the monk's garb. He pulled the trigger of the .45.

The blast tore a hole in George's chest, knocking him to the ground. Fred turned to run, but a second shot took him in the leg. He fell face forward. Before he could move, the warm metal of the gun barrel pressed against the back of his neck.

"Tell them," a cold voice whispered, "The Grey Monk is here. Then confess. If you go free, I will find you. You will suffer, then die."

Fred felt the gun withdraw as sirens sounded in the distance. When he turned, he was alone in the alley with the dead. When the police arrived, it was only seconds after they finished with his rights that he told them everything.

The man who had called himself the Grey Monk watched from distant shadows. He had been haunting these alleys ever since discovering the common link in the brutal deaths of several women, deaths that the police had not even connected. Now the victims were avenged, and their killers brought to justice. It was a good start.

THINGS LEFT UNDONE

*We have left undone those things which we ought to have done; and
we have done those things which we ought not to have done.*

Morning Prayer, General Confession, Book of Common Prayer
(1662).

There's a street like it in every city. Sometimes it has a name – the
Strip, the Block, the Walk. Other times it's nameless, but everyone
still knows it's there. Here it was called the Miracle Mile, by the cops if no
one else. They called it that because if you had anything to do with the girls
who walked it and came away with your health and money intact, well, that
would be a miracle.

She called herself Lola, from a song she had heard and liked a long
time ago. She'd been walking the Mile for a few months now. She didn't
like it, but it was what she did to get by. She'd done two already that
night but needed a few more. I hope they come soon, she thought, smiling
bitterly at the wordplay. And as if in answer to some corrupt prayer, a truck
stopped in front of her.

The truck was a pickup, she noted with another bitter smile, brand
new and shiny. "Hi, she said, "Looking for a date?"

"No, Ma'am," came a country voice from the cab, "But I would like
some sex."

Well, this one's no cop, she said to herself. Lola leaned in a little to
get a better look at her would-be client. It was hard to tell by the streetlight,
but he seemed young, clean and not bad looking. The hick voice could be
a put on – that, the truck and his T-shirt and jeans all part of a fantasy the
man needed to be doing this. It didn't matter, her street sense telling her
that he was probably harmless.

She told him what she could do for him and what it would cost.

"That'd be just fine," he said and opened the side door for her. She
got in and directed him to the place she used, a parking lot between three
downtown buildings, all closed and dark for the night. It was a well-used
area, one pointedly ignored by the police. She took his money and then in
the darkness did what he had paid her to do. Then she heard the clicks of
the automatic locks closing.

"What …" was all she got out. She couldn't see him in the blackness of the cab. She didn't see the Mayberry demeanor drop away and a different kind of delight than the one he had just experienced appear on his face. She did feel the knife slide into her chest, but not for long. She died so fast she didn't have time to bleed.

The automatic locks clicked again. Lola's now satisfied client took what he needed then got out of the truck, quietly, so as not to disturb any other couples parked on the lot. He just as quietly closed the door, and in the darkness walked away from the stolen truck.

***

The small confessional was quiet and dark. No sounds came in from the outside. He imagined that this would be how a coffin felt. He heard the priest slide shut the panel on the other side. The other penitent had said his piece, been forgiven and had received his penance. Now it was his turn.

He knelt quickly. As his knees hit the pre-dieu they depressed a switch, turning the amber light inside the box to a deep violet. Nice touch, he thought. The priest slid the panel on his side open. A heavy metal screen kept either man from seeing the other's features too clearly.

"Bless me, Father, for I have sinned. It's been ... well, it's been a long time since my last confession."

"That doesn't matter," he heard the priest say. He sounded young. "The important thing is that you're here. Now then, what's troubling you?"

"I've killed someone, Father, a woman."

There was no sound from the center of the confessional. The man imagined the priest thinking about what he had just heard, wondering if he had heard correctly, quickly praying to God that he hadn't.

"Father, are you all right in there?"

"Yes, I am. You said that you'd, you'd hurt someone."

"I said that I'd killed someone, Father."

"When was this?"

"Last night, not far from here."

He heard the priest settle back in his chair. The initial shock over, he was back into his pastoral role. He was again the shepherd, and he would bring this lamb back into the flock.

"Last night and you're here now. That's good." The voice from behind the screen was soothing, the concern genuine. The priest was saying all the right things. He almost wished it mattered. He let the sound wash over him, not caring what was being said. "… shows you're troubled and regret what you've done. Let's talk, tell me what happened and together we'll find the best way to resolve this."

Next he was supposed to say how he didn't mean for it to have happened, and how sorry he was. Then he'd be told that, to be truly forgiven, he had to confess not only to God, but to the police as well, so that his victim's family could find peace, so that the wrong man would not be punished.

No, that was not why he was here.

"I'm not troubled by what I did, Father. The woman was a harlot, defiling His temple, betraying Him for pieces of silver. I stopped her sinning, and sent her to God to be punished. I'll send Him more when I can." Let him think about that.

"That's not what God wants you to do, my son." The priest's voice was now higher, the words more rapid, a little louder.

"He does, Father. You told me, last Sunday."

There was no reply. He waited as the priest went over in his mind all that he had said last week, knew he wouldn't get it.

"In the Gospel, Father, 'Let he who is without sin cast the first stone.' I've always obeyed, never swore, never lied. I'm sinless, it's up to me." That wasn't true, of course. He had sinned many times in his life, and he would keep on sinning. But no need to tell this priest that. Let him think it's partly his fault. Just another way to prolong the fun.

"Of course," he added, "I used a knife, not a rock."

He stood up, the violet changing back to amber. From the screen came the question, one last desperate try.

"What about the commandment, 'Thou shalt not kill?'"

"It's not a sin if God tells you to do it." He opened the door and left the church, knowing the priest would not, could not, come after him.

Father David Scott watched helplessly as the man stood up and walked away. He fought down the urge to jump up, rush out of the box and confront the man, to hold him for the police and tell them what had just been said. What was heard in the confessional stayed in the confessional, kept in the mind, held in the heart. To break the Seal was a grievous sin, far worse than anything else, even – murder. Father Scott found himself praying that the man had been delusional, just one of the poor confused souls this city had too many of. Then he said a quick prayer for the police, that if the man had been telling the truth, the real truth and not just a fantasy that seemed real, that the police would have their best people on the case, and solve it before another woman died, and another and …

"Father?"

At first Father Scott thought that the man had come back, maybe to tell him that it was all a joke. But no, it was just a boy, a regular from the parish.

"Father, are you all right?"

That was how the last one started.

"I'm fine, it's just a little hot in here. Are there many more out there?"

"Just a few."

As the boy began the ritual, Father Scott put aside his thoughts of what had just occurred, and took some comfort in the more familiar litany of uttered "hells" and "damns," of lies told to teachers and parents, and the surreptitious watching of forbidden cable movies and afternoon talk shows. Somehow, he got through the rest of the afternoon.

When confessions were over, Father Scott hurried back into the rectory. He found himself almost running into the kitchen where he had left that morning's paper. He didn't recall reading any articles about murders or recently discovered bodies. Still, he went through the paper again to be sure and almost missed it this time as well. The story was small, no more than a paragraph on page three of the local section. A woman believed to have been a prostitute had been found stabbed to death in a stolen pickup truck. Police were investigating. A location was given, some place downtown. Father Scott knew the general area but not the exact location.

It means nothing, Father Scott thought. The poor soul could have read the article this morning and in his confused mind believed he had committed the act. And if not, what can I do? Even if I were to call the police, what could I tell them? That a voice from the darkness confessed to a crime then ran away. They'd be no closer to solving the murder than before.

All week it worried him. Was it just a troubled soul, driven to confess sins he hadn't committed. He understood that the police got them all the time, people coming in and confessing to the crimes of others. Maybe this was one of them. He hoped so.

Confessions the next Saturday went smoothly – nothing more serious than a woman feeling lust for a man other than her husband. When no one came in for fifteen minutes Father Scott thought about ending the session early. Then he came in.

"There were others, you know."

It was the same voice. Father Scott froze. This was not something taught in the seminary. "Others?" he finally asked, keeping his tone as level as possible. "How many?"

"Eight, I think. One or two may have survived."

"And were they, were they all ..." He couldn't think of a proper word.

"Harlots? Sinners?" The voice from the darkness laughed. "I just said that last time to get your attention, have a little fun. No, I may have sent them all to God, but not for any particular reason."

"Who were they?" Keep him talking, Father Scott told himself. Look for something you can use to turn this man away from his path.

"Hitchhikers, homeless, someone who took a bad turn in the wrong neighborhood. I take them where I find them."

"And you've come to me, why?"

There was another joyless laugh. "Not because I'm sorry, and I'm not asking for forgiveness."

"Not yet, anyway." Father Scott had to make the effort, plant the seed.

"Or ever," came the cynical retort.

"Then why come to me?"

The answer that came back through the screen was the one Father Scott didn't want to hear. "It adds to the spice, someone else knowing, someone who can never tell."

There was silence. Before Father Scott could form a reply he heard the click of the pre-dieu and the closing of the door and knew he was alone. And for a long time afterward he sat in the darkness, praying for help and wondering how it would arrive.

None came. Every morning after that Father Scott read the local section of the paper, looking for news of recent murders, ones that could have been caused by his penitent. A week went by, then two. People died by the gun, in arson fires and from savage beatings. They died because of domestic violence, from street robberies gone bad and as casualties in the never-ending drug wars. Whatever the reason for their deaths, none seemed to be the victim that Father Scott was looking for.

***

Her shift over, Delores walked to the Metro. She hated night work, but it was the best she could find. Mopping hospital floors didn't pay that well and wasn't the most glamorous job in the world, but it was steady and the benefits included free medical for her and her family.

Delores checked her watch. No need to hurry, there was plenty of time to catch her train. Then twenty minutes later she'd be home. Her husband would have the kids up and dressed, and the four of them could enjoy breakfast together. She'd get the kids off to school, and then just maybe she could convince her husband to be late for work. Lord knows they didn't have that much time alone anymore. One day, she thought, things will be better.

Delores held on to this hope as she crossed the hospital parking lot and headed down the street to the Metro stop. If she saw the parked van she didn't pay it any attention. Nor did she notice the man seemingly asleep behind the wheel. She certainly didn't see him get up from the driver's seat as she approached. When the van's side door slid open as Delores passed she might have turned and tried to run, but by then it was too late. After she was pulled inside, a sharp knife eventually ended whatever dreams she might have had.

***

As soon as Father Scott read the paper he knew that his penitent had been at work again. He also knew that the next Saturday he'd get another visit in the confessional. What he didn't know was why he felt the need to visit the crime scene.

That afternoon found Father Scott walking the same path that Delores had taken, from the hospital across the parking lot and down the street where she had met her death. There wasn't much to see – chalk markings where the van had been, stray bits of crime scene tape still tied to light poles, a pair of rubber gloves left by a careless police officer. Father Scott spent an hour there, wandering up and down, concerned about what he could do next. Most anyone who saw him would think that he was just another gawker; one of many who were drawn to scenes of brutal crime for the vicarious thrill it gave them. And except for one who kept to himself in the relative darkness of an alley, no one took any special notice of the priest.

Saturday. Each time Father Scott heard the confessional door close, each time he slid open the panel he thought he would hear the killer claim another victim. Not this time. Sins of pride, avarice and lust were confessed, but no one mentioned murder.

Another week, another death – this time of a young boy, a teen who had been missing for two days. A drug user, a sometimes prostitute, and presumed to be a runaway, the boy's body was found along a jogging trail in Patterson Park. This time news of the murder was accompanied by hints that this death might be connected to others in the area. And while the police department had no official comment, no denial was issued.

And again Father Scott was drawn to the scene. Why, he asked himself, did I come here? I'm not a detective. I'm not going to find the one clue that the police missed that will lead me to the killer. And even if I did, could I use it against him? As he walked the scene he prayed. He prayed for the souls of those who had died. He prayed for the killer to be captured or to turn himself in. He prayed for himself, that he would find the right words to say when the killer came to him again. And finally, and with some amount of shame, he prayed that he might never have to face the killer again. As he finished he thought of Gethsemane and added, "But Your Will be done."

***

Confessions started late that next Saturday, and it was only through Father Scott's sense of duty that they started at all. Midway through he thought guiltily that maybe his last prayer had been answered, but then he heard, "Do you want to know what I do to them, Father?"

"No, I don't," Father Scott said with a calm he didn't feel. After the last time he had thought long and hard about what he was going to say and do if the killer came back. Before he could reply the priest went on. "If you're here to confess, if you're sorry for what you're doing, if you need my help in any way, then I'm here for you." Father Scott hoped this would work. "But if this is just part of your twisted game – well, I'm not playing any more."

He moved to slide the panel shut. As he did so, he heard the man on the other side say, "Wait."

Father Scott paused, the panel half closed.

"You're in a bad mood today, I'll come back when you're feeling better." The man stood, but didn't leave the confessional. His voice came out of the darkness. "And the next time I hope you're feeling better. It would be a shame to have crime scene tape littering your schoolyard."

Father Scott sat back in despair. Other penitents came in, were ignored and finally left, leaving him alone and surrounded by his own darkness.

Things grew worse the following week. Two more people, another young boy and an older man, were killed in a manner similar to the other deaths. The police had ceased any pretence of denial. At a press conference, the commissioner announced that a task force had been formed some time ago to investigate this series of killings and that the department was devoting all of its resources to bringing the killer to justice.

Father Scott continued going to crime scenes. He now saw these visits for what they were – penance for his weakness, for his lack of faith, for his inability to be anything other than a living victim of this beast. His prayers were now for the police, that they'd soon find and stop the killer. He had little hope that these prayers would be answered.

It was the day after the week's second murder, that of the older man, and Father Scott was walking the levels of the parking garage where the body had been found. He wondered if he should just keep walking, away from his duties, away from his vocation, when a voice called to him from the shadows between two parked vans.

"Are you lost, Father?"

Yes, Father Scott thought, but not in the way you mean. "No," he answered, "just walking back to my car."

"You look like a man in need of direction," came the whispered voice.

No kidding, Father Scott thought bitterly to himself. He looked up, but whoever had addressed him had gone. It wasn't until he returned to the rectory and took off the street clothes he always wore on such outings that Father Scott wondered, "How did he know I was a priest?"

Whoever it was hadn't been one of his parishioners; Father Scott knew that for sure. He would have stopped to talk. And it wasn't – him. Father Scott knew the voice of the killer all too well. He heard it in his sleep, in dreams that taunted him for his failure as a priest. Who then, and how had he known?

The murders were now the lead story on all the TV news shows – each of the city's four local stations selecting a different victim to profile, each story complete with exclusive interviews with families and friends of the deceased. The city's daily papers published a list of all the known victims – fifteen in all, the police had finally admitted. The dead were young and old, male and female, killed in no discernable pattern except maybe opportunity.

Experts were hired, by both the media and police task force. Called in were FBI profilers, renowned crime scene specialists, a psychic or two and even a prominent mystery author whose popular series of novels were written from the killer's point of view. All of them had an opinion as to the type of man who would commit such crimes. None of the opinions matched, none of the experts helped. And the one man who knew enough about the killings to give the police any kind of a lead sat alone in his rectory, watching the news every night and reading the paper every morning, praying for a miracle and slowly losing his faith in God.

Another week went by, another body was found – number sixteen if the official count was to be believed. Father Scott put off his usual visit to the site, there was no longer any need. He had seen all he had needed to on television. And soon it was Saturday again. The killer didn't come last week; he'll be here today, Father Scott thought as he dressed for morning Mass. During the Service the readings seemed to mock him, speaking as they did of the Lord's divine justice and mercy. One line in particular, from Paul's Letter to the Romans, stayed with him.

"'Vengeance is Mine, I will repay' says the Lord." Like the tune of a too familiar song, the line stayed with Father Scott as he walked through the empty church after Mass. "When?" he shouted toward the altar. "When will You stop this? If vengeance is Yours then take it."

Father Scott's words echoed through the empty church as he looked around, hoping no one was there to hear him. Seeing no one, he walked into the sanctuary and knelt before the altar. Saying nothing, thinking nothing, he waited for an answer. And again, none came.

How long he knelt there Father Scott didn't know. When he finally stood up he said, "It's not Your way anymore, is it? No more Divine Intervention? You put us here and gave us the Word, and now the rest is up to us."

And then it came together. It is up to us, to me. And what was the Word? "Vengeance is Mine?" Father Scott knew what he had to do.

Buying the gun was easy – the city had yet to establish waiting periods and record checks – he just handed over his credit card and walked out with a .38 revolver and ammunition.

He returned to the church just in time, thirty minutes before confession was to start. He took out the gun, opened the cylinder and loaded the cartridges. Could he do it? He'd never fired a gun before. Just point and shoot, he thought. I'll be close enough that marksmanship won't matter. What if there are other penitents? He put that thought aside. What happens, happens and then I'll call the police.

And tell them – nothing. They'll arrive. I'll hand them the gun and admit to the killing. I'll say nothing after that. The Sanctity of the Confessional extends after death. With luck they'll link the dead man to the murders. If not, at least the killings will stop.

I wonder if I'll be allowed to practice some sort of ministry in prison, Father Scott thought as he took his prayer book out of its black leather case and replaced it with the gun. He zipped up the case. All set.

"You won't be needing that." Father Scott looked up. Stepping out of the darkened doorway that lead from the basement stairs was a man in a charcoal grey monk's robe, the cowl pulled forward to hide his face.

"I told you once," the man continued, "that you were in need of direction. I see that I was right."

Father Scott recognized the voice. This was the man from the garage. "Who are you?"

"I am called the Grey Monk."

Father Scott remembered reading something in the paper about this man, some sort of vigilante who had just appeared in the city.

"I've been watching you, Father. I watched you from an alley after the death of Delores Smith and again when you visited the park. I thought at first you were the killer. Later I learned otherwise. He confesses to you, doesn't he? And now you mean to stop him." A gloved hand pointed to the leather case Father Scott was still holding.

"So, what if I am? You of all people should understand. It's what you do, isn't it?"

"It's what I do," The Monk admitted. "The gun, once taken up, is hard to put down." The whisper of the Monk's voice grew softer. "I was once like you, a man with souls in his care. One day to save those souls I used this …" In the Monk's hand there was suddenly the biggest gun Father Scott had ever seen, some sort of automatic the priest supposed. "A deadly answer to a terrifying problem, but at the time the only one I could find. After that my path in life was set. And so will yours be if you don't turn aside."

Father Scott heard the chimes mark the hour. Time for Confession. He knew this man was offering to take the burden from him. Of course, Father Scott would have to identify the killer, and there was only one way to do that. It was tempting, but so are most sins.

"I can't help you."

"You'd kill rather than violate the sanctity of Confession. Which sin is greater, do you think?" The Monk quickly moved forward. "Forgive me, Father."

Which sin is greater, the Grey Monk thought as he sat in the darkness of the confessional. Assaulting a priest and leaving him tied and gagged in a closet, or impersonating him and hearing confessions. The Monk felt no guilt about either. Lesser sins to prevent greater ones. Father Scott would never have cooperated willingly. And to whom did people confess, the priest or God? If God, then did it matter who sat in the box? And if to the priest, then they were wasting their time. Besides, it wasn't as if this were the first ... no, that part of his life was over, best not to think about it.

There were few penitents that day. Not like it used to be, the Monk remarked to himself, remembering the days when the line for confession was five or six people long on both sides of the box. Of course, that was when the Mass was still in Latin and mystery and ritual surrounded all the sacraments. He listened to those few who came to recite their minor offenses and transgressions and gave out penances appropriate to the sin. Much like my real life, he thought, momentarily glad to be dealing out Pater Nosters and Ave Marias rather than punishment and death.

An hour went by. Will he come, worried the Monk. That Father Scott was bringing a gun into the box suggested that the priest was expecting him.

The Monk waited. In came a girl who had been mean to her sister, a man who had cheated at cards, a wife who had cheated on her husband. The Monk heard them and sent them away with prayers to say and amends to make.

Fifteen minutes left. The church would be empty by now. This tactic had failed. Maybe the killer had decided not to come; maybe he had heard someone remark that "Father Visitor" was hearing confessions today. Maybe ...

The Monk heard the door of the confessional open and close, then the click of the pre-dieu. He slid the panel open.

"They're wrong, you know," came the voice from the other side. "It's only fourteen. The other two weren't mine."

Mimicry was not one of the Monk's gifts. Keeping his voice low and trusting to the darkness of the confessional, he hoped to pass for Father Scott just long enough. "Which two?" he whispered through the metal screen.

"The guy in the garage and that old woman last week. I didn't do them."

"But the other fourteen, they are yours? You take responsibility for their deaths?"

"That's right. Good to hear you're in a better mood, good for both of us."

Not understanding the reference, the Monk ignored it. "And are there any bodies not yet found?"

"Not yet, but there's always …" The killer paused in sudden realization of the deception. "You're not Father Scott." The pre-dieu clicked as the man stood.

The Monk was already in motion. He was out of the box as the killer was opening his door. The Monk shouldered it hard, forcing it shut. He heard the man inside fall to the floor.

.45 in hand, the Monk opened the door and quickly stepped back, prepared for the killer's rush. Instead, he found him sprawled half on the floor, half seated on the pre-dieu, bathed in the violet light of the confessional.

"Don't," the Monk whispered. The killer, who had been about to stand, looked at the automatic pointing at his head and obeyed.

The Monk kept his attention on the man in front of him. He hoped that the church was empty, and prayed that anyone present would flee rather than try to interfere.

"You have made a mockery of this holy place. There is time for one last, true confession." He would give the man in front of him that much of a chance.

Hands raised, the killer smiled. "Nothing to confess. Whatever the priest told you, whatever I told you, can't be used. And when the police get here, I'm just a poor sinner attacked by a crazy man."

Time was short. The police would be here soon. And there was no reason for them to hold this man, this poor sinner. And sinner he was, the Monk reflected, but one who won't repent in this life. So let him be judged in the next.

"Forgive me, Father," the Monk said aloud, and pulled the trigger.

One more sin, the Monk thought as he fled the church. A greater one this time. If he had time, he'd ask Father Scott for absolution. But it was better to leave the man tied up in the sacristy, the better to absolve the priest of the murder committed in his church.

As he drove back to his small, downtown apartment, the Monk wondered if the dead man would ever be linked to the serial murders. He hoped so, but it really didn't matter. The killing had been stopped, and the Lord's Justice and Vengeance meted out. There was more work to be done, but for today it was sufficient.

DEN OF THIEVES

After leaving work, Harry Smith turned left and walked toward the police station. It wasn't right, he thought. No matter how much they offered him it wasn't right. Then the thought of the money made him reconsider going to the cops. It was a lot and he could use it for his kids. Food, clothes, school – all of it cost, and the cost kept going up. The only thing going down was his salary. His hours had been cut at the museum and he was worried about paying the bills. A security guard didn't earn that much to begin with, and now he would be making even less. The money would come in handy, and all he had to do was be somewhere else when …

No! Harry had tried to raise his kids to always do the right thing. He wouldn't preach one thing and do another. He'd go to the district station and tell the cops. That would stop things cold. Maybe then the museum would restore his hours, even promote him, at the least they might give him a raise.

Going to the police was starting to look like a very good idea as Harry crossed the street. He didn't hear the truck that had been following him speed up, and didn't see it until it was on top of him. Then there was darkness.

***

Lester Nash knocked on the office door. He heard a muffled "Come" and let himself in. The man behind the desk wasted no time on the niceties.

"Well?" he asked Nash. "Is it arranged?"

"Everything's fixed, Boss. You were right about Smith. The other two guards went for the deal, a payoff for their cooperation. With what they make, they were eager for the dough. Smith wouldn't go for it at first. He finally agreed to call in sick that night. I could see he wasn't happy about it so I had Scott follow him in the truck. When Smith passed the Metro station and headed for the cop house, Scott ran him down."

"What about the truck?"

"Stolen to begin with, with cold plates. By now it's crushed and sunk. No come back."

The man behind the desk thought about this development. "The other guards, they'll be okay with this?"

Nash shrugged. "Who cares? With Smith dead, they're in too deep, accessories to murder now, at least that's what I'll tell them. I'll also remind them what happens to squealers."

"We'll push things up," the man said. "The exhibit next week, the paintings will be here Thursday. Have everything ready. We'll move then."

Nash stood to go. "What about Smith? Should I put one of my people in his place? The other two would go for it."

Nash's boss considered then rejected this suggestion. "Too risky. A new man just before the job and just after Smith is killed would be the first one the cops would look at. Leave it at two. With the museum cutting costs, no one will worry about filling the position."

"Thursday, then. I'll call you when we're done."

"Do that, Mr. Nash. I'll be waiting for your call."

***

"Eternal rest grant onto him, O Lord,"

Of all his duties, Father Richard Harper liked officiating at funerals the least. It wasn't saying the Mass that he disliked. The ritual of the Mass was comforting and familiar. He knew what to do and say then. Rather, it was the before and after where he felt awkward.

"And let perpetual light shine upon him."

He never knew just what to say to the people who had lost a loved one. True, the deceased was presumed to be with God, but that was little consolation to someone grieving for a lost parent, child or spouse. Father Harper always found himself falling back on the clichés, the tired expressions that everyone expects and accepts as honest attempts at comfort.

"May he rest in peace."

He's in God's hands now, he's in a better place, it's God will. All of these are true, yet they all seemed so inadequate in consoling the survivors.

"May his soul and the souls of all the faithfully departed, through Your mercy, rest in peace,"

In this case, especially. As Harper finished the prayer for the dead, he tried to think of what words he could offer the family of Harry Smith. There were none that would make things better for them. Harry's family was barely making it on his salary as it was. Rent, food and clothing left little for savings. His wife had no job skills. After nine years spent raising children, her office skills no longer matched today's needs and technology.

"Amen."

As family and friends passed by the coffin one last time before it was lowered into the grave, Harper tried to think of what he would say. Then the motto of his academy class came back to him. "Deeds, not words," it had proclaimed. He knew what to say.

The service over, the widow came over to him.

"Thank you for a lovely service, Father."

"Estelle, next week, after you're settled, call me. I think I can help." Harper made a mental list – Catholic Services for temporary financial relief and job retraining, he'd see if the diocese could come through with a job, he'd talk to the school about a needs scholarship and after school care for the children.

"Thank you, Father." She moved on. He could tell that Estelle Smith had taken his words for the usual "call if you need anything" that most people say. If she didn't call, he'd call her and get her the help she needed.

As Harper walked back to his car, he heard a voice call out to him. "A minute, Father?"

Harper looked over at the face of an old friend. "Amos, what are you doing here?"

Amos Hoffman was a friend of Harper's from his time on the police force. He hadn't seen him for ten years or so, since just after his decision to give up the badge for the Cross. They had meant to get together, but his studies and Hoffman's schedule had never coincided. They lost touch.

"Rich, I mean, Father, I ..." Hoffman seemed at a loss on how to address his old friend. It was something Harper encountered from time to time. He usually let people call him whatever they were comfortable with.

"Rich is fine, Amos. What can I do for you?"

"I knew you were a priest, but I never expected to run into you. Listen, I have to talk to you, and I guess we have a lot of catching up to do. You got time today, we can meet at your church."

"St. Sebastian's," Harper gave him the address. "Is this about ..." He inclined his head toward the gravesite. At Hoffman's nod he said, "I thought it was an accident."

"It was, a hit and run. There's just some things I need to ask before I send the case over to traffic."

Harper looked at his watch. It was almost noon.

"Come for lunch. I have a few hours free."

Over lunch, the two old friends talked shop. Hoffman brought Harper up to date on department politics and gave him news about his former co-workers. They discussed the outcome of some cases they had worked on together. Finally, as the conversation was winding down, Hoffman asked him the question Harper had known was coming.

"You were a good cop, Rich, with a promising future. You had just made detective. Why'd you quit?"

"I didn't quit, Amos, I got called away." Harper smiled, remembering back ten years ago. "I really wasn't all that happy as a cop. I was good at my job, and I was content, but I wasn't happy. It seemed that all I did week after week was arrest the same people for the same crimes. Nothing I did seemed to matter. Even after I made the homicide unit, everyone brought in had been picked up before for murder, or assault with intent, or some other violent crime. I couldn't help but think there was a better way.

"The one Sunday morning after work, I was walking home and passed by a church. I hadn't been to Mass for years. For some reason I went in. Then for some reason I kept going, first on Sundays, then every day I could. Soon I realized what was, for me, the better way."

"Do you miss being on the force?"

Harper answered honestly, "On the whole, no. But sometimes I find myself wishing I was back with the department. I've run into some situations where I wished I was both cop and priest."

"Wouldn't work, Rich, as soon as they confessed you'd have to forgive them."

"Only if they were sorry, Amos."

"Aren't they all, once we catch them?"

"Sorry they were caught maybe." Harper looked at the clock on the wall. "I hate to hurry you, Amos, but I have a meeting at four. What did you need to know about Harry Smith?"

"Just routine with any violent death. Did he talk to you about being in any kind of trouble? Was he having any problems? Was anything worrying him – the kids, the wife, a girlfriend maybe, money problems?"

"You mean was there any reason that he'd walked in front of a truck?"

"Or for someone to deliberately run him down."

Harper slowly shook his head. "No, none that I can tell you."

Hoffman noticed the way Harper answered. "That you can tell me. Are we talking about something you can't tell me?"

Harper laughed slightly. "Oh you mean the box. Sorry to disappoint you, Amos, but we're not talking the Seal of Confession here. Harry hadn't, well, let's just say that few people go to confession these days. Those that do confess regularly don't really need to, and those that should don't go at all. There's nothing to tell about Harry."

"Well then, that leaves it as a simple hit and run. Smith was in the wrong place at the wrong time, that's all."

The two said their good-byes, promising to keep in touch. Harper wasn't sure if Hoffman would make the effort, but he would. The priest had been wanting to make contact with some of his old co-workers, and Amos had appeared as if in answer to someone's prayer.

That night, his meetings over and his Office read, Harper took his nightly walk through his church. Lewis, his sexton, had cleaned up and gotten things ready for tomorrow's Mass. Harper sat in a front pew to think.

A priest and a cop. What was I thinking, saying that to Amos? It was true, but a little too close to the real truth to be talking like that, even if he might need Amos's help one day.

Harper's thoughts turned toward the reason for Amos's visit. The detective had no suspicions; he had just been following procedure. That's all Amos ever did, Harper recalled, followed procedure. He was a plodder. As long as an investigation proceeded along regular lines Amos was on sure ground. However, if things took a turn and required imaginative thinking or leaps of intuition, he was lost. Amos could connect the dots but not fill in the empty spaces.

This was not necessarily a career flaw. Most crimes were solved by following routine, homicides especially. You followed the book – gathered evidence, interviewed witnesses, talked to snitches – put it all together and your murderer fell into your lap. A detective who mastered this routine would clear most of his cases, and please his superiors. At year's end they looked at how many murders you solved, not how cleverly you solved them. Amos was very good at what he did and that was why he was still in homicide.

Sometimes, however, things didn't all come together, and that's when a detective needed a little something more, something that Amos didn't have.

This explained why Amos had not raised the one question that the priest had expected. Harry had been in the wrong place at the wrong time, but why? Why had he passed the subway station and continued down the street? True, he could have been walking home, but he always took the subway. Why had he walked passed it? What was there? Harper closed his eyes to remember. Bars, strip clubs? Possible, but those weren't Harry's sins, at least not the ones he confessed to. Besides, Harry couldn't afford it. What then, pawn shops? A city ordinance kept them from staying open that late. The only thing left was the district police station.

Had Harry wanted to talk with the police? And was there someone who had not wanted him to? If so, why and who?

Harper thought about the charcoal grey habit that hung in the back of the wardrobe where he kept his vestments. No, it was too soon for that. He'd do some quiet investigating first, see if his suspicions were right, or wrong. If so, only then might the Grey Monk be needed. Just the same, he'd better talk to Lewis and tell him to get things ready.

The next day Harper came out of the Metro station Harry should have gone down into. The museum had just opened. Harper walked through the front doors and over to the information desk.

"You pay over there, Father," said the woman at the desk, pointing to the other side of the room.

"Actually," Harper replied, "I'm not here to see the paintings, although that would be a pleasant way to spend a few hours. I'd like to talk to someone in your Personnel Department."

"Why, the bishop lay you off?" she asked with a smile.

Harper returned the smile. "I think my job is safe. I want to talk to someone about someone who used to work here, Harry Smith."

"Oh, he was the guard who was killed the other night, wasn't he?" At Harper's nod, she picked up the house phone. "I'll get someone to escort you."

"Afraid I'll steal something?"

"No, it's just that we have a major exhibit starting, and security's being extra careful."

"What's coming, the Crown Jewels of Britain?" Harper asked after she had placed the call to security.

"No, the Eli Jacobs Collection of Early Post Impressionist Miniatures." She handed a brochure about the exhibit.

Harper took the pamphlet and nodded as if he understood. "Worth a lot of money, I guess."

The woman shrugged, "Everything in this place is worth a lot of money, to the right person. The Jacobs Collection is worth more than most."

Just then, Harper's escort arrived. He thanked the woman and followed the guard. On the way he looked at the paintings they passed.

"Don't look at too many, Father, or you'll have to buy a ticket."

This must be a nice place to work, Harper thought, everyone seems to be in a good mood.

"What if I look, but don't understand them?"

"Then you'd be no different from most of the people who come through here, only more honest for admitting it."

They passed the hall where the Jacobs Collection would be displayed. "I guess you're busy with the new show coming in?"

"Oh that. It's coming in Thursday, and will be set up Friday. Saturday night's the big reception. Well, here we are."

The guard took him through a door marked "No Admittance" and led him to the Personnel Office.

"Will I need an escort back?"

"No, Father, they'll probably let you out through the business entrance. It's quicker than going back through the galleries."

Harper thanked the guard and went through the door. He found the person responsible for employee benefits and sat down to try to get some money for Harry Smith's family.

An hour later, Harper left in frustration. The Lord had said that faith could move mountains, but maybe the Lord had not met Mr. Krasner, the museum's personnel officer and somewhat more immovable than any mountain Harper had climbed.

"I'm sorry, Father, but there's absolutely nothing I can do."

Harper was trying to get a pension, death benefits, something to help Harry's family. He had been trying for twenty minutes.

"Surely there's something that can be done, Mr. Krasner. Harry's family really needs the help."

Harper could tell that Krasner was becoming exasperated with him. But like the woman in Luke 18 with the judge, he persevered like the Lord told him he should. It did him little good.

"Father," Krasner said with an air of finality, "I've told you and told you there's nothing. I feel for Mr. Smith and his family, but he was not on duty, he was not acting in the museum's interest, and as I told you, technically, he was not an employee here. Mr. Smith worked for the agency we use to guard the museum. The head of security is the only full time, salaried employee we have that actually works for us."

"Despite being a contract worker, had Harry been acting in the museum's interest, could something be done for his family?"

Krasner shook his head, he was not getting through to this man. "Maybe, Father, *if* he had been, something could be done, but that's not the case here. Mr. Smith died in a traffic accident. Anyway, that would not be my decision to make."

"Whose would it be?"

Krasner saw a chance to get Harper out of his office. "That would be

Mr. Anthony Cambridge, the museum's director. Would you like to talk to him?"

To Krasner's relief, Harper quickly agreed, and the priest soon found himself in the director's office, with much the same results.

"Mr. Krasner was right, Father, there's little we can do."

Harper pulled the brochure on the Jacobs Collection out of his pocket and held it up. "I'm sorry, Mr. Cambridge, I just can't understand how it is that you can afford to mount a multi-million dollar exhibit of paintings yet can't spare money to help someone who worked for you."

"We can't afford it. We are in desperate circumstances ourselves. We've raised our entry fee, cut back hours, laid off staff. We may have to start selling parts of our permanent collection just to stay open. An art dealer we've worked with, Noel Black, heard of our financial straits and offered to help. It was he who arranged for Mr. Jacobs to lend us his collection. We're hoping that the exhibit will bring in needed revenues, and will encourage other collectors to help."

"That was most generous of Mr. Black, considering the commissions he would be giving up by helping you sell your paintings."

"Well, if the exhibit is a success, we may be in the position to start buying art again. And if not, we'll still have to sell. Either way, we'll remember who our friends were. Now if there's nothing else, Father."

Harper left the museum with part of what he had come for. From there, it was a short walk to the library. He took the time to visit it and learn what he could about the Jacobs Collection and its owner. He found one fact he could use. Mr. Jacobs was Catholic. So when he got back to the rectory, Harper called a friend at the diocese business office.

"Eli Jacobs is in town and in a charitable mood," he told his friend. "I'm thinking of hitting him up for a contribution, but first I wanted to check him out – previous donations, types of charities he likes, what approach to take. Can you help me? No, he's one of us. Right, who'd have thought it?"

His friend promised to find out what she could about Jacobs's previous generosity. Harper had one more call.

"C.I.B." he said, asking for the detective bureau once he reached the police department. He hated to call Amos so soon, but maybe it was better to get him used to being a source now rather than later.

"Amos Hoffman, please. Richard Harper." He waited until the detective came to the phone.

"Rich, what a surprise to hear from you so soon." From the sound of his voice, Amos hadn't expected to hear from him again.

"Sorry to bother you, Amos, but something came up and you were the only one I could think to help me."

"What is it?"

Father, forgive me for the lies I'm telling today. "I have the chance to buy some religious art for the church, both as devotional inspiration and as an investment. Some lesser known modern pieces, done in the classical style. They're not worth anything now, but should appreciate in value. I'd like to know if the dealer is on the up and up. If it were my own money I wouldn't bother you, I'd just take the chance, but this is Church funds I'd be investing."

There was a pause at the other end. Harper knew what Amos was thinking. Who can I ask? Who owes me this kind of favor? Who do I want to owe? More importantly he's thinking, is this worth it? It will be Amos, if I'm right about Harry and you were wrong.

Finally, "Sure, Rich, what's the guy's name? I'll check him out for you."

"Noel Black."

"Okay, I'll get back to you as soon as I can."

"Thanks, Amos, I owe you one."

"Just put in a good word for me with your boss. I need all the help I can get."

That's done, Harper thought after hanging up. Now all I have to do is wait for them to get back to me. His calls for the day weren't finished though. He spent the rest of his morning trying to arrange aid for the Smith family. He had a full schedule after lunch, and this would be his only chance.

Harper told Lewis of his suspicions the next morning after Mass. He waited until the altar servers had left then called the sexton into the sacristy.

"If it's the art they're after, it has to be done Thursday, after the paintings arrive but before they're hung. It would be too difficult to remove them once they're on the wall." Harper said, after reviewing everything with Lewis

"If there is anything to these suspicions of yours, Father." In his usual quiet voice, Lewis quietly expressed the doubts that Harper shared. "It could be that Mr. Smith just decided to walk home, or stop for a beer. It may be that he had sins he did not confess. Some people do."

Harper shook his head. "I may be wrong about the museum, but not about Harry. That's why the Monk has to go out tonight. If I am right, and the robbery is tomorrow, they'll be nervous. They'll talk about it, and maybe give us the man behind it."

"What about your sources?" Lewis asked. "The detective and Hilda in the Diocesan Office. Their information should have pointed you to the one behind this."

Harper shook his head. "I thought so too, but yesterday afternoon Hilda faxed me with the information on Jacobs. Right now, he's having rich man's problems. He made too much money too fast. Then he tried to make more. His investments have left him overextended just when the Justice Department and the IRS are starting to take a good long look at him."

"So he might be planning to steal his own artwork. He could collect on the insurance and keep his pretty pictures. What about Black?"

"Amos called me last night. Black doesn't have a record, and there are no active investigations involving him, but Amos's source told him that Black may not inquire too closely about where a piece of art comes from before he sells it. It is also rumored that if you are looking for a particular piece that may not be on the market, Black may be able to 'arrange' a private sale."

Lewis stood up and walked over to the wardrobe where the Grey Monk's habit hung. He half opened the door and turned to Harper. "Black's hands are not clean. Jacobs is in financial difficulty and Director Cambridge is looking at having his museum close down. Then too, Cambridge might be the cause of the difficulty. Any or all of them could be involved." Lewis removed the few vestments that were in the wardrobe and hung them on the hook that was on the inside of the door. He pulled at another hook at the back of the wardrobe. The inside back panel swung out. In a hidden compartment hung the robes and guns of the Grey Monk.

"I think you are right, Father. The Grey Monk should investigate."

***

As is the case on the days before a major exhibit opens, the museum did not have as many visitors as it usually did. Still there were enough of them that no one noticed that one less person left than had paid admission to enter.

It had been a simple matter for the Grey Monk to hide himself in the museum. Just before closing, he found himself alone in one of the many exhibition halls. As he entered, he heard an announcement over the museum's loud speakers.

"The museum will close in five minutes. All visitors are requested to leave via the main entrance. We hope that you have enjoyed your stay."

The Monk listened for any footsteps coming his way. He heard none. The hall he had chosen was toward the back of the building. It was not likely that any of the museum's guests would be passing through it on their way to the exit.

There was a small utility room in the back of the hall. The Monk had noticed it the first time he had passed this way. With the door secured only by a simple knob lock, it was a matter of seconds for the Monk to slip the lock with a knife blade and hide himself within the room. Then he waited.

"The museum is now closed. Please exit via the main entrance. Anyone found in the museum will be escorted out."

Fifteen minutes after this last announcement, the Monk heard footsteps coming his way, their echoes off the museum's marble floor making them seem closer than they really were. He heard the clicks of the guard's shoes stop at what he judged was the middle of the room. Then the footsteps began again, this time walking away from him. Another five minutes, and the light coming from under the door of the utility room went out. The Monk carefully opened the door and stood in the darkened exhibition hall.

He slipped out of the bulky overcoat he had worn to conceal his habit. He left it draped over a chair, just another item for the museum's lost and found. He pulled the bottom of his robe from his rope belt and let it drop to the floor, then he pulled the cowl over his head to conceal his features.

His way guided by the small red emergency lights that state law required always to be lit, the Monk glided through the museum. He paused only when he heard the footfalls of one of the guards. Determining by the sounds of the footsteps the direction in which way the guard was moving, the Monk made his way toward the guard.

With his own footsteps silenced by the rubber soled shoes he wore, and the dark grey of his habit allowing him to blend with the darkness of the museum, the Monk easily trailed the guard, sometimes going ahead of him, sometimes staying just behind him. It was not long before the man that the Monk was trailing met up with his fellow guard in the museum's main hall. The Monk stayed in the shadows and listened.

"Relax, Ray," said the guard that the Monk had followed, "after tomorrow it will all be over."

"Then I'll relax tomorrow, Danny. I wish we had never agreed to do this."

"Too late now, even if we wanted to back out, or do you want to wind up like Harry?"

Ray shook his head. "I'm not backing out, I just don't want to go to jail. No amount of money's worth that."

Danny threw up his hands, the light from the flash he carried making weird shadows on the museum walls. They had obviously had this discussion before. "I keep telling you, there's nothing to be worried about. Nash said that all we had to do is be down in the warehouse when they come through the loading dock. Nash says the alarms will be taken care of from the outside. We'll get roughed up a little, then tied up and left in the warehouse. It will look as if we discovered the burglary and tried to stop it."

"And the cops will believe that, on our say-so?"

"Look, Ray, what's going to happen is that we'll be checking the shipment when these armed men come in. They'll have guns and wear masks. They'll tie us up, take the collection, load it into a truck and drive away. The cops ask, that's what we tell them, and it will be the truth. That way, even if they give us a polygraph, we're okay. Nash has it all worked out."

"I'll still feel better when this is over." Ray looked at his watch. "Time for our second walk through."

The two guards parted. The Monk, who had heard all, quickly made his way back to the utility room.

The next morning, among the early patrons walking through the museum was a man carrying what appeared to be carrying a dark grey overcoat. Had anyone asked to see his admission ticket, they would have found it to bear the previous day's date. He stayed until noon. As he left, the guard at the door wished him a nice day and asked him to come again soon. The whispered reply was that he intended to, very soon. The man with the grey coat took the Metro back to St. Sebastian's for some much needed rest before the night's activities.

That night, a dark panel van pulled into the alley behind the museum. Four men got out and went to the loading dock. One guided the van's driver into a docking bay while the others opened a side door and entered the museum's warehouse. The driver of the van got out and joined the man on the dock. Words were exchanged, and the driver also disappeared into the museum. The fifth man stood watch outside, a portable radio in his hand, ready to alert those inside at the first sign of trouble.

Once the four men were inside, a shadow detached itself from a doorway in the alley. Avoiding the cone of light cast by the one street lamp in the alley, the Grey Monk glided quietly toward the museum. He crossed the alley and, staying close to the walls, silently made his way toward the loading platform. He paused once as the man on the dock glanced his way, pressing close against the wall. The guard, expecting to see nothing, did not notice a thicker patch of darkness on that wall. He turned away, and the Monk moved forward once again.

The next time the man turned in the Monk's direction it was too late. A leather-covered sap came crashing down on the guard's and he collapsed on the floor of the loading dock. The Monk bent over the unconscious man, first to check that he was still breathing, then to bind him with cord he brought out from inside his robes. Once the man was tied up, the Monk moved to the warehouse door. He examined the door's lock and alarm system, then without a sound, the Grey Monk was inside the museum.

While the Monk was approaching the museum, Ray and Danny came down from the exhibition halls and joined those who had come to steal the paintings. Ray went over and greeted Nash, who was directing the recrating of the miniatures.

"Any trouble getting in?" he asked the gang leader. He did not notice two of the gang coming up behind him and his friend.

"Obviously not," Nash said. "I told you, everything was fixed ahead of time."

It was then that Danny noticed something that was not in the plan. He could plainly see their faces of each member of the gang. None of them were wearing their masks.

"Nash, your masks, where are they?" he asked. Just then, he and Ray were grabbed from behind.

"About the masks, fellows, sorry, but it was decided that you two were just too much of a risk." Nash nodded, and there were the muffled reports of two small caliber revolvers. Ray and Danny dropped lifeless to the floor, both shot from behind by the men holding them.

By the time the Monk had made his way to that part of the warehouse where the miniatures were stored, the bodies of Ray and Danny had just hit the floor. Too late to save them, he waited in the darkness until all the men but Nash were busy packing up the paintings, then he stepped forward and announced himself.

"Do not move," the Monk said in a cold, emotionless whisper. He emphasized his command with the .45 he held in each hand.

The men froze at the unexpected interruption, but quickly recovered.

"Who the hell are you?" asked one.

"Never mind that," Nash commanded, "take him down."

The two men who had murdered the guards were the first to draw their guns. But the Monk's weapons were at the ready. He shot them down, the explosions of his automatics echoing through the warehouse. Then he turned to the other three.

Of those, only Nash was armed. He was drawing his gun as the Monk turned his way. "Don't," came the whispered command from the hooded figure.

Nash hesitated, weighed his chances. With his hand just an inch away from the grip of his gun, he looked over at the specter before him. It was Death, Death with two enormous .45s pointing right at him, ready to blow him to Hell. He wasn't ready to take the trip. Slowly, carefully, so that his intentions would not be mistaken, he removed his piece with just two fingers and laid it on the floor. Then he joined his surviving gang members with his hands up.

"Who is your leader?" the icy voice asked Nash.

"No one," Nash tried to bluff, "we're working alone on this."

The Monk slowly lowered one of his automatics until it was pointing at Nash's left knee. "If you ever want to walk again, you will tell me the truth, for whom are your working?"

Nash said a name, the Monk nodded. It was as he had reasoned. One of the Monk's weapons disappeared inside his robes, to be replaced by a cell phone. He pressed a button, and said to the voice that answered, "It's done, make the call."

The Monk gave Nash rope and ordered him to tie up his two accomplices. He then produced handcuffs and had Nash secure himself to a rail.

The Monk checked the bindings of the men. "The police will be here soon. Tell them everything." He faded back into the shadows of the warehouse. The police did not find him when they arrived minutes later.

Within the hour, the police had taken over the warehouse. It was bright with lights. Crime scene techs were taking photographs and making measurements. Medical examiner personnel were bagging the bodies of the four dead men lying on the floor, and detectives were making notes and planning their reports.

This activity was presided over by Detective Amos Hoffman, who had received the tip that led the police to the museum. He would talk to the source of the tip later, on his own. As far as the department was concerned, it would forever be the usual anonymous informant. Right now, he was talking to Anthony Cambridge, the museum's director.

"The men you captured didn't say anything, Detective?"

"No, sir. As soon as we read them their rights, they clammed up and asked for a lawyer. They'll talk soon enough though. With four bodies to account for tonight, and if I'm right a fifth one from earlier on, they'll want to make some kind of deal, if only to save themselves from a lethal injection."

Cambridge excused himself. He wanted to go up to his office for the documents relating to the art. Hoffman went back to directing the crime scene activities.

Cambridge did go up to his office. He did gather some papers, but instead of returning to the warehouse, he left through the business entrance and went home. It would be an hour before Hoffman missed him, and another thirty minutes before he sent someone to check on him.

At home, Cambridge opened the safe in his study; from it he took a supply of cash and his passport. He could be out of the country by morning. Fortunately, most of his funds were already in offshore accounts.

"Going somewhere, Cambridge?" A shrouded figure stepped out of the shadows. In one hand it held the biggest gun Cambridge had ever seen.

Who are you?" asked Cambridge.

"I am the Grey Monk, the messenger of He whom you have angered." Cambridge had read of this man in the papers, a masked vigilante who showed no mercy to criminals.

"If you've come to tell me about the museum robbery, I already know. It was you who stopped it and called the police?"

The Monk ignored the question. "Nash and his men entered without trouble. The alarm had not been tampered with, nor had the door been forced. The murdered guards were to have been blamed for that, but only you could have supplied the means to accomplish it. Nash gave me your name. He will give it to the police to save his life."

"Let him, what's the word of a thief and a killer against a respected member of the community like myself? Let the police arrest me," Cambridge picked his passport off of his desk, "if they can find me. My lawyers will keep me out of jail."

The museum director moved from behind his desk and sought to leave the room. The Grey Monk moved to block him.

"It will be days before Nash gives up anything to the police or D.A. You plan to keep me here until then? Call them now; see if they have any grounds to hold me. Face it, Monk, unless you're willing to shoot me, there's no way you can stop me from leaving."

The Monk brought his gun up. "If you are not willing to be judged by man, then there is no other choice. 'Vengeance is Mine,' says the Lord. And I am His instrument." The Monk pulled the trigger.

It was just before dawn. As he often did the nights that the Grey Monk walked, Father Harper had spent the night in the Eucharistic Chapel, praying for the success of the mission, praying that Lewis would return safely, praying that they were doing the right thing.

Harper was on his knees at the prie-dieu when he caught the movement of a shadow behind him. It was Lewis. The sexton had come from the sacristy. He was dressed in everyday clothes, the robes of the Monk put away for another time.

"It went well?" Harper asked.

"Somewhat," came the whispered reply. "The robbery was stopped, but the guards were killed. Their killers paid the price, as did Cambridge." To Harper's unspoken question, Lewis added, "He gave me no choice."

"He was behind it?"

"Yes, and now Nash and his men have nothing to bargain with. They too will pay." Lewis checked his watch. "It is almost time for Mass."

Harper came up off his knees. "I hate this."

"It is necessary. When no one else can act, we must. What did you tell Hoffman?"

"What we discussed. He'll have questions later."

"You can deflect them?"

"I'll tell him that what I know is under the Seal. He won't like it, but he'll have to accept it. Which reminds me, we have just enough time."

Lewis, who that night had walked as the Grey Monk, knelt on the prie-dieu. He began the ritual that was so familiar to both men.

"Bless me Father, for I have sinned. It has been a week since my last confession."

CRUSADE

*F*ather Richard Harper sat alone in his church. It was night, and again the Grey Monk stalked the streets of the city. Who his target was tonight, Harper did not know. He helped the Monk on many of his cases, but there were times when the man kept his own council. Some nights the Monk would leave with no specific goal in mind, but rather lurked in the darkness where crime occurred, so as to prevent the rapes, robberies and murders that might happen there.

Harper had first been a cop and was now a priest. He knew much about the human heart, mind and soul. He had heard countless confessions and knew how people could lie to themselves about their true feelings and emotions. He also knew how honest others could be about the motives for their actions. Sitting in the front pew, in a darkness relieved only by the sanctuary lamp, he again wondered about his own motives and feelings. He supported the Grey Monk, gave him shelter, and assisted him in his mission. Was he right to do so, or was this crusade, like so many others, misguided and doomed to failure? He thought back to how it began for him.

***

It had been almost a year ago. The vigilante calling himself the Grey Monk had been operating in the city for a little over three months. The police had no clues as to his motives or identity. The few friends from the force with whom Father Harper still kept in contact privately admitted that no one was actively looking for him either. There was no Grey Monk task force, or anyone assigned to track him down. There had been no public outcry for his arrest. As long as he kept to targeting criminals, the department was content to let him be. Right now, he was a media darling – a Lone Ranger, a Batman, a Shadow. He'd eventually make a mistake. He'd be shot down in the street, or target someone who had connections, or bring down a member of a politically active group. Only then would the police go after him.

Harper had mixed feelings about the vigilante. On principle, he disapproved of anyone taking the law into his own hands. But back when he wore a badge, he had seen too many guilty men go free. Lack of evidence, murdered or intimidated witnesses, mistakes by judges, juries and prosecutors – all left people who should be locked up free to commit more crimes. Those that were convicted of all but the most serious crime served little if any jail time. Back then, there had been many times that Harper had been tempted to tip the scales of Lady Justice.

He had not, of course. Harper stayed true to the oath he took, not breaking the law he had sworn to uphold. Still, his feeling of helplessness had led to his calling to the priesthood.

Harper was committed to serving God, a God whose commandments including forgiving enemies and refraining from killing. Still, the Catholic Church was not pacifistic. One could fight in a just war and defend himself from attackers. God was all Merciful and would grant forgiveness to those that sought it. He was also all Just, and those who refused His Mercy would suffer His Justice.

The Grey Monk was one who brought vengeance to those who had avoided justice. The cop in Harper approved of this. The part of him that was a priest prayed that no innocents would be taken along with the guilty.

Father Harper was cleaning the church. His sexton had quit two weeks ago, and he had not yet found a replacement. He had finished sweeping and was getting ready to dress the altar, when there came a pounding on the side door of the church. Harper looked out the small window, and saw only the face of a man in pain. Not stopping to worry about his own safety, he unlocked the door. As he opened it, a man dressed in a dark grey monk's habit collapsed in his arms.

"Sanctuary," was all the man said as he passed out.

Harper gently lowered the man to the floor. He then got up to lock the church door against whoever might be coming after him. As he turned the bolt, he saw that his hands were covered in blood.

Looking down at the man on the floor of the vestibule, Harper recognized him as the Grey Monk, the man who had been in the papers and on TV for the past few months. His first thought was to call 911, to get needed help for the wounded man. Then he realized that to do so would cause the man to be arrested and jailed for the killings ascribed to the Monk. This he could not do. The man had come to him for help, had cried sanctuary in his church, and Harper would not turn him in.

"You know what you're asking me to do?"

"I know exactly what I'm asking you to do – cover up a crime, fail to report gunshot wounds, harbor a fugitive, in short, break the law. But it's for the best of reasons."

Dr. James Sayers had to agree that that might be the case. He had hurried to St. Sebastian's after receiving Harper's phone call. The priest met him at the rectory door and led him to the wounded man. Sayers managed to revive the man long enough to get him into the guest bedroom of the rectory.

Harper and Sayers had first met when the priest was a rookie cop and the latter a second year resident at Hopkins. Their friendship was formed over emergency room patients that Harper would bring the fledging physician. They remained close friends after Harper left the force and entered the seminary. Harper was counting on this friendship.

"Call in the cops, and this man goes to jail," argued Harper as Sayers examined the man on the bed. "Not much of a reward for what he's done for the city, and what he still might do."

"He's been hit three times – right leg, left shoulder, left arm. All wounds through and through." Sayers wasn't ignoring Harper. He had heard every word, but his primary focus was on his patient. He talked aloud to himself during his examination, and as he cleaned, treated and bandaged the wounds. "There's some blood loss, give him fluids and keep him rested. There might be some muscle or nerve damage, but I don't think so. Your new friend is terribly lucky. First he escapes whoever was trying to kill him, then he finds his way here, where you have a friend who doesn't want to see you go to jail. Your Boss must be watching over him."

"So you're not going to turn him in."

"I should, but you might go with him for calling me instead of the police. Why didn't you?"

"Jim, he asked for sanctuary ..."

"A medieval concept, one the law does not recognize."

"But I do. No one who asks for God's help should be turned away."

"It's late and I'm too tired to argue," Sayers said as he put away his instruments. "He's in your hands now, Rich."

"And His," said Harper, gesturing upwards. With the Grey Monk sleeping, he escorted his friend to the front door.

"I appreciate this, Jim," said Harper, offering his hand.

Sayers took it. "Wait until you get my bill. One big favor with interest."

The Monk woke up the next day, early in the morning. Harper went in to check on him and found him conscious but still in bed.

"Where am I?" the injured man asked in a low voice.

"Saint Sebastian's."

The man nodded as if he had already surmised that, and was just checking his conclusions.

"Why did you come here?" Harper asked him.

The Monk raised himself into a sitting position against the headboard, wincing from the effort. Harper moved to adjust his pillows but the man waved him off.

"Here to this church, or here in general?"

"To this church for a start."

The Monk sighed. "There was no place else to go. A hospital or the police were out of the question. Just after I escaped my attackers, I saw the lights on in the church. I took the light as a beacon of hope. If you cannot hope in the Lord, you are truly lost."

"What happened to you?"

"I was too clever, or not clever enough. I went after the men who were selling drugs in this area. I confronted the dealers, forced information from them. This information soon led me to what I believed to be their headquarters. When I broke in to confront them ..."

"It was a trap?"

"Correct. I had been led to a vacant house. There were no drugs, but there were men with guns. I entered through the basement, quietly I thought. However, anyone waiting and listening would no doubt have heard me. As soon as I was inside they attacked."

"What happened?"

"They used bright flashlights to blind me and take away my advantage in the dark. Fortunately, I already had my gun out and fired immediately. This surprised them enough that most of their first shots missed. One did strike my left side." The Monk raised his hand to the bandage on his shoulder. "Unable to use my other gun, I did the only thing I could, the one thing they did not expect."

"Which was?"

"By now, they probably had my retreat blocked off. There would have been men waiting to cut me down if I left the way I had come in. So I charged them. Once I was on the move in that dark basement, they had difficulty finding me with their flashlights. On the other hand, their lights made excellent targets."

"You fought your way out then," asked Harper.

"To the first floor. By then, my gun was empty. The two men on the first floor were not expecting me to make it up the stairs. I brushed past them. They were firing as I went out the front door. They were better marksmen then those in the basement."

"Your other wounds."

The Monk nodded. He was getting tired. "Once I was outside, they tried to follow, but the darkness permitted me to escape. I found my way here."

Talking had exhausted the Monk. Harper let him rest and went about his duties. That night after dinner, their conversation continued.

"What is your name? I can't keep calling you 'Monk.'"

The Monk was silent. "I haven't used my real name for some time, it was part of my old life. Call me 'Lewis.'"

"Why the get up?" Harper asked the Monk. "Why do you do it?"

"I do it because I must. Like you, I was once a man of peace. Then ... let us just say that something happened that reminded me not of the Good Shepherd, but of the One who judged and punished Sodom, the Egyptians and the merchants in the Temple."

"An eye for an eye," said Harper.

"Life for life, eye for eye, tooth for tooth, hand for hand, foot for foot, burning for burning, wound for wound, stripe for stripe," Lewis quoted from Exodus, then added, "'Vengeance is Mine, sayeth the Lord.'"

"And are you His agent?"

"It would seem so."

The next morning, as Lewis ate the breakfast Harper had brought to him, the priest surprised him with an offer.

"I think you should stay."

Lewis stopped eating. He looked at Harper. "Stay here, with you?"

"Yes?"

"And continue being the Grey Monk?"

"Yes." Harper let out a sigh, and expelled all the turmoil and doubt that he had been feeling since the Monk collapsed in his church. Having voiced his decision, he now felt that it was the right one. "I believe that you were brought to my door for a reason. You need help in your mission, help that I can give you." Harper told the Monk about having been with the police, both as a patrol officer and a detective. "I still have some contacts on the force who may be willing to help us. I can help in other ways. Alone, you'll become lost in your mission. You may ... lose perspective."

"You mean lose control." Harper nodded. "And you'll be what? My conscience?"

"Your conscience, your advisor, your partner."

"And if I do lose control?"

"Then I'll be the one who stops you, however I can."

The Monk thought for a moment, then asked, "What do you get out of this?"

Harper smiled, "A new sexton."

Over the next few weeks Lewis healed and grew stronger. He began to help Father Harper, first around the rectory and then in the church. One night over dinner, he told Harper, "It's time for the Monk to go out again."

The priest nodded agreement. "You're ready. Sayers had given you a clean bill of health." Harper was quiet for a while, then asked, "You're going after the drug gang, aren't you?"

"I have to. The Grey Monk cannot be effective if he can be attacked with impunity."

"I thought you would, so I called a friend from the old days. I told him that I was concerned about drug activity in the neighborhood. Asked him how bad it was and what, and who, I should watch out for."

"And what did he tell you?"

"He said that things are bad all over the city, but especially around here. He said that if I hear the name 'Tremaine' that things have gotten as bad as could be. Tremaine is a coming player in the city. Was small time, now big time. In the last few weeks, he's taken over the east side drug market. Word is he's smart, ruthless and has a major rep."

"Did your friend say how this Tremaine acquired his rep?" Lewis's voice came in an icy whisper, one that Harper supposed he used when he was the Monk.

"Yes," Harper told him. "Word on the street is that Tremaine killed the Grey Monk."

"Well," came the reply. "We'll just have to see if this Tremaine is afraid of ghosts."

Over the next few weeks, the Grey Monk haunted the shadows. Unlike his last outing, the one that led to his being wounded, he stayed in the darkness. He did not reveal himself to the dealers he watched. He did not confront them and order them away from the area. He did not overcome them and leave them tied up for the police to find. This time he just watched, and followed.

He followed the dealers to learn where they picked up the drugs they sold. Each led him to a different location. The Monk watched as money and drugs were traded between dealer and supplier.

"There seems to be an infinite number of dealers," he told Harper one night before going out. "Each has his own corner, each pretends to be selling a better brand of poison."

"When in fact it all comes from the same source – Tremaine."

"It would seem so. I have identified only four suppliers in this area. After each transaction, they get into their cars and drive away, either to the next drop or to meet with Tremaine."

The part of Harper that was still a cop asked, "Could the suppliers be working for more than one man?"

"No," replied the Monk. "All four operate in the same manner. They meet with the dealer, they transact their business and then they presumably give the dealer the location of the next meeting, since no dealer returns to the same site more than once a week."

"The sites are random, then?"

"Yes, but different suppliers use the same sites, which convinced me that they all work for the same man."

Harper nodded. "What's your next move?"

"Tonight I follow one of the suppliers, to see where he leads me."

"Will you need the car?"

"No, I think I can catch a ride."

"Hiding in a back seat is too risky."

"I'll need the car."

It was very early in the morning or very late at night. It depended on whether you were just waking up or had not yet been to bed. For Kevin Little it was very late. The man called "Little Kev" had spent the night, as he spent almost every night, making deliveries for his boss. This was his last drop. Little Kev parked his ride in the back of an apartment house. He waited until he saw the boy he knew only as "Spicy" walk up to the dumpster, then he got out and joined him. Little Kev carried a blue plastic grocery bag. He handed it to Spicy and in return received a brown paper bag. Neither man checked the contents of the bag he received. If Spicy ever shorted Little Kev, he'd soon be mourned by the few friends he had. If Little Kev failed to deliver the right amount of product, word on the street would soon reach Tremaine and the mourning would then be for Kevin Little.

The transaction took less than five minutes. When Little Kev drove off, he failed to notice the car following him.

The Grey Monk had shadowed only one dealer that night, Spicy. He knew from past times that Spicy got his drugs just before dawn. The Monk hoped that, because of the hour, it would be the supplier's last drop of the night. He could not spend the night following a supplier in a car. He would soon be spotted.

Little Kev led the Monk into a better part of the city. Once a middle class neighborhood, the closeness to the city harbor and nearby redevelopment had caused property values to skyrocket. Tremaine would not have them report to his house, would he, wondered the Monk.

He wouldn't. Little Kev drove past newly built and restored houses and continued to a nearby self-storage facility. Makes sense, thought the Monk. The new houses were being built without basement or attic. The residents needed a place for everything they think they cannot live without. So they store it blocks away, and live without it for most of the year. It is private, secure, well lit – a perfect place for Tremaine to do business. As Little Kev drove onto the lot, the Monk drove past it.

"Do you think they all use the same storage area?" Harper asked him that morning.

"No, Tremaine probably has one for each of them, all in separate areas. That way, there is little chance of his suppliers meeting each other by accident."

Harper agreed, "And if one falls, the rest stay in business. You'll be waiting there tonight?"

"Yes," Lewis said, "Eventually, the trail will lead to Tremaine."

"And when you find him?"

"He will regret ever having met the Grey Monk."

"Just try and make sure that he lives to regret it."

Lewis gave Harper a brief smile. "Yes, my Conscience. No one will die unless they insist upon it."

That night, as Little Kev drove into the storage facility, the Monk watched from the darkness. Seeing which unit the drug supplier used, The Monk waited until after Little Kev drove off, then went over to it. It was built like a small garage, a cinder block structure sharing side walls with the units on either side. A sliding metal door was the sole means of access. The Monk inspected the lock. He had been expecting a simple padlock, one easy to pick and even easier to cut off. Instead, the lock was electronic, with keycard access and a code to punch in. He would not be entering the unit tonight. Tremaine's secrets were safe for a while longer.

During the next week, the Grey Monk tracked the rest of the suppliers to three other storage facilities on the east side of the city. He was ready.

Davon Williams was the first supplier to fall. After his first delivery of the night, he had his car door open when the Monk came out of the shadows. Davon would have gone for his piece, but the sight of a .45

appearing out of the Monk's robe halted this action.

"Say nothing," the Monk ordered. "Keys, gun. Remove them carefully, place them on the ground."

Davon dropped his keys. Very carefully, he reached into jacket and took out a 9mm pistol. He slowly leaned down and placed it next to the keys.

"Good. Now, the access card for the storage locker." The facility that Davon used was run by the same company as that used by Little Kev. The same security system was in use in both places.

"It's in the car."

The Monk thought for only a moment. Then he decided. "Get it," he said, and waited to see if Davon Williams chose to live or die.

Davon slowly got into his car. He turned his back on the Monk. He reached into the glove compartment not for the access card but the .32 semi-automatic pistol he had put there for just such an emergency. He turned quickly in his seat and fired two shots at where the Monk had been standing.

The Monk was no longer there. Expecting this move by Davon, he had moved to a point slightly behind and to the left of the supplier's car. As Davon fired his two shots, the Monk fired once, the roar of his .45 drowning out the sounds of the .32.

Davon's lifeless body slumped in the front seat. The Monk looked at it with regret for the wasted life. He said a quick requiescat, thinking however that considering how Davon had lived, he was unlikely to rest in peace.

Sirens in the distance told the Monk that the shots had been heard and called in. He left, knowing the police would find the body.

The next two suppliers proved to be more cooperative. These the police found sitting calmly in their cars, money and drugs in plan view on the front seat. The Monk had confronted them both, threatening each with death if they did not cooperate. He had them place their product and profits on the seat next to them, and their hands on the steering wheel. He then stood near the shadows watching them, his gun pointing menacingly at their heads as he called the police on his cell phone to report a drug deal in progress. He waited until the police cruisers were less than a block away, then faded into the darkness.

The Monk then paid a visit to the storage facilities used by those dealers. Different storage companies, simpler security. Cutting off their locks, he found a quantity of drugs and a large amount of money. The drugs he left. He would tip off the police as to the locations in the morning. The money was a different story.

The Monk and Father Harper had had a long argument about what to do with the proceeds of Tremaine's drug trafficking, if any were found. Harper had argued that any such money was tainted, stained by the misery and deaths the drug trade had caused. He wanted no parts of it.

The Monk had countered that money had no conscience. However it was obtained, it could be put to good use. The police would seize it, then eventually use it in the fight against drugs. It could also be used, the Monk pointed out, to feed and clothe the poor of St. Sebastian's and other parishes. It could also be used to defray the costs of the Grey Monk's campaign against crime.

While The Monk had capitulated to Harper's wishes to reduce the level of violence he visited on criminals, he had prevailed on this issue. Leaving half the money he found for the police to seize, he took the rest, to be put to better use than Tremaine would have.

It was almost dawn. The Monk waited for Little Kev outside the storage unit the drug supplier used.

Little Kev's car pulled up. The supplier parked next to his unit. He got out and gave a cursory look around. He saw no one, but then, he never did. This early in the morning, everyone was either still asleep or too busy getting ready for work to bother with things they wanted out of sight anyway. Tremaine's idea of storing the product in low crime areas, where police never bothered to look as long as there was no trouble had been a good one.

Little Kev swiped his card through the reader and punched in the code. He pulled up the door and started to go in.

"Stop," came a whispered command.

Little Kev, both hands up in the air holding up the sliding door of the unit, turned and saw a man step out of the shadow of the neighboring structure. The man was wearing a dark grey monk's habit, the cowl of which was pulled forward so as to hide the face. From the right sleeve was thrust a gloved hand holding a very large gun. "If you want to live, you will stay as you are," the man told him.

"Damn!" Little Kev exclaimed. He recognized this man. It was the Grey Monk. This man was supposed to be dead. He had helped Tremaine ambush him, and Tremaine had sworn that the Grey Monk was dead. Here he was alive again, and pointing his gun at him.

"What do you want?" the drug supplier asked the Monk. His only answer was silence as the Monk searched him. The unit's access card, a cell phone and a 9mm pistol from Little Kev's pocket disappeared inside the Monk's robes.

The Monk stepped to the side. His left hand went up and supported the sliding door. His right hand kept the gun trained on Kevin Little. "Go in, switch on the light." The supplier complied. As soon as the light came on, the Monk entered the unit. He pushed the button to let the door shut behind him.

The inside of the unit was almost identical to that of the other two the Monk had visited that night. Shelving lined the walls. A table was in the middle. On the shelves were drugs, cutting agents and paraphernalia. The table bore the scales, vials and bags used to weigh and package the product.

"Now what?" asked Little Kev.

The Monk produced a set of handcuffs. He had the supplier cuff himself to an upright support of one of the back shelves.

"Where is Tremaine?" the Grey Monk demanded. Little Kev was silent. The Monk straightened his arm and pointed his .45 right at the supplier's head. "Where is Tremaine?" he repeated.

"You can kill me if you want," came the reply. "I give up Tremaine, he'll kill me worse, me and my family. You don't give up Tremaine."

To Little Kev's surprise, the Grey Monk put up his gun. "I believe you," the Monk said in his icy whisper. "I believe that you would rather die here today than betray your employer. Either that, or you know my threat to be but a bluff."

Little Kev knew nothing of the kind. Still, he felt he should display some bravado, now that his life was spared.

"Yeah, I knew you didn't have the heart. Guys like you don't kill. That's why Tremaine always wins. Hey, where you going?"

While Little Kev was talking, the Monk had moved over to the unit's door. "I am leaving. Since you will not tell me where to find Tremaine, I will seek him elsewhere. Perhaps tonight one of his other employees will be more cooperative. If not, I will be back to see if you have changed your mind."

Little Kev pulled at his cuff. The shelf it was attached to didn't move. He started to pull harder, but then realized that to do so would bring the entire shelving unit down on him.

"And if you do find out where he is?" The Monk did not answer. "You can't leave me here."

"Why not? You will be of no further use to me. I will not kill if I can avoid it. However, I have no problem leaving you here."

"But, I can't get out."

"So?" Monk pushed the button that raised the door.

"Wait!" Little Kev shouted so as to be heard over the sound of the door going up. "If I tell you where Tremaine is, you'll let me go?"

"Eventually." The Monk did not shout. Somehow, Little Kev could hear his whisper over the noise of the door.

Little Kev nodded. The Monk pressed the button to stop the door. The supplier gave the Monk the address of a house on Monument St. "That's where we meet him. We give him the money, he tells us where to pick up the stuff."

"When is the next meeting?"

"He's there every night."

"Does he ever come here?"

"No, never, he never wants to be around the dope."

"Then I hope you have told me the truth."

The Monk pressed the button to close the door and quickly stepped outside. As the door closed behind him, he heard Little Kev shouting, "The code, you need the code to open the door again, it's ..." The door finished closing and cut off the supplier's voice.

Let him worry, thought the Grey Monk, who already knew the code. He had watched from the shadows as Little Kev punched it in.

It was light when the Monk came out of the storage unit. A quick glance around showed no one in the area. He stripped off his habit and walked over to the next row of units. There he got in his car and headed back to St. Sebastian's.

"I thought that you were going to follow the suppliers back to Tremaine," commented Harper over lunch. Actually, it was breakfast for Lewis, who had slept through the morning and into the afternoon.

"I tried that the last time, it did not work out well. The suppliers may be watched more closely as they approach the house."

"So now what," asked Harper. "Tip the police off as to where they can find Tremaine?"

Lewis shook his head. "It would do little good. According to the man I have locked up in that shed, Tremaine avoids being anywhere near the poison he has them sell. If the police were to break in, they would find nothing there to incriminate him."

"Just guns and money."

"There is no crime against having either, not inside your house."

"So you're going to go in there with guns blazing, and bring them to justice yourself."

Lewis gave Harper a rare smile. "That's one plan. I have another." He explained his to the priest. Harper agreed that it would probably work.

Little Kev was surprised when he heard the door start to rise. He hoped that it was somehow Tremaine, come to release him and tell him that this time, the Grey Monk was well and truly dead. Instead, he barely saw the dark form of the Monk as he slipped inside and closed the door behind him.

The light came on, and the Monk approached him, his gun drawn.

"Back against the wall," the Monk ordered. Little Kev was quick to reply. After he did, the Monk placed a paper bag on the floor. Once he allowed Little Kev to move, it would be within the supplier's reach.

"Food and drink," the Monk explained. "It will last you until tomorrow. If all goes well tonight, by then you will be in a more conventional prison." The Monk stepped back to let his prisoner get to the food.

Little Kev started in on his meal – burgers, fries and soda from a fast food chain – but soon stopped when the impact of the Monk's words hit him. "What if things don't go good?"

The Monk did not reply. Instead, he busied himself taking things off the shelves and placing them in a canvass bag. Little Kev suddenly realized that if the Monk did not survive the night, then he would slowly starve to death. He started chewing his food more slowly, taking time to enjoy what might be his last meal. Idly, he wondered what the Monk wanted with the stuff from the shelves.

The lights suddenly went out, and Little Kev heard the sound of the door going up. The Monk slipped out, and the door closed. Little Kev stood chewing in the dark. He never thought that he'd look forward to going to jail.

The house that Tremaine used as his headquarters had been carefully chosen. It was not in the best of neighborhoods but neither was it in the worst. The police patrolled regularly but were not a constant presence. There was little crime compared to some parts of the city, but few people ventured out at night if they did not have to.

The Grey Monk approached the house carefully. He had parked his car several blocks away, and traveled the side streets and back alleys. The alleys were safer, the only light coming from back windows. When he had to be on a street, he stayed close to the sides of the houses, avoiding the cones of light that came from the street lamps. If the few pedestrians who did pass by saw him, it was only as something in the corner of their eyes that was not there when they turned around.

The Monk was a block away from the alley running behind Monument St. and he had yet to see any guards. This was as he expected. The presence of loitering men in the neighborhood would only draw attention, attention that Tremaine did not want. Any guard would be inside the house. The Monk entered the mouth of the alley, and began counting houses. "3400, 3402, 3404 ..." the Monk whispered house numbers to himself. He found the house he wanted. He looked at the houses on either side of it.

The houses in this block all had covered back porches. The high porch roofs were wider than the porches themselves, so as to keep the rain off anyone sitting out back. From the roofs, one could easily climb into a second floor window.

The Monk quietly entered the yard to the right. This house was dark – either vacant or its occupants were out. More importantly, the porch roof extended out far enough to allow the Monk to easily cross over to Tremaine's house.

The Grey Monk stepped on to the porch and tested the wrought iron holding up the roof. It felt solid. He quickly scaled it. Once on the roof, he paused to catch his balance, then he stepped across the gap from one roof to another.

The roof of Tremaine's porch was a bit more sloped than the other and the Monk stumbled slightly, dislodging some debris that had accumulated on the roof. It fell noisily into the back yard.

His back pressed against the wall between the two second floor windows, his hands holding tightly to the window frames, the Monk watched as a man with a gun came out into the yard. He looked to his right and left, then in the alley. If he looked up when he turned around to go back inside, he saw nothing but a thicker patch of darkness.

With one hand still holding tight to a window frame, the Monk slid a thin piece of metal between the upper and lower sashes. He worked the metal until the window lock unlatched. He then lifted the bottom sash, and slipped into the darkness of the second floor.

In the darkness, the Monk made his way by feel. His hands found a dresser in the back bedroom. In the top drawer, he left a packet he took from beneath his robes. He moved out into the hall, his gun out, ready to use if he were discovered. Now his way was guided by the light coming up the stairwell from the first floor. He stopped in the middle bedroom to leave behind another packet.

The Monk stopped at the top of the stairs, and listened to the voices coming from the floor below.

"I still think we gotta go from here. Davon dead, Little Kev missing, the others down at Central, the cops gotta be coming here." The man's normally voice sounded high, his words hurried. He would have been the man who came out to investigate the noise.

"Kevin is as probably as dead as Davon," replied a much calmer voice – Tremaine's, the Monk hoped. "Someone is making a move, Darrell. When we find out who, we will deal with him."

"But what if they talk?"

"If the police were coming, they would have been here by now. The two who were locked up know better than to talk, especially after what happened to the family of the last man who tried to give us up."

Now was the time. The stairs to the first floor bisected the house. There was a bend partway down, a natural platform for the Monk. He eased down the stairs, stopping at the bend. From this position, he could see two men sitting in the living room. He waited until they saw him.

"Oh hell!" shouted the larger of the two men, the one with the nervous voice. He went for his gun.

"Don't!" came the Monk's whispered command. He drew his second .45 and covered both men.

"The Grey Monk, I presume?" The smaller man's voice was as calm has it had been a few minutes ago. He did not seem dismayed by the specter standing above him.

"Slowly take out your guns. Lay them on the coffee table." As the pair complied, the Monk warned, "Any move in my direction by either of you will bring the death of both."

"And now what?" asked the smaller man.

"And now, Tremaine, justice."

The larger man braced for a bullet. Tremaine kept his composure. "Relax, Darrell, if he was going to shoot, we'd be dead by now. He means to turn us over to the police." To the Monk he said, "Call them. There's nothing here for them, except maybe you."

One of the Monk's guns disappeared. Out came the third packet that the Monk had taken from the shelves of Little Kev's storage unit. It was a large zip lock plastic bag containing a white powder. He threw it down to Darrell. Instinctively, the big man caught it. As soon as he saw what he held, Darrell dropped it as if it had burned his hands.

Little Kev's cell phone replaced the packet in the Monk's hand. "Now," whispered the Monk, "I will call the police." He dialed 911, then pressed send. When the operator answered, he gave the address, then added, "An officer's been shot, hurry." He broke the connection.

None of the three moved, the Monk keeping the other two in place with his gun. The tableau remained until the Monk saw blue flashing lights in the front window. "I would strongly advise against any sudden moves," he warned them. He fired a shot into the ceiling, then fled up the stairs.

As the Monk had expected, police burst through the front and back doors. None of them saw him, but those coming in the front saw both Tremaine and Darrell. Then they saw the guns on the table and then the dope on the floor.

Tremaine remained calm, heeding the Monk's advice against sudden moves. Darrell panicked. As the police came in, his first thought was to hide the dope, then the guns. He was reaching for both when police bullets cut him down.

The Grey Monk was at the upstairs back window when the officers below fired. He watched from this window as the officers who job it was to watch the back ran toward the house at the sound of the gunfire. Once they were out of sight, the Monk went out the window. With no one watching anything but Tremaine's house, the Monk crossed several porch roofs until he could descend in safety. More police poured into the alley, but they all were concentrating on getting to the crime scene. The Monk hugged the shadows as they passed, and soon slipped out of the neighborhood.

Before returning to St. Sebastian's, the Monk paid a visit to a relieved Little Kev. He returned the supplier's cell phone to him. "Your release is in your own hands. You may call the police, or you can remain here."

"And what if I call someone else?"

"Davon is dead," the Monk replied. "Darrell is dead. Do you wish to join them?" The Monk watched as Little Kev dialed 911. He left him still handcuffed to the shelving, leaving the door open for the police to find him.

Harper was waiting for him when he came home. "How did it go?" asked the priest.

"Tremaine has been arrested. The police will find the drugs that I planted in his house. It is sufficient quantity to charge him with distribution. With him in jail, Little Kev and the others will soon turn against him. His drug ring is broken."

"Any deaths?"

"None that I caused."

With Tremaine's organization shattered, there was very little drug activity in the area for the next two weeks. Gradually, new dealers moved in, and the drug sales began anew. The Monk resumed his fight, but the dealers and drug lords he took down were always replaced. There came the realization that as long as there were people who wanted to use drugs, there would be people willing to sell them.

One night after a mission, the Monk asked to confess. It soon became a regular habit. He did seem to truly regret his actions when they led to death, Harper reflected. However, a small voice reminded him that by hearing those confessions, he was forever prevented from testifying against the Monk. If the police ever traced the Monk to his church doors, Harper would be more likely to go to jail than his sexton.

***

Harper's reverie was broken by the sound of the outside sacristy door opening and closing. Lewis was back. Harper left the past behind and went to hear of the Grey Monk's night.

SOULS ON FIRE

And Hell the Shadow of a Soul on fire
(Omar Khayyam – Rubayat, verse lxvii)

The first bottle shattered against the stonework of the church, the gasoline it once held running down the wall. The wick went out on impact, leaving nothing to ignite the flammable liquid.

The second bottle was better aimed. This one struck the window. But rather than breaking, the bottle just bounced off the heavy leaded glass. It smashed down on the sidewalk, the burning rag in its neck causing the gasoline to catch fire. Cement, however, doesn't burn, and the fire quickly went out.

Someone threw a rock, then another. The window finally broke. A third bottle was thrown through the broken glass. The bottle shattered on a back pew, gasoline beading up on the varnished surface, fuel for the rag that was the fuse. The wooden bench caught fire, a fire aided by the varnish coating. Then the next pew started burning, then the next, and the fire spread from back to front.

This was not a neighborhood where noises such as broken glass are a concern. Gunfire often went unreported in this neighborhood. So it was not until the stained glass windows began exploding from the heat that anyone called in the alarm. By then it was too late. The Fire Department arrived only in time to contain the blaze to the one building. By the time the fire had burned itself out, St. James Episcopal Church was just a memory in the minds of its parishioners.

***

"It's the fifth church fire in a month," Amos Hoffman explained. "All predominately black parishes, all obviously arson."

Father Richard Harper sat back in his chair. He and Hoffman were in the priest's office in the rectory of St. Sebastian's Catholic Church. The police detective had telephoned Harper this morning and asked for a meeting.

"I know," Harper replied. "The story was in this morning's paper, and the news shows haven't stopped talking about it since the last fire."

"Then you know what kind of a spot the department's in. This has the highest priority. The mayor could be murdered, and that would take second place to this. You were a cop once, Rich, you know what a red ball case is like. I've got the brass, the City Council, a half dozen community and minority groups and the Black Ministers Alliance all screaming at me to solve this yesterday."

"Any leads?"

"If you means suspects, any and all the white supremacist and skinhead groups in this state, Virginia and Pennsylvania. As far as evidence, I can tell you what kinds of bottles were used for the Molotovs and maybe the brands of gasoline. That's it. The thing about arsons is that your evidence tends to burn up. And what the fire doesn't burn, the fire department washes away."

Hoffman reached into his briefcase and pulled out several manila files. Harper recognized them from his days on the force – case folders.

"Here," the detective said, "It's all in here." He threw the folders on to Harper's desk.

The priest ignored them. "Why you, Amos? I thought you were homicide."

"Rich, after the first fire we called in the State Fire Marshall. After the second one, the FBI and ATF got involved. Now that St. James has gone up, the Commissioner's desperate. So he put me on it."

"You're a good cop, Amos, but you never did Arson, did you?" Hoffman shook his head. "So why you?"

"Because, Father Harper, I got you. You're an ex-cop who's a man of the cloth. You understand both sides and can mediate between them. And right now we need someone like that."

"Don't lie to a priest, Amos. That's a good first answer, but what's the real reason you've come to call, in an official capacity no less?"

Hoffman hesitated a minute. "I got you, Rich, and you got a direct line to the Grey Monk."

Harper nodded. He had expected this ever since Hoffman had called and asked to see him. Hoffman knew that the priest was somehow connected to the vigilante who called himself the Grey Monk. Twice now Harper had passed messages from the Monk to Hoffman, messages that had led to the arrests of people the Monk had caught committing crimes, the ones that the Monk had left alive that is.

After the first time, Hoffman had accused Harper of being the Monk. The priest had calmly pointed out that he had called Hoffman from the rectory phone at the same time the Monk was seen leaving the scene of a museum robbery. Harper forestalled any further questions by telling Hoffman, "Amos, the man calls me with information, I pass it on to you. That's all I can tell you." When Hoffman persisted, Harper invoked the Seal of Confession, a religious confidentiality more sacred than that between a lawyer and client or a doctor and patient.

Harper picked up the folders Hoffman had thrown on his desk. He leafed through them.

"They're copies," Hoffman told him, "but everything we have is in there – Lab reports, witness statements, crime scene photos, everything."

"The brass know you're doing this?"

"Rich, why do you think they've left the Monk alone? It's not because he's *only* killed the bad guys. It's not because officially he's some kind of urban myth. And it's not because he's solved crimes we didn't even know about. It's because the Department knew that sooner or later a situation would come up where someone like the Monk was needed, someone who can do the dirty work we can't." Hoffman took a breath and continued. "I was ordered to come here today. Offically, to tell you that the department would appreciate any help you could give us as a liaison between church and state. And off the record, to let you know that should your friend manage to end this in his own unique fashion, well, let's just say not too many questions will be asked."

The priest took the folders and stacked them neatly on his desk. "I'll look these through, Amos. If I come up with any ideas, I'll call you. I'll also call on my fellow ministers and ask the usual questions about threats, suspicious calls and the like."

Harper stood up and extended his hand. Hoffman rose to take it. "What about the other, Rich?"

"You mean the Monk? Amos, I don't control him, and if I did promise you anything, then later on that might be interpreted as having criminal knowledge of a wanted man. But I wouldn't be surprised to learn that he was already working on it."

"I'll have to settle for that, then."

Harper showed the detective out. When he returned to his office, Lewis, his sexton, was waiting for him.

"You were listening from the other room?" Harper asked. Lewis nodded. "Are you working on it?"

In addition to being the church sexton, Lewis was also the Grey Monk. "I've been out twice since the third fire." Lewis answered. "None of my sources had any information. I also checked the Internet."

"For what? Arson.com?"

"Hate groups, Father. The Internet is a breeding ground for anyone with a cause. Set up a web page for your agenda and others will come to it."

"Did you find anything?"

Lewis shook his head. "Only that there are a great many people with hatred in their souls. The forums I visited were full of the vilest talk I had ever thought ..." Lewis put a hand over his eyes. "Never mind. Suffice to say that despite wading through that filth for several nights, there was nothing about the fires in this city. I even joined in some of the discussions, heaping praise on the arsonists, hoping someone would claim credit."

"Any luck?"

"Most expressed approval at what was being done, but no one admitted doing it."

Harper picked up the case folders from his desk. He offered them to Lewis. The sexton declined. "You read them, Father. Tell me what they say. I'll be going out tonight."

Later, after dark, the Grey Monk drove through the city. Behind the wheel of a nondescript black sedan, collar pulled up and hat pulled down, he drove to the area where the fires had occurred. He passed St. James. He noted the police guard and the yellow tape around the building, both keeping the curious away. They would be there until the crime scene investigation was finished.

The Monk drove past the other three damaged churches. None were guarded. No need, afterwards. The Monk kept driving, looking for other churches, those still standing and not yet victimized. Many of these had guards as well – off duty police officers, private security or simply volunteers from the congregation. All of these were quite visible and were there more for deterrence than detection. Finally, the Monk found what he had been looking for - a church without any visible guardian, one off a main road, but close enough for a quick getaway. Parking a few blocks away, he moved through the darkness back to the church. Taking up a position in the shadows across the street, he waited. Dawn found him still waiting. Before the light could reveal his presence, he made his way back to his car and returned to St. Sebastian's.

After Mass, Harper reviewed the case folders for Lewis over breakfast.

"Five fires, four different methods of starting them. The first a Molotov through the window, just like the last one. The second a break-in with gasoline poured everywhere. For the third, another B&E, with someone igniting rags found in the basement. The fourth, someone poured lighter fluid into the mail slot and tossed in a lit pack of matches."

"Then we have a group rather than an individual," Lewis observed.

"Right," agreed Harper, "And probably amateurs. Their methods certainly aren't professional. Two of the churches were not even damaged that badly."

"The police investigation?"

"The police seem to be covering all investigative angles," Harper told him. "They've checked out the hate groups, known pyros, anyone with a prior record of crime against a church or clergy."

"In the photographs," the Monk asked, "Are there any burnt crosses?"

"You mean other than on the churches themselves? No. I guess whoever this is feels that a burning church sends a better message."

That afternoon, Harper visited the pastors of the vandalized churches. He went to the First Church of Jesus the Savior, a storefront church on Lanvale St. One of the front windows was boarded up. It had been the first to be hit. There he found the Rev. Thomas Mosely getting ready for evening services.

"We were lucky, Father," Mosely told Harper after the priest had explained that he was helping the police with the investigation. "I live upstairs. I heard the glass break, then the smoke alarm go off. I was down here before the fire could spread too far. I put it out then called the police. It's a good thing I'm a light sleeper or I'd be with Jesus now."

"And you hadn't had any threats or warnings of any kind?"

"None," Mosely walked him over and showed him the burn mark still on the floor. "Came right through there." The minister pointed to the boarded up window.

"Have you had any threats or have any prowlers been seen around the property?"

Mosely thought a minute. "Nothing out of the ordinary. Like I told the police, there's always people out and about around this neighborhood. And too many of them have mischief or worse on their mind. But none of them would hurt the church. Before this, we never even had a break-in. No wait, I'm lying, and in church yet." The reverend chuckled at this. "Several years ago there was a man who was breaking into God's houses both here and further up in the northwest of the city. He hit us once. The police caught up with him soon after that."

"And you can't tell me anything else about the fire?"

"No, sir. I just thank Jesus that no one's been hurt, and pray it will stay that way."

"Amen to that, Reverend, amen to that."

St. Michael the Protector Church was the next to have been burned. Where the church had stood was now a semi-vacant lot. The burnt out structure had been torn down and now heavy moving equipment was busy clearing the debris.

"Going to rebuild?" Harper asked the former pastor, Darryl Greaves. The reverend's house was detached from the church. Harper found him there, watching the backhoes and cranes from a window.

The Reverend Greaves shook his head. "Not here," he told Harper. "There are enough churches in this area to take care of the faithful. A lot of my people are moving out to the county. They don't like coming all the way into the city for services anymore. It's past time I followed."

"What will you do with the land?"

"A supermarket chain made me an offer. That money and the insurance will make a nice start on a new building fund."

Like Mosely before him, Greaves could not think of anyone who might be starting the fires. His church had had several burglaries in the past few years, but all had been the smash and grab types – junkies looking for something to sell.

Nor could the pastor at the Madison Church of Christ. She was busy running a pre-school class when Harper called on her. She left the class in the care of an aide and took him down to the basement.

"There used to be classrooms down here." The Reverend Louise Jackson told Harper as the two stood at the bottom the basement steps. "Not no more. Praise Jesus that the Fire Department arrived when they did. They saved the rest of His house for Him."

Like the others, Jackson was a member of Black Ministers Alliance. Before Harper left, she invited him to their next meeting.

"Thank you, Reverend. At the least I can tell them what precautions to take and what to look for."

The fourth church on his list, The Temple of God's Soldiers, was another storefront. Despite having suffered minimal damage, it was shut and locked when Harper arrived.

"They done moved, Reverend," said a woman coming out of the beauty shop next store. "After the fire the pastor decided it was a sign from heaven that he should move back to Alabama. He had been praying on the move for a week, and he took the fire as God's answer." Harper thanked the woman and moved on

Unable to contact the pastor of St. James, Harper returned to his own church. He joined Lewis in the kitchen where the sexton was busy making dinner.

"I see you had as much luck as I did," Lewis remarked.

"That obvious?"

"A downcast look is not a sign of success, Father."

Harper started setting the table. "Are you going out again tonight?"

"What choice do I have? The police are doing the investigating. The best I can do for now is to pick a likely target and pray that the arsonist picks the same one."

After dinner, the Grey Monk left for his vigil. Harper cleaned up. Then prepared his church for the next day's Mass. As he worked, he went over the day in his mind.

Could the fires all be coincidence, he wondered. Some caused by burglars, others by simple carelessness on the part of someone inside. From his days in homicide he remembered a series of deaths that everyone thought were connected. TV and the papers made a big deal about them. When the investigation was over, two of the seven deaths had not even been murders. The remaining five had all been committed by separate people.

No, the two Molotovs argued against that. Both bottles had once held the same brand of beer and analysis of the liquid residue suggested that the same gasoline had been used in both. If nothing else, those two fires were connected.

There was something else, something Rev. Mosely had said. It was about the series of church burglaries that had occurred years back. Harper remembered the case. The burglaries had been plotted on a map, showing the pattern the burglar had followed.

After another fruitless night, the Grey Monk returned to find Harper in the office, asleep on the couch. The Monk shook him awake.

"Morning already?" the priest asked him. "I just laid down for a minute." Harper wiped the sleep from his eyes. "I've something to show you."

He walked over to the desk and turned on the computer monitor. Putting a CD in the drive, he called up a mapping program. Soon, a map of the city's western district filled the screen.

"Here's where the first fire was." Harper moved the cursor to the spot. He clicked the mouse and a marker appeared. "And the second." Another click, another marker. He continued until the locations of all five fires had been plotted. "Suggest anything?"

Lewis looked at the screen. In the center was the site of the last fire. Almost equally spaced around it were the other four sites, once each to the northwest, northeast, southwest and southeast. He watched as Harper drew two lines to connect the five scenes.

"An X."

"Or?" Harper rotated the image 45°.

"A cross. Have you told Hoffman?"

"I'll call him after Mass. But I'm sure they've figured that much out. But watch."

Harper changed the map back to a north orientation. He then drew lines 90° out from ends of the cross.

The Monk nodded agreement. "A swastika. If this group is not content with making a burning cross, then this makes sense." He touched the screen, his finger stopping near the end of one of the new lines. "The church I'm guarding."

"Then be ready, Lewis. I'm not sure Amos will buy what amounts to a guess on my part. If he doesn't, there's a 25% chance that you'll get to end this yourself."

"I don't know, Rich, sounds like kind of a stretch to me," Hoffman told Harper over the phone the next day. "We'd already figured out the cross pattern, but that's not enough to make that into a swastika."

"Amos, if they were just going for a cross, they'd have picked different churches," Harper countered, "ones that ran north-south-east-west instead of on the diagonal. They'd also be done and announcing their accomplishment – turning the west side into one big cross burning. I don't think they're finished. An X means nothing, a swastika makes a statement."

"I still think it's nothing better than a guess, but you might be right. We're having a task force meeting tomorrow. I'll bring it up and see what the experts think. Maybe I can get them to deploy some troops around the churches you pointed out."

"Tomorrow might be too late, Amos."

"Other than ask the Western District commander to increase patrols in those sectors it's the best I can do."

Harper hung up. "It's up to you, Lewis – for tonight anyway. The best Amos can do is try for something after tomorrow."

For the third night the Grey Monk drove to Sinai Lutheran. Again he checked the back and, seeing that it was still secure, took up his station in front. Then, alone in the shadows, he waited.

It was just past one when his wait was rewarded. A red sports utility, some foreign make, pulled up in front of the church. Though it was hard to see through the tinted windows, it appeared to the Monk that two white men were inside it. The Monk dropped further back into the darkness, a .45 in his hand.

The car drove off. County boys looking for drugs, the Monk thought. He had seen enough of that during his crusade against crime in the city. As pervasive as drugs might be in the black community, there were just as many whites who drove into those communities to buy them. As the SUV drove off, the Monk started to holster his weapon. Then he heard a slight squeak of brakes, and a car door slam close. He kept the .45 in his hand.

Two young white men walked up to the front of the church. One was carrying a clear glass bottle. From his post the Monk could see the liquid sloshing back and forth inside it. He could also see the rag stuffed in the neck. The other man carried a rock.

The young men studied the church front. The one carrying the bottle transferred it to his left hand. He reached into his jacket pocket with his right. He brought out a lighter and lit the fuse of his firebomb.

The Monk watched as the other man prepared to throw the rock through a church window. He stepped out of the darkness.

"You do not want to do that," he said in a low cold whisper.

The two men turned as the figure robed in a charcoal grey habit stepped from the shadows. Neither moved. The flame of the bottle's wick burned brighter.

"Put down the bottle," ordered the Monk, "and the rock."

The rock hit the street. The man with the bottle bent over to his right. In that position, his movements were partially concealed from the Monk's gaze. With his left hand, the man carefully put the bottle on the street, the wick still burning. His right hand, however, snaked into his jacket and found the revolver in his waistband.

The young man with the gun straightened suddenly and fired a shot where the Grey Monk had been. The Monk, however, had moved. The .38 bullet smashed harmlessly against the wall.

The Monk's bullet did not. Discharging his .45, he struck the man in the chest. The man fell, knocking over the bottle, breaking it. Flame from the wick ignited the spilled gasoline, some of which had splattered on the fallen man. His clothing caught fire instantly and soon the air was filled with the stench of burning flesh.

The Monk made no move to help the man. Instead he turned to his accomplice. "It will be hotter still where he is going. If you do not want to join him in Hell, tell me why."

Stunned by the horror of his friend's death, the surviving arsonist was at first unable to speak. Only when the Monk put his gun against the young man's head did he find his tongue.

"It was to join ...to join The Fellowship ... you had to burn a church, a black church. Oh, please don't ... don't kill me ... it wasn't my idea ... Danny talked me into it."

Sirens sounded in the distance. "Quickly now, where is this Fellowship?" The young man gave the Monk an address.

"You will wait for the police. Tell them everything. If you do not ..." The Monk did not finish his threat. Instead he simply looked over at what was left of Danny. The young man got the message.

As police cars pulled on to the scene, the Grey Monk faded back into the shadows. If any of the responding officers saw him, they kept that fact out of their reports.

Leaving the area, the Monk called Harper on his cell phone.

"You were right," he told Harper when the priest answered. "It will soon be over." He quickly told Harper what had happened and gave him the address.

"I know the area," Harper said. "It's down in Essex." He gave the Monk directions, adding, "Be careful." A click was all the acknowledgement he got.

Driving into the county, the Monk knew from what Harper had told him of police procedure that he had at least an hour before the man he had left alive gave the police the address of the Fellowship, whatever that was. The investigators would have to be called in from home. The man's rights would be read to him. He might still talk after that. Or he might feel safe enough from the Monk's vengeance to remain silent or ask for a lawyer. Assuming that he did talk, a warrant would have to be obtained for the house in Essex. At least an hour before the county police were asked to guard the house to make sure no one entered and to detain anyone leaving. More than an hour before anyone entered. Enough time for the Grey Monk. The part of the county into which the Monk drove was mostly rural. Houses were set apart from one another. Streetlights were rare, and mostly only at intersections. Perfect conditions for a man at home in the darkness.

The Monk stopped his car a block away from the address he had been given and made his way on foot. He found the house. Lights were on inside, on the first and second floors. The basement was dark.

No police were around. That did not mean that they would not be there soon. Not wanting to be there when they arrived, the Monk silently made his way around the back.

With gun in hand, the Monk moved slowly and carefully into the back yard. He found the steps to the rear basement door. There was no deadbolt, only a passage lock keeping him out. A quick pass with a knife blade, and the Monk was inside.

In the darkness of the basement, the Monk risked a flashlight rather than trip over something and betray his presence. The flashlight's beam revealed that the basement was fitted out as a meeting room. There was a podium against the far wall with three rows of folding chairs lined up facing it. Behind the podium hung a flag, one whose device was a swastika over the letters P.R.F. Near the desk along a side wall was an open set of steps leading to the first floor.

A map hung on the wall opposite the stairs. Walking carefully around the set up chairs, the Monk went over to it. The map was of the city's west side. Nine circles were drawn on the map, with crosses covering five of the circles. The circles marked the locations of the churches were there had been fires. The other marks indicated churches that had not yet been attacked. Sinai Lutheran was one of those. The Monk supposed that Danny and his friend were to have drawn their cross on their return.

Looking at the map, the Monk realized that Harper had been right. Taken together, the marks on the map did make up a swastika.

Hearing no sounds from upstairs, and careful to make none of his own, the Monk continued to prowl the basement. There was a desk in the corner. Flyers on the desk exhorted loyal whites to join the Pure Race Fellowship. Near the leaflets was a small file box. Index cards in the box bore names, addresses and phone numbers – no doubt the members of the Fellowship.

There was enough here for Hoffman, the Monk decided. He was about to leave when he heard footsteps above him. They were muffled enough to tell him that they were people descending from the second floor to the first. Then he heard voices.

"I don't like it, Debbie. They should have been back by now."

"Some of the others were late, Joe. Give 'em some more time." The tone of the woman's voice sounded like she was trying to convince herself more than Joe.

"What if the cops grabbed them? What if they talk?"

"One, the cops won't grab them. Most cops in the city are white.

Most of them are on our side, whether they know it or not. So they're not going out of their way over some colored churches. And if some *other* cops grab them, those two know enough not to talk."

"I still don't like it, Deb," the man said.

"After tonight we can stop," the woman said soothingly. "Start over in another part of the city. Pick new targets."

"But what if ..."

"To Hell with the cops, Joe. If they come, well, we can hold them off long enough to get rid of the evidence."

Hearing that, the Monk decided not to wait for the police to break their prisoner. He carefully made his way around the chairs again. Raising a foot, he kicked out at one of the chairs in the back row. The metal chair collapsed and fell in the one it front of it, which in turn knocked over a third. "What the hell was that?" the Monk heard Joe shouting once the din in basement quieted.

"Someone's down there," Debbie yelled. "Grab your gun."

Bright lights clicked on, illuminating the entire basement. With no darkness to hide him, the Monk stood where he was, and waited for the two to come to him.

Feet stamped hard down the wooden stairs. Debbie was in the lead, with Joe close behind her. They were not expecting to find anyone still in the basement. With all the noise he had made, the intruder should have fled.

The pair came to the bottom of the steps and turned toward the rear. As they did, they stopped at the sight of the figure before them. The Monk, his cowl raised, his dark grey habit covering all but his hands, stood there with guns drawn, a dark specter of Death.

Before he could warn them, both Debbie and Joe raised the shotguns they were carrying, giving the Monk little choice. His .45s spoke. Debbie and Joe fell to the floor. Neither would move again.

The Monk checked the fallen pair. Finding them both beyond help, he went over to the desk, picked up the phone and called Harper.

"It's over," he said when the priest answered. "Call Hoffman and have him come to this address. He'll find everything he'll need to close the case." The Monk hung up before Harper could reply. Then he disappeared into the darkness of the night.

The next day found Hoffman back in Father Harper's office. "The case is closed then," the priest asked him.

"Yes, it's closed." The detective did not seem pleased. "What we found down in Essex was more then enough. Right now we're rounding up everyone who's name was in the file box."

"What about your witness?"

Hoffman made a sound of disgust. "The one from outside the church? Got nothing from him. He's so scared he's practically catatonic. Not more than a boy, really." Hoffman paused. There was something he had to say, but had to work up to it.

"Listen, Rich, I know I brought you into this, you and the Gre … your friend. But I never … I didn't … Hell, Rich, did he have to burn that guy alive?"

Harper had been expecting that question. He of course knew what had really happened. He wasn't sure, however, that he should let Hoffman know that. He wanted to maintain the fiction that he was merely a contact man for the vigilante, and not a close confidant.

"I don't what happened out there, Amos, and neither do you. Could be the Monk had no choice and things simply happened. I do know that when you play with fire you can expect to get burned."

If Harper had meant that as a joke Hoffman didn't find it funny. He looked long at the priest and saw that he wasn't laughing either.

"And there's the woman he killed," the detective finally added.

"You mean the Nazi with the shotgun?" Harper countered. "The one she was probably pointing at the Monk? What was he supposed to do, Amos? Shoot the man and politely ask the woman not to kill him? Or should he have withdrawn and left them for the police?" Harper went on before Hoffman could answer. "They'd have seen the county cops pull up. Or seen the news about Sinai Lutheran. Either they're gone or you got a nice, well-publicized barricade situation during which they'd get rid of all the evidence."

"You done?" Hoffman asked. At Harper's nod he said, "Look, Rich, I'll admit that I dragged you and him into this. Even knowing what he'd done in the past, well, I thought I needed his help. I was wrong. There are rules and the Monk plays too far outside them. If ever I ask again, please tell me no."

Both men were quiet for a time. Hoffman broke the silence. "Forgive me, Rich. I've been working too long on this and now it's suddenly over. A man in a grey robe did in one night what I couldn't do in a month. It's like you said. I played with fire. Now I'm mad I got burned. I'm going home, wash up and get ready for the press conference. The Chief's going to let the city know that their churches are safe again. Don't worry; the Monk's name won't even come up. We plan to take all the credit and lay all the blame on the bad guys."

Harper and Lewis watched the press conference on the noon news. The mayor and police chief both spoke, each praising the combined task force and their work in tracking the terrorists to their lair. The death of the group's leaders was attributed to an unknown assailant, probably a disaffected member of the Fellowship. With the other members rounded up, the threat to the city's houses of worship was over.

Two weeks later, Sinai Lutheran burned to the ground.

No Molotovs this time. Incendiaries were set inside the church, gutting the interior. The ceiling gave way when the support beams burned through. The walls fell next. By morning what had been a House of God was a pile of rubble.

The same press that had previously lauded the police for their efforts in bringing an end to the terror now called for an investigation of those efforts. It was suggested that the case was closed too soon, that not all of the Fellowship had been rounded up. Lawyers for those arrested claimed that the evidence against their clients had been manufactured, citing the burning of Sinai Lutheran as proof that the real arsonist was still at large.

The mayor and police chief quickly responded to these attacks. Where two weeks ago they had accepted the plaudits for a job well down, they now defended themselves by blaming the man responsible for the investigation, Detective Amos Hoffman. Whereas two weeks ago he was on the verge of becoming a detective sergeant, Hoffman was now castigated publicly by his own commander, who questioned his competency for relying on "outside sources" to work his cases for him. Instead of a promotion, it was likely that Hoffman would be busted back to patrol.

Harper tried to talk to the detective, but none of his calls were returned. He and Lewis discussed the situation, looking for ways to both help Hoffman and find the arsonist.

"The churches are staked out," Lewis told him. "Last night, I went by those that were marked on the map. All had police protection. If they strike again, it will be elsewhere."

"Then there's nothing else for us to do. The leaders are dead, the followers aren't talking."

"Not to the police," Lewis said. "Their lawyers will free them, either on bail or they will use this last fire to get the charges dismissed. Good. Let them go home, feel safe. Then the Monk will visit them and they will talk."

"Will they, Lewis? These aren't your average street thugs, afraid of a dark avenger coming out of the shadows. In their own way they are as committed to their beliefs as we are to ours. And if they do talk, what can they tell us? That they were told to burn this church or that one. According to Amos, every member was accounted for. Whoever took down Sinai Lutheran wasn't a regular part of the group."

Harper got up out of his chair. "Maybe I can learn something at the Ministers Alliance Meeting tonight that will help."

"You are still going?"

Harper nodded. "I told them I'd be there. Might as well take my lumps. Maybe I can put in a good word for Amos."

Harper had expected to face an angry crowd. Instead, all the ministers present thanked him for his efforts.

"I only wish I could have done more," Harper said, deflecting the gratitude he didn't feel he deserved.

"What more could you have done?" the Rev. Jackson asked him, "except get out there and try and catch them yourself."

"I just feel sorry for Detective Hoffman," Harper added. "He did all he could too."

This comment lead to a general debate about the way the police handled the case, with some ministers siding with the press and others seeing Hoffman as a scapegoat.

Finally, Hoffman asked, "Where's the pastor of Sinai Lutheran. I had hoped to talk to him tonight, if only to express my condolences for the loss of his church."

"He's gone," Pastor Mosely told him. "He got an offer for the land and took it. He and the church board are busy looking for a new site in the county."

"Let's hope he and Rev. Greaves both don't pick the same site," Jackson offered, and the talk turned to the common problems every pastor has in the fight for souls in the 21st century.

"It would be interesting to learn just who the buyer is," Lewis commented after Harper returned to St. Sebastian's rectory and told his sexton what was said at the meeting.

"I thought so too," the priest agreed, "but a supermarket bought out Greaves and a chain drug store is taking over the Sinai property, so it might just be a stray member of the Fellowship."

"You may be right, Father."

Lewis left the rectory right after Mass, not coming back until just before dinner. "I'll be going out tonight," he told Harper.

"As the Monk?" Lewis nodded. "The church fires, or is this something new?"

"Still the fires, there's something I have to check."

The house in Essex was empty this time. Its owners were dead and the county police had finished their search and left the scene. Only tattered bits of crime scene tape remained, fluttering from the bushes where it had been tied.

The police had made their entry through the front door, forcing it open and nailing it shut when they left the scene. Again, the Monk slipped the lock on the basement door and entered.

From the light of his flash the Monk could see that the chairs he had knocked over were still on the floor. They were black with fingerprint powder. The map and flag were gone, as was the file box on the desk.

The Monk searched the desk, but did not find anything that he wanted. He moved upstairs, hoping that the police had confined their search to the crime scene in the basement and items with obvious Fellowship connections.

Keeping his flash pointed to the floor to avoid shining its light through a window, the Monk searched the rest of the house. There was nothing for him on the first floor. Just a little used living room, dining room and kitchen. As he looked through them, the Monk noted how few personal touches there were – no photos, no statues or knick-knacks sitting around, few books or magazines. The kitchen cabinets were mostly bare, containing just what two people might use on an occasional visit. The dining room and living rooms were likewise empty – no DVD or cable connection, nothing in the drawers of the furniture, which itself looked old and far past well used. It was as if Debbie and Joe had rented the house as was, or had just taken over an abandoned property. Either way, it seemed as if they had not been living there.

On the second floor, only the bathroom and master bedroom bore any signs of use. The bathroom had the necessary hygiene products and that was all. In the bedroom, a few items of men's and women's clothing were hung in the closet and folded away in the drawers. The Monk went through everything, looking for papers, bills, receipts, anything with a name, address of phone number. Nothing he found was of any help to him.

The other second floor rooms were bare, only stripped beds and empty closets. The Monk found only a few "For Rent" signs thrown carelessly into the back bedroom closet.

His visit a failure, the Monk started to return to the basement when he turned and picked up one of the rental signs. He folded it and tucked it into his habit. Then he left as carefully as he had arrived.

The next day, using the computer's criss-cross directory, the Monk found an address for the phone number printed on the sign. The property was being leased by Albert Harden Realty.

"It's in a strip mall up in the northern part of the city," Father Harper told him. "I walked a post in that area back when I was a patrolman. Much harder to break into than a private home," He added, knowing what Lewis was thinking.

"But not impossible," Lewis replied.

"No, not impossible," the priest agreed. "These places are usually alarmed, but brute force always works for a quick smash and grab, if you don't mind waking up the whole neighborhood and can get away before the cops come."

"That will not do." Lewis thought a moment then asked, "Father, if you own a business and there's a break-in at night, what do the police do after they have arrived?"

"They make their own entry, and either catch the burglar in the act or not. Then they notify the owner to come down to make a report and secure the premises."

"That is better. The police will leave the owner while he waits for repairs?"

"Usually. It's just too busy for them to wait."

"Good."

The homeless are invisible; people choose not to see them. So no one noticed the man who huddled against the strip mall fence next, bedding down for the night covered in what looked to be a charcoal grey blanket. It could be that no one saw him because he had positioned himself at a point of the fence where the parking lot lights fell short, leaving that area in darkness. If anyone did see him they were probably grateful that he was far across the lot and not camped in their doorway. They may have thought that he was a sign that mall management should look into private security.

From his position against the fence, the Grey Monk watched the stores of the shopping center close for the night. At nine the store lights started going out, by nine-thirty, most shop owners had locked up and gone home.

The Monk was waiting for Albert Harden to leave. He'd wait an hour; give the realtor time to get home. Then when no one was in sight, he'd throw a rock through the window of the realty company and quickly depart. The alarm would go off and the police would arrive. They would investigate, find nothing, and call the owner back to repair the broken window. Once Harden was there and the police had left, the Monk would appear, confront the owner and find out just what his connection was with the PRF. At least, that was the plan.

Harden did not leave. His storefront was dark, with only a small light on in the front office, but realtor had not yet left.

A car pulled up and a man got out. He walked straight to the realty office and opened the door, as if knowing it would be unlocked this time of night.

Seeing no one about, The Monk stood up, pulling up his cowl, the "blanket" that was his habit falling around him. He crossed the parking lot, moving from one island of darkness to another until he came to the storefronts.

From the small light in the outer office the Monk could see that there was no one in there. Looking through the window, he could barely make out a door leading to a back room. A strip of light was coming from the bottom. Harden and his visitor must be in there.

The Monk carefully opened the door. He had not heard any chimes or bells that announced customers but he was taking no chances. Once inside, he drew a .45 from beneath his robe and silently approached the back room.

Almost at the door, the Monk heard voices from the other side.

"So tell me how this scam works again?"

"It's simple, Brook. Businesses like these chain groceries and drug stores have finally figured out that they can make money in the inner city. People need food and medicine, and the closer the stores are the more they're gonna shop there. The only problem is that there's no place to put them."

"So you find a good site, burn it out, and come in and broker the deal. Good thinking. But why'd you pick on churches? You had to know you get the wrong kind of heat."

"Churches get built where the people are. They're prime locations. So when those Fellowship idiots came to me looking for a headquarters I offered 'em the dump in Essex. Then I made my pitch, showed 'em how they could advance their 'cause' and make some money. Pointed out the churches I wanted out of the way. Told 'em to take out as many more as they wanted, long as they didn't stop until mine were toast."

"Still a risk," Brook said.

"But worth it. Those two preachers saw me as an angel sent from

God, showering money on 'em. The chains don't ask. Show 'em a good site and their checkbooks are out. Then those two fools had to get caught outside that church."

"The one I burnt for you?" There was a pause. The Monk imagined Harden nodding his head, because Brook continued. "At least those two at the house got themselves killed by the cops."

"Yeah," agreed Harden, "They would've talked. But listen, Brook, The reason I asked you here, I need you to torch one more church."

"Another drugstore?"

"No, I just don't want to stop with one of mine. If another one goes the cops will keep looking for Klansmen and skinheads. All I need is for one smart cop to make a connection."

"Got a church in mind?"

"No, just pick one, maybe draw a swastika or paint 'White Power' on the wall before you go."

"I got it." The Monk heard a snap of fingers. "I'll pour out the gas in the shape of a cross. That'll leave a nice burn pattern for the hate crime cops to play around with."

"Brook, it's nice to deal with a pro. Here's the second half from last time, and another half for this time."

"Thanks, Harden. I'll pick a place and torch it. Give me a call when you read about it in the papers."

Footsteps coming toward him told the Monk that the men had finished their business. He stepped back toward the front window. When Harden and Brook emerged from the back office, there before them stood the Grey Monk.

Coming from the bright office into a darkened room, all the two men saw a dark figure silhouetted against by the light from outside. It did not speak or move. Not knowing who or what it was, neither did they.

As their eyes adjusted to the dark, they saw the shape before them become the figure of a man wearing a monk's robe, a figure that was holding a .45 in each hand.

"You have two choices," the Monk said in a cold tone. "One of you can pick up the phone, call the police and confess what you have done. Or you can face my judgment, here and now."

Brook saw Harden start to move toward the phone. "Hold it," he told his partner. "I've heard of this guy. Calls himself the Grey Monkey or something like that. A do-gooder in a costume." To the Monk he said, "What you going to do, kill us? That's not the way you guys work. We're not resisting, and we haven't killed anyone. So what you going to do, Mr. Monk?"

"Three people have died," came the whispered reply. "And you, Harden, are involved in their deaths. Brook, you are now with him, with him in his crimes and with him in his sins. And the wages of sin is the damnation of Hell."

In the dark room, the two men saw the shadowy figure move a bit forward. The gun in his right hand extended as if to fire. Whether this was a just a second warning of their possible fate or not, Brook wasn't taking any chances. His hand swept the lamp from the desk, and he ducked down. At the same time he pulled his own gun. Firing blindly toward the window, all he did was break the glass.

The lamp did not go out when it hit the floor, so its light still shown, revealing Brook's position. As his opponent looked for him in the dark, the Monk fired once. Brook crumpled and hit the floor.

Knowing the police would soon be responding to investigate the gunshots, the Monk was about to leave Harden to them. Instead, he asked the realtor, "Is there a back door?"

"Yes, but?"

"I no sooner want to be here when the police arrive than you. Go."

To save himself, Harden thought that the Monk was going to help him escape as well. He started to think of a way to explain the shooting to the police. He need not have bothered.

The shopping center employees parked in the rear. By the time the police arrived, the Monk and Harden were driving away in the realtor's car.

"Pull over here," the Monk told Harden once they were a safe distance away. His gun was still out, although both men knew the folly of shooting the driver of a moving car. Still, the gun made a point, since Harden knew he'd have to stop sometime. The realtor pulled over, expecting the Monk to get out. He did not expect the Monk to hit him in the head with the gun. As blackness fell over him, Harden remembered what the Monk had said about the wages of sin.

"Everything is ready. Make the call," the Grey Monk told Father Harper over his cell phone sometime later.

The phone next to Amos Hoffman's bed rang. Unconsciously the detective picked it up. Long used to late night calls, his wife slept through it.

"Hoffman," the detective mumbled.

"Amos, it's Rich Harper."

Hoffman was instantly awake, "Listen, if this is about the Monk, I want no parts of ..."

"Amos, look out your front window." Harper hung up.

Hoffman moved to put on a light then thought better of it. He knew what he'd see once his eyes adjusted, his police uniform hanging on the closet door. He had been told to make sure it still fit. After the church arson debacle, he was assured that he would be wearing it soon. Besides, to see outside he'd need the light off.

Hoffman went to the window. Parked across the street from his house was a strange car. Next to the car, just under a streetlight, stood a man in a charcoal grey monk's habit. On seeing Hoffman appear in the window, the Monk waved once to indicate the car, then again with a farewell gesture. Then he faded into the darkness.

I should call a unit and have that checked out, Hoffman thought. The he remembered the uniform hanging on his closet door. Maybe it could go back in the closet. He got dressed and went outside.

Harden looked around. He had been conscious for several minutes now. His car was parked in a residential neighborhood, with houses on one side of the street and a very nice park on the other. His head still hurt. He was alone in his car, not bound in any way. The passenger's side window was down. Harden watched as the front door of a house opened and a man came out. "Remember," came a voice from the darkness outside the open window, "tell him everything. Leave anything out and I will find you. Brook, Debbie, Joe, Danny – you will join them in the shadows of Hell if you do not obey me. Now get out slowly, keeping your hands in sight."

Hoffman approached the car carefully, his service revolver at the ready. He raised it when the car door opened and a man got out. The man quickly raised his hands. "I'm responsible for the fires," he told Hoffman. As the detective began to read Harden his rights, he heard the sound of police cars responding to provide back-up. Harper must have called them, he thought. With his prisoner handcuffed, Hoffman risked a glance into the dark woods where he knew the Grey Monk was watching. That's where he'll always be, Hoffman thought. Just inside the dark woods, walking that fine line between it and the light.

THE GREY MONK'S JUSTICE

I

The minute Dyson walked into the kitchen he knew it was up. The crew should have been packing rock. Instead they were just sitting there, no product on the table.

"That him?" asked a tall, dark-skinned man he didn't know.

"That the Diceman," was the reply from the one called Dray. The other two men at the table nodded.

Dyson didn't wait. With no time to go for his piece, he pushed his way out the storm door just as the guns were being drawn.

The first bullet hit the doorframe where Dyson had been standing. By then, he was in the back yard. He almost made it to the gate. A shot from the door hit him in the arm. He kept running. To stop now was to die. Out of the yard, he turned left into the alley. He'd have a chance if he could get to the street.

The way was blocked. A man was standing at the mouth of the alley with his gun already out. He turned and saw the other end blocked as well. He was trapped and boxed. By the time he got past either one the gang from the house would be on him. In one last useless gesture he drew his own piece, hoping to tag at least one of his killers. He didn't get the chance. He was cut him down before he got his nine clear.

The tall man came out of the house. He walked down the alley and stood over the fallen man. The Diceman's chest was still going up and down.

"Finish him," he said calmly and walked away. Gunmen gathered around the helpless man and emptied their clips.

Multiple calls to 911 of shots being fired drew police into the neighborhood, too late to be of any help to Dyson Jones. Officers working a two-man car found his riddled body in an alley in back of N. Carey St. Following procedure, they roped off the scene with yellow tape, called for Homicide and the Crime Lab and began the search for evidence. Officers arriving later began a canvass of the houses backing the alley, looking for witnesses.

Detective Amos Hoffman had been helping to work a double stabbing on the Eastside when he got the Carey St. call. By the time he arrived, the Crime Lab was already at work. Periodic flashes from the tech's camera lit up the alley. Yellow numbers marked where cartridge cases and other evidence had been found.

Hoffman walked up to the barrier tape and showed his badge. "What have we got?" he asked the officer standing by the tape.

"John Doe under the sheet there got shot more times than was good for him."

Hoffman noticed the notebook on the officer's hand. "You the primary?"

"Yeah, lucky me." Hoffman got the needed information from the officer. He caught the lab tech's eye and motioned for her to come over. With all the evidence in the alley he didn't want to cross the tape and disturb any of it.

Careful not to step on anything, the tech gingerly made her way to Hoffman. "Evening, Detective, how are things?"

"They've been better, Carol. Run it down for me."

"This one's a mess. Victim's got multiple gunshot wounds. There's a blood trail leading into the yard of the fifth house back on the right. There's a bullet in the back doorframe. There are more cartridge cases and bullets out here than I have numbers for. From the looks of things they stood over him and fired until he stopped twitching. Once the M.E. moves the body we'll probably find additional bullets under him."

"Any witnesses," Hoffman asked the primary officer.

"The usual number for this area."

"In other words, everybody heard it, nobody saw it."

"That's the way it is around here, detective. The smart ones, they hear gunfire, they drop and hope that a stray doesn't come through their window. Anyone who does see anything knows if they talk to us they're the next one under the sheet."

Hoffman shook his head. He left the alley and walked around to the front of the block. Five houses down he saw an officer standing in the front doorway. He identified himself and went inside. In the kitchen, he found another lab tech dusting for prints. He nodded a greeting and went out the back door, pausing to look at the bullet hole in the frame. In the yard, he saw the beginning of the blood trail that ended in the alley under the sheet. Having reviewed the entire scene, he went back inside and began the routine of investigating yet another drug murder.

The next day, after returning from the medical examiner's office where he had witnessed the autopsy, Hoffman was called into his lieutenant's office.

"Any progress on last night's murder?" his superior asked him.

"Bullets and casings from the scene, no witnesses. Prints but no matches yet. I'm waiting for the victim's prints to come back from Ident. Once we know who he is I'll have an idea of where to go next."

"His prints are back." The lieutenant handed him a report. Hoffman read it with surprise. This wasn't just a drug murder anymore. The victim, identified as Dyson Jones, had been a trooper with the State Police, detailed to the city for undercover work.

"He was a cop," Hoffman finally said.

"That's right, and you're telling me that we don't have lead one."

Hoffman nodded. In his mind he quickly went over every step he had taken last night. Was there anything he hadn't done that he should have? No, he decided. The investigation of what had been believed to be a drug dealer had been as thorough as if everyone had known the dead man was one of their own.

"Do what ever you have to, Amos," his boss told him. "Sweep the streets. Search every vacant house. Hell, search all the houses if you think that will help. Bring in every junkie, dealer and hooker in the area – sweat 'em, buy 'em or break 'em. Just find the bastards."

II

The evening news told the story of the murdered officer. Dyson Jones was brought in from the Eastern Shore as part of a drug task force. His undercover identity was somehow revealed and he was murdered by the gang he was trying to infiltrate. Police were following every lead and expected an arrest shortly.

"That means they don't have any idea who did it," Father Richard Harper told his sexton when the commercial break came on. "I see Amos has the case," he added as almost an afterthought. The TV station had run the footage its cameraman had taken the night before on the scene. After a quick pan of the alley showing the covered body, the camera focused on the activities of the investigators – the officers knocking on doors, the crime lab taking measurements, Amos Hoffman in the alley studying the blood trail.

"Lewis, I know that you're reluctant to go after drug dealers, especially after ..."

"I am not reluctant," interrupted the sexton. "It is just that it does little good. Destroy one gang and another takes its place. The drug trade will not stop until people no longer want drugs. Until then, it is like trying to stop the tide from coming in." Lewis was silent a minute then added,

"This case, however, has less to do with drugs than with the murder of a police officer and the viciousness with which he was killed. I'll start tonight."

"First you should find out what Amos has," Harper suggested. "If the case is going good, then back away. If not, then the Grey Monk should intervene. Do you want me to call him?"

"No need. It's past time that he and I met."

III

Another long night. Hoffman had spent part of it going over evidence from the Lab, what little there was of it. Blood from the scene was being prepared for DNA comparison, in case someone other than Dyson had been injured. But from the blood trial it looked like Dyson was the only one bleeding. Ballistics results told him that three different guns had been used, two 9mms and one .380. An open case search revealed that the bullets and cartridge cases from the scene matched those from previous shootings and murders in the area. None of those crimes were close to being solved either. And while the Lab had recovered plenty of fingerprints from the house, no names came up when they were run through the Ident Computer.

"Give us a name or a gun, we'll match them for you," the Lab people had told him. "No miracles this time."

If I had a name or a gun, I wouldn't need you, Hoffman thought bitterly. He looked at the phone. It had been strangely silent all night. No one calling in any tips on this one. No witnesses coming forward. Hoffman had a folder thick with Lab and police reports, crime scene photos, diagrams and canvass statements. He would have traded it all for a single sheet of paper with just one name on it.

It was past midnight, Hoffman finally noticed. He wasn't doing any good sitting in the office. He'd go home, start fresh tomorrow morning.

As the detective went down to the Headquarters garage, he mentally made a list of what he had to do. Check back with the Drug Enforcement Unit for their list of local drug gangs. See if any of the neighborhood bad guys had been in trouble over on the Shore. Get with the Task Force members to see if Dyson had left any notes behind or made any kind of report. All that, and he had to meet with State Police detectives tomorrow as well. It was their man who had been killed and they wanted in on the investigation.

Hoffman paused at the door between the HQ building and the police garage. As usual, he paused to take several deep breaths, willing away his stress and calming himself for the ride home. He had promised his wife that he'd never bring the job home, and this ritual helped him start to leave what worries and concerns he had about his case behind him. It was never entirely successfully, but he usually did manage to arrive home in a better mood than when he left work.

Once he began to feel more relaxed, Hoffman opened the door and stepped into the dark garage. Not for the first time did he think that if this were commercial parking, he'd have his hand on his gun until he was safely strapped in behind his wheel. The Department had not overspent on its parking facilities. The fluorescent lights were dim and widely spaced. Some had missing or burnt out tubes. It made Hoffman wonder just where the millions of dollars in the police budget went. It certainly did not come anywhere near this place, he thought.

Since he parked in or near the same space every day, Hoffman found his car more by habit than by sight. He had his key out and was unlocking his door when an icy whisper called,

"Detective Hoffman."

Hoffman straightened. He turned left and right, looking up and down the garage ramps. Nothing there, nothing but darkness and shadows. Then one of the shadows stepped forward.

The figure that emerged from the darkness was clad in a charcoal grey monk's habit. The cowl covering its head was pulled forward so that even in good light it would be difficult to see the face it hid.

The Grey Monk. Hoffman didn't know whether to admire the audacity of the vigilante for daring to invade police headquarters, or to cry out and raise the alarm. No, at his first yell the Monk would be gone. There was no way for Hoffman to hold him alone without using his weapon, and the Monk had helped the police too many times in the past to deserve that.

"What do you want?" Hoffman asked the hooded man before him, and instantly answered his own question. "The Dyson case." The Monk's cowled head bowed in a nod. "I thought I told Harper that I wanted nothing more to do with you."

"I do not answer to the priest or to you," came the whispered reply. Despite its low tones, Hoffman heard every word clearly. "I've come to offer my services. However, if they are not needed, if you are so close to an arrest that an extra pair of eyes on the street, one more man looking for the killer, one more gun to bring him down cannot help you, I'll be gone."

The Monk took a step backwards, and the shadows began to envelope him. Let him go, came a voice inside Hoffman's head. You don't need his kind of justice. Hoffman remembered the last case on which he was helped by the Monk – a woman killed and a man burned to death, both at the hands of the Grey Monk.

But the Monk had solved that case, as he had others that had stymied the police. And with no witnesses, no suspects and no real evidence, Hoffman needed all the help he could get. Hating himself, he called to the fading specter.

"Wait!" The Grey Monk paused. "I could use your help, whatever you can do. But leave the killers for us. You find them, you tell me where they are. Dyson was a cop."

"I understand, Detective," whispered the Monk. "You wish to avenge your own." The two men heard a car start on a ramp above them. "Call Harper," the Monk said quickly. "Tell him what you can." Then he disappeared into the darkness.

Hoffman took a step after him, then two, then he stopped. And what, he thought, would I do if I caught him? He went back to his car. A few deep breaths later, he was ready to drive home.

From police headquarters, the Grey Monk drove to Carey St. Parking on a secluded side street, he stayed with the shadows until he was standing in the alley where Dyson Jones had died. What few houses were not boarded up appeared abandoned. For all the signs of life he saw, he could have been on an old movie set, one in which they were shooting a story about a plague that had robbed the city of its inhabitants. The filming had ended and the crew had gone home without striking the set.

No movie, thought the Monk, but the plague was real. Drugs had taken the life from many parts of this city, some areas more than others. Here it was worse, with those who had not fled huddled behind closed doors, afraid for themselves and their children.

The Monk had tried to end it once, a crusade that ended in frustration and near disaster. At war with the drug gangs, the Monk had been led into a trap and almost killed. He recovered and in turn sprung his own trap. Tremaine, the dealer who had tried for his life, was arrested and his organization shattered. All to no avail. Within weeks, new dealers had arrived and taken over the area.

Walking through the alley, the Monk made no attempt at concealment. There was no need. The alley was poorly lit, with light poles at either end and one in the middle. The dim glow from these lights did more to deepen the shadows than banish them. No lights shone from any of the houses. No one would be watching.

The beam from the Monk's flashlight broke the darkness. Rats scurried away as the Monk found a fading blood trail. He followed it to the house where the trap had been sprung.

Other than pulling the door shut and letting the knob lock catch, the police had not bothered to secure the building. A moment's work with a knife blade and the Monk was inside.

Use the flash or risk the light? The Monk tried the wall switch and found that the power was out. His flashlight beam played around the room. He noted the hole in the doorway from where the police had dug out a bullet. Black powder covered all the smooth surfaces. Looking through the rest of the house he found nothing but the signs of a police search.

Returning to the kitchen, the Monk reflected on how close he had come to Dyson Jones's fate. He too had once entered a house only to be met with gunfire. His gun already drawn, the Monk had attacked rather than retreat. Had he retreated, the Monk had no doubt that, like Jones, he would have been cut down as he left the building. He had been lucky. Although seriously wounded, he had escaped Tremaine.

"There but for the Grace of God," the Monk whispered, again giving thanks to his Creator for having delivered him from the same kind of trap that had snared the fallen officer.

The crime scene now fixed in his mind, there was nothing more for the Monk to do. He left the house the way he had entered, pulling the door shut after him.

Something bright suddenly flashed. Still on the back porch, the Monk stopped. Slowly, his hand reached for the doorknob. Ready to force his way back inside should a haven be needed, the Monk waited for the flash to repeat. He heard nothing but the scurrying of rodents. He saw nothing but the shadows. A minute, then two, then five went by. Nothing. Ten minutes and still nothing. Just as the Monk felt it safe to leave, there was another flash. And this time he caught what it was.

The west end of the alley opened on to Lafayette Ave. Like those on Carey, the houses on this block were dark. But someone in one of those houses had pulled back a curtain, letting light from the bedroom shine out on the night. Anywhere else in the city this light would have been swallowed by the general glare of the street. Here, it shone like a beacon.

The curtain dropped back and the light went out. Again the Monk waited and again after ten minutes the light appeared. Someone was watching the alley.

A member of the drug gang that killed Jones? No, why would they watch a house they had abandoned? The police, waiting to see if anyone returned to the house? The light flashed again and the Monk realized that neither group would be so careless. He laughed quietly to himself when he realized who the watcher might be. If he was correct, it might be the first break in this case.

Timing his movements to the flashes of light, the Monk walked down the alley toward Lafayette. He moved only when he was sure the watcher was at the window. Although he could have easily avoided the area lit by the center alley light, as little illumination it put out, he made a point of passing under it, allowing himself to be seen. Soon he was at the west mouth of the alley. Hugging the darkness, he made sure that the street was clear then crossed when the light again appeared. Going up to the house, he mounted the steps to the front porch. Then he knocked on the front door.

The Monk waited. He could hear no signs of movement inside. He knocked again and again waited. He was considering whether it was advisable to force entry and risk startling the resident when he heard the sound of someone approaching. The door opened. An elderly woman answered the door.

Standing there, she looked the Monk up and down, mostly up, as he towered over her five-foot height. "I saw you," she said in a voice graveled with age. "I watched you go into that house of death. You're Him, aren't you?"

"Who?" replied the Monk.

"The Angel of Death."

"I have been," the Monk said honestly, "but not tonight, and not for you. Tonight I seek those who bring death. May I come in?" The woman stepped aside and let the Monk enter. "Thank you, Miss...?"

"Watkins, Dorothea Watkins. And it's Mrs. Been widowed for ten years now. You took my Joe in a car accident. You after those men what killed the police officer?"

"I am. Did you see them in the alley?"

Mrs. Watkins nodded her head. "Not much left to do but look out and watch the world go by. I saw them, every other night or so they were in that house. They weren't selling out of it. But men would go in and out. Sometimes one or two, sometimes more. But they're not there no more. Of course you know that. Can I get you something? Coffee? Tea?"

"No, thank you. Where else have you seen these men?"

Mrs. Watkins went to the living room window. The Monk joined as she pointed out to the street. "Fourth house up from the far corner, across the street. They started going in there a few nights before the shooting. Haven't been back since, but they will. They're just waiting for the police to stop coming around."

"Thank you, Mrs. Watkins. You've been a great help." The Monk started to leave, then said, "You should really turn out your bedroom light when you look out."

Mrs. Watkins smiled. "I normally do," she said. "But then how would you have known to come here?"

Leaving Mrs. Watkins, the Monk would have liked to have taken the time to search the house she had pointed out. But it was near dawn and time to return to St. Sebastian's. Father Harper would need help in setting up for Mass, and afterwards there were his sexton duties to perform. And having chosen darkness as his ally, the Monk felt uncomfortable in the daylight.

IV

It was almost four when Lewis woke up and joined Father Harper in his study. The priest was behind his desk, studying a police case folder. "I see Hoffman's been here."

"Yes," Harper replied holding up the folder. "He left this, along with a very pointed message for you."

"I can only imagine." Lewis sat down in front of Harper desk, taking the offered folder.

"Let's see if I can recall what he said." Harper leaned back and closed his eyes, remembering the detective's brief visit. "He came in here, threw the file on my desk and yelled, 'Here, I'm sure that spook's called you. He's helping with the Dyson Jones case, and tell him to make sure that's all he does – help. I want his killers alive. If the Monk takes them down, he becomes my next project.'"

"And if it can't be helped?" Lewis asked.

"That's what I asked. And to that Amos said, 'He better help it. I mean it, Rich. I don't like the Monk. He's a loose cannon that's going to roll back on you one of these days.' There was more, but all along the same lines."

"If he doesn't trust me, why use my help?"

"Because, Lewis, he has a dead cop and nothing to go on. He needs you, and he hates needing you. He hates that you can do things he can't, that you're outside the law he's sworn to uphold."

Harper gestured to the folder. "Look in there and you'll see why he's frustrated. Six months ago new product began to flood the West side. Better quality, cheaper price. All the junkies wanted some. The other dealers couldn't compete. Some joined up, others fought back in the usual way. A few of the new sellers were killed, shot down in the street. Retaliation followed." Harper shook his head. "Business as usual in this city. Within a month things settled down. Word was there was a new boss on the street and there were only three ways to go – work with him, get out of the game, or say goodbye to your loved ones."

"Who is this new boss?" Lewis asked.

Harper shook his head. "If they knew that, Hoffman wouldn't need you. The street dealers only know their suppliers. The suppliers get their instructions by cell phone, pager or email. The enforcement team is separate. Arrests were made, but they didn't lead anywhere."

"They must have made some arrests. Haven't they been able to trace them through the phones or pagers?"

"They're all using pre-paid phones – use them and toss them. No accounts to access. Either that or it's stolen phones with cloned numbers. Same with the pagers. The emails are all from Web-based services, accessible from any computer."

"And the computers used to send the emails?" Lewis already knew the answer. It was how he was setting up his network of informants and contacts.

"They had to go to the State Police Computer Crimes Unit. They traced two – a public library and a community college. Both available to anyone who walks in."

"Why was Jones brought in?"

"After three months the Task Force had nothing. As is usual in these cases, they had someone from outside brought in, a new face that no one should know. Jones passed himself off as just coming down from New York. He made the right connections and was supposed to be brought into the gang. Somehow his cover was blown."

"Tremaine."

"What about him?" asked Harper.

"He's involved. He plans things out very well, remember? And the trap he set for Jones, identical to the one he caught me in."

"But you can't be sure. For all you know Tremaine is still in prison. He should be, he went up for distribution. It's been less than two years."

"No, Father. I followed his case. Tremaine's lawyers cut a deal. He pled to possession. He could be out by now."

Harper picked up the phone. "I'll check with Hoffman, he should know."

Lewis stopped him. "Don't. I'd rather Hoffman not know, not yet. I'll check with another source."

"Another source?"

"You seem surprised, Father. There are others beside yourself who aid me. Some are those who know that if they do not, their minor sins will be reveled to the police. They'd rather help me than be arrested. Some of those I have helped in the past have offered to return that help. Finally, there are those like yourself, people willing to risk their jobs and freedom for the sake of justice."

"And where do you find these people?"

"Like Mrs. Watkins, sometimes they find me. When the need is there, the Lord provides."

A phone call later, Lewis had his information.

"Tremaine is out. He was paroled eight months ago."

"Long enough to set things up," Harper observed. "What will you do now? Call Hoffman and give him his suspect."

Lewis gave a dry chuckle. "I wish it were that easy. Beyond our suspicions, there is no proof that Tremaine is the one. Once it's dark, I will go out and see if I can learn more."

As evening faded into night, Lewis went into the church sacristy. He opened the wardrobe where the vestments hung. Moving them aside, he pressed a hook in the back. A hidden panel opened to show an inner closet. There hung the habit of the Grey Monk. A brace of .45 automatics hung next to it. Lewis quickly dressed.

Going down the steps into the basement church, the Monk entered a tunnel that lead to the rectory. A side door let him out into a darkened alley. The Grey Monk walked out into the night.

V

It had been a long day for Kim Yung. But then, every day was long. The early morning hours were spent at the markets, finding the best produce, meats and fish at good prices, and trying not to get cheated by those fools who thought that Asian meant stupid. Then back to his Lanvale St. grocery store by nine to stock the shelves and freezers and wait on the deliverymen. Open at ten, close at six, leave at seven to spend a few precious hours with his family before doing it all over again. Kim would be glad when his children were old enough to help. Not because the work was hard. He enjoyed hard work, but because it would give him more time with them.

There was a time when Kim would not have thought to bring his family into the store. While it was the best he could afford, it was not a safe place. In the first year he had been open, he'd been robbed six times, beaten twice and shot at once. He was saving to buy a store in a better neighborhood and hoping he'd survive until he could. Then things changed.

It was last year. He was leaving the store late, even for him. Problems with the beverage cooler had caused Kim to stay past nine p.m. As he locked up, he felt rather than saw the two men approach. He turned slowly, knowing what was going to happen, again.

They stood on either side of him. With his back to the store, there was no retreat. "You know the drill," the taller one said in a young man's voice. "Give it up." Both men were wearing dark clothing and black knit caps pulled low. Even if he could see their faces both he and they knew he'd never describe them to police, if he even bothered to call them. He'd called many times before and nothing ever got better.

Moving slow, Kim reached into his pocket and took out his wallet, hoping it would be enough. The store receipts were in an inner pocket of his coat. He could not afford to give them up, not again.

The smaller one took the wallet and looked through it. "Not enough, slant." From somewhere he pulled out a pistol. "You better have more."

Unwisely, Kim said, "There is no more." His voice was pleading, apologetic. To beg thus to such as these shamed him, but would not give up the money his family needed.

"Then you're no more. Too bad, slant." As the pistol leveled in his direction, he realized that his family needed him more than the money and in seconds would have neither.

The shot came, but from a distance. The man with the gun fell at his feet. The other began to run but froze when a whisper from the far side of the grave issued a single command, "Stop."

The would-be robber stood still. He knew what had killed his buddy. He had heard talk of a ghost that haunted the night, one who showed little mercy to those who broke the law. As he felt the cold barrel of a large pistol against the back of his neck, he knew the talk was true.

After the shot had felled the gunman, Kim looked up to see a shadow leave the darkness. A man in a hooded grey robe walked up and put his gun up against the head of the other assailant.

"Listen carefully, and you will live. This store, this man will be left alone. He and all his fellow merchants are under the protection of the Grey Monk. If any harm comes to them, I will find the ones responsible. I am not the police. My justice is swift, sure and final. If you doubt me, look down at your friend. You do not want to share his fate."

The Grey Monk pushed the robber away from him.

"Go," came the whispered order, and the man fled.

From the depths of his cowl the Monk addressed Kim. "I doubt if one warning will be enough." He looked at the corpse at his feet. He might have sighed. "It will take more deaths before they understand." Then he stepped back into the night.

There were more deaths. From what he heard, both from customers in his store and from other grocers, three other men were killed trying to rob stores in the area. Kim Yung did not know how much effect these deaths had on crime. He only knew that since that night, he had not been robbed.

Kim was not thinking of the Grey Monk as he closed out his register. The first he knew of his visitor was when a shadow fell over him. He looked and saw the man who had saved him a year before.

Though surprised, Kim felt no fear. The Monk had saved him once. He would not harm him now.

"What do you hear of drugs, Kim Yung?" the Monk asked. "Who is buying, who is selling?"

Kim owed this man a life debt. He would gladly repay it as often as needed. "I know little directly, sir. No one speaks to me about it."

"But they talk while in your store. They talk and in their ignorance may assume you do not understand. What have you heard?"

Kim shook his head. "Not very much. I have heard about a new gang, one that now controls much of the street. Sometimes strangers come in. Nice clothes, full wallets."

"Nothing else? No names, places?" If there was disappointment in the voice Kim did not hear it.

"No, nothing" The Monk started to leave. Kim searched his memory for something that might help. Finally, he called out, "Wait."

The Monk turned back to him.

"A few months ago, I think two of these men came in. They were talking about someone. The 'tree man' I think they said."

"Thank you," said the Monk as he left through the back.

VI

When he woke up, Harper had been surprised to find breakfast on the table. Lewis had had an early night. Over pancakes the sexton told him of what he learned.

When Lewis finished, Harper said, "'Tree man.' It's close to Tremaine, I'll give you that."

"Close enough, Father," Lewis said. "Close enough that I'm now sure with whom we are dealing."

"But you still don't want me calling Hoffman?"

"No. One more night. The house that Mrs. Watkins told me of – I want to check it out. It may be another trap."

"Which you'll walk into – again."

"Not again," Lewis corrected. "Is a trap really a trap if one is ready for it? This time I'll be walking in prepared."

"And if it's not a trap?"

"Then I will wait, and watch, and learn. When I know enough, I will act."

"Just make sure," Harper reminded him, "that when you act it's to call Hoffman. And not just to come pick up the bodies."

"Of course, Father. Dead men cannot tell me where to find Tremaine. I'll have to leave one of them alive."

That night the Monk watched from Mrs. Watkins's window as two men, then a third went into the house on Lafayette Ave. He waited a while longer then handed the binoculars he had been using to his host.

"Keep these," he told her. "With them you'll see more."

"I couldn't," she protested.

"Yes, you can. Keep watch for me, tonight especially. Watch that house after I go in. If others come, call me." He handed her a cell phone. "The red button will alert me. After tonight, use it if there is something I should know, if you're willing."

"You might just be the Angel of Death, Mr. Monk – my death if this comes out. But I can't sit by and do nothing." She took the phone. "Give 'em Hell."

"If necessary I will give them to Hell," he assured her.

Mindful of a trap, the Monk carefully made his way across the street. Feeling Mrs. Watkins's eyes on him, he entered the house. Guns drawn, ready to fire at the slightest movement, he found himself in a long hallway. In front were the stairs to the second floor, to his left a doorway to the living room and the rest of the house. He went through the open doorway.

Light from the outside street lamps came in the front window. It was just enough for the Monk to see back to the kitchen. Beyond that was blackness. Moving slowly, feeling his way across the rubble covered floor, relying on senses other than sight, the Monk moved towards the back of the house. At the end of the living room he passed a small passage that led back to the stairs and the longer hall. He crossed the dining room by feel, his sandaled feet sliding across the floor, his arms out in front of him, feeling for objects that might block his path.

Reaching the kitchen, he stood in the doorway. A closed door was to his right – the basement stairs. The Monk risked a light, the beam from his flash sweeping the area. No one there. The back door, he noted, had long ago been boarded shut. No one could leave or enter by that route.

Up or down, the Monk wondered. If not here, then they were on the second floor or in the basement. Either could be an ambush, with the basement the better choice. There, gunmen could be waiting, with more upstairs ready to close the trap. Unlike an upper floor, there would be no windows to jump from. No doubt the squeaking of the basement door as it opened would warn those below. Steeling himself for what was to come, even if it was his own final judgment, the Monk opened the basement door.

He had been wrong about one thing. The door didn't squeak. It opened silently on well-oiled hinges. The Monk peered down the stairway. Again there was nothing but darkness. Stepping lightly down the open stairs, ready to return fire each time a tread creaked under his weight, the Monk made his way down. Midway, he flashed his light first to the front, then the back. The back door was boarded over. The grime-encrusted windows in front were thick with cobwebs. On the dirt floor in between were puddles of stagnant water, rodent droppings and odd pieces of brick and wood.

The second floor then. He'd have the advantage. With no one at his rear, he could face his foes without worry. If necessary, a line of retreat was open. But there were only three of them. He did not expect to have to retreat.

He also did not expect to find the upstairs as vacant as the rest of the house. Searching the second floor with the same care as he did the first floor and basement, the Monk found it just as empty. Somehow the three men had departed without his noticing.

Had they left when he was in the basement? No, he had anticipated that and was listening for sounds of their leaving. The basement door had been as secure as the kitchen door. They had not left that way. There was no exit from the second floor. How then had they left?

The Monk decided to ask Mrs. Watkins. The widow had no doubt been watching from her window. She could tell him how and when they had left. The Monk started down the stairs when he heard the sounds of footsteps coming up from the basement.

Impossible. The Monk had thoroughly checked the basement. It had been empty. But impossible or not, there was more than one man coming up from there now.

The Monk stood midway on the stairs to the second floor. Hidden in the darkness, he waited for the men to come up to the first floor.

The footsteps below ceased. There was a pause, then a slam. One of the men must have pushed opened the basement door. Then he heard footsteps coming toward him.

"So when's the boss coming to see the new digs?" The Monk heard one of them say. Making no effort to be quiet, they obviously did not know he was there. His guns were drawn. From his position on the steps, he could rain death down on them if he chose to do so. Instead, he moved further back into the shadows and listened.

"Not for a while," another answered. The men had by now passed by the stairs and were going down the front toward the front door. "Tremaine's doing the 9 to 5. He's playing it straight, keeping his PO happy. Works the day, stays home at night or goes to the library or movies. He ain't gonna give 'em any excuse to violate him back to the Pen."

"Smart," said the third voice. "Another few months of that and he be free and clear. Then he can …" The men left, closing the door behind them.

Leaving the mystery of how the men came up from an empty basement for later, the Monk moved rapidly to the entrance. He opened the door and carefully peered out in time to see two of the men walking east while the third walked west. He followed the lone man and watched as he got into a car parked around the corner. Noting the license tag, he then returned to the house.

Once inside, the Monk paused to call Mrs. Watkins. The woman answered on the first ring. "Yes?" She sounded worried.

"Everything is fine," the Monk assured her. "What did you see?"

"I saw you go in, then a short while later I saw the three men come out. You followed one of them. Then you went back in again."

"Thank you, Mrs. Watkins. I may be in here for some time, if you wish to get some sleep."

"Plenty of time to sleep when I've passed over. I'll be watching. I'll call if they come back."

The Monk closed the connection and returned to the basement. Again the light from his flash cut through the darkness. Again there was nothing but the skittering of insects and rodents disturbed by his light.

He played his light around the walls. All of them seemed solid. There was nothing there but some 4x8 paneling propped up against one of the long walls. He descended to the bottom and turned his attention to the floor.

The dirt floor was damp. It held the shoeprints of the men who had walked on it. The Monk saw several sets from different shoes leading from the steps towards the front of the basement. Following them, he was led to the wood paneling.

Could it be? The wood was leaning against the wall at an angle. He shone his light behind it. Rather than reflecting off the wall behind it the beam of light showed him a large hole cut into the wall.

The Monk pushed the paneling aside. With his light, he traced the opening. Properly shored up, so as to support the weight of the wall above it, it formed a doorway to the house next door.

Crouching down, the Monk entered the passage. When he turned to move the paneling back in place he found that handles had been attached for that purpose. The hole covered, he stood to examine his surroundings.

By the light of his flash the Monk saw that this basement was just as empty. Standing in one place, he looked for and found more shoeprints. These led him to the stairs. Following them, he carefully made his way to the first floor.

Bright lights greeted him when he opened the door from the basement stairs. The Monk was momentarily blinded. He quickly pulled back to the stairwell, pulling the door shut behind him. Hearing no sounds of anyone approaching, he cautiously opened the door again, this time more slowly, giving his eyes time to adapt to the light.

The house had been fixed up as a workplace. Shielded from the outside by the boards that covered the doors and windows, it was as remote as if in the country. The living room seemed to be storage – small envelopes, vials, jars of cutting agents and other chemicals the modern drug dealer needs to prepare and package his merchandise. Everything there but the drugs themselves.

The Monk went further back into the house. What would have been the dining room was now the packaging area. Scales and glassine envelopes were on the table, waiting for the poison to be weighed and bagged. In the kitchen was the laboratory, where pure drugs were diluted to street level product.

On the second floor were a bathroom and two serviceable bedrooms. Wet towels showed that the bathroom at least had been recently used.

Very nice, the Monk thought as he returned to the basement, and very safe. A boarded up row home was above suspicion. And should the police investigate any activity next door, they would do just what the Monk had done – take a quick glance through a seemingly empty basement before moving on. He wondered how many other places like this Tremaine had throughout the area.

The Monk had not discovered any drugs. He supposed that Tremaine's men carried it in with them and carried the finished product out for distribution. Safer that way. Should the house be discovered, nothing important would be lost. And the penalties for possession of drug paraphernalia, in whatever amount, were far less than that of possession of narcotics with intent to distribute.

Before leaving, the Monk again called Mrs. Watkins. "You may rest now," he told her. "I am through here for the night."

VII

After Mass that morning, Lewis explained to Harper what he had found.

"So, we call Amos and have him set up a stake out inside the vacant house. Tremaine's boys come in, they get busted and rat out their boss. Case closed."

"I wish it were that simple, Father. But there is no proof that the men who came out of that house were involved in Jones's murder. Nor is there any guarantee that once arrested they will implicate Tremaine. He would no doubt reward such a betrayal with violence, either against the men or their families. And there is another consideration."

"Which is?"

Lewis shook his head. "A suspicion of mine, one that should be tested before voiced. Call Hoffman, give him the license number of the car the one man was driving. Let us see where that leads. If back to the house, well and good. It might be as you said. No, wait." Lewis said as Harper picked up the phone, "Call later. Let me first prepare the way."

McHenry St. – a mile south from where Dyson Jones was gunned down – a slightly better neighborhood. This was where the Grey Monk's contact at the Motor Vehicle Administration told him Lamont Turner, the owner of the car, lived.

The car the Monk had seen drive away from Lafayette Ave. was parked in the middle of the block, only two doors down from the house he wanted. From an areaway across the street, the Monk had watched it pull up and Turner get out. He waited as the man went into the house and watched the light in the front bedroom come on and go out.

Going around to the back, the Monk counted the back yards until he came to the one he needed to enter. A dark alley, no signs of a dog in the yard, a cheap lock on the door – the Monk's entry was quick and easy.

Silently, the Monk crept to the front bedroom. Turner was alone in bed, asleep. He quickly searched the rest of the house. No one else was there. The Monk returned to Turner's room.

Lamont Turner was dreaming the dreams of the unjust. A gloved hand covered his mouth and nose, interrupting his images of women, money, liquor and more women. He woke, gasping for breath. A bright light shone into his eyes, which he quickly shut. He groped under his pillow, looking for a gun that was no longer there.

An icy whisper called his name. "Lamont Turner."

Turner froze. He knew that voice, knew it from talk on the street. It was the voice of the Grey Monk. Few had heard it and lived.

Slowly Turner opened his eyes. As they adjusted to the light he first saw a dark shape. This resolved itself into a man, if man it was, who wore a grey robe. His head was covered. Turner made no effort to look into the hood. Word varied as to what was under there – scars from acid or fire, a skull bare of flesh, an ugliness enough to scare a man to death. There was even a rumor that if you could look past the hood, you would see your own face staring back. One thing was sure, to see the face of the Grey Monk was to die. Turner made no sudden moves.

"Tremaine, where does he live?" the Monk demanded.

Turner shook his head. "He'd kill me."

The Monk brought up a 9mm, Turner's own gun. He held it before Turner's face. "Die now. Die later. Choose." Turner sputtered an address. He let out a breath he didn't know he had been holding as the Monk moved the gun away from him.

"The police will be here soon. You will wait for them here, in your bed."

"I ain't talking to them."

"I do not care," came the surprising reply. "Talk or remain silent. Protect Tremaine or give him up. That does not matter to me. His days are almost at an end. I have numbered them. You will remain in bed and await the police."

The Monk moved to the doorway. He placed the nine on the dresser. A .45 quickly replaced it. With his free hand he took out a cell phone. "Make the call," he said into it. Then he left the room.

No sooner was the Monk gone than Turner moved to get out of bed. If that ghost thought he was just going to wait for the cops he was – he couldn't move his leg, not far. It was only then that he felt a ring of cold metal around it. He lifted the blanket and saw the cuff that shackled him to the bedpost. He looked over at his gun, the gun that he had used to blow away that cop, the gun that he knew would be just out of reach. Turner had been done and done good. He laid back on the bed and waited for the cops, wondering if they'd believe him when he claimed that the gun had been planted.

VIII

The news the next day was not good. Lewis and Harper sat watching a picture of the front door of the house on McHenry St. as the TV anchor did her voice-over of what had happened there after the Monk had left.

"Acting on a tip from an anonymous informant," she began, "police today raided the home of Lamont Turner. The caller had informed police that Turner was one of the men involved in the shooting death of State Trooper Dyson Jones, who was gunned down in an alley not too far away from where Turner lived. According to a police spokesman, when members of the Drug Enforcement Task Force broke into the house, they were met by Turner in an upstairs bedroom."

The police department's public information officer then appeared on the screen.

"The Task Force," he explained in a most sincere voice, "led by Sgt. Brian McKenzie entered the suspect's home at four a.m. They were confronted by the suspect in the front bedroom. He produced a gun, a 9mm semi-automatic pistol, and pointed it at them. Sgt. McKenzie was in the lead. To protect his men, the sergeant had no choice but to shoot and kill the

```
suspect. Subsequent test on the gun showed that it was one
of the weapons used in the murder of Trooper Jones."
```

A voice off camera asked if the killing was necessary, if the police had not just gunned Turner down for killing a fellow officer. The spokesman dismissed this charge.

```
    "Of course not. First of all, there was no proof that
Turner was involved in Trooper Jones's death, not at that
time. There was just the word of an informant. Secondly, if
he was involved, we definitely wanted Turner alive, to be
questioned as to who else was involved."
```

The spokesman went on to say how the officers involved had been placed on administrative leave pending a review of the shooting. A reporter started to interview Turner's neighbors. Some of those believed that he had got what was coming to him. Others held that despite being a drug dealer and a cop killer, the police had no right to gun a man down, no matter if he was pointing a weapon at them. They should have given him a chance to surrender. The remainder told of how this was always a nice neighborhood and they couldn't believe that this was happening here. Harper switched off the set.

"Turner could not have reached the gun," Lewis said. His voice was calm, almost analytical. "He could not have freed himself."

"You're saying that Sgt. McKenzie killed Turner in cold blood, that he executed him for killing Jones."

"Father, there was a reason that I asked you to call in that tip from a pay phone, and to the Task Force rather than Hoffman. Jones was an experienced undercover officer. While it is possible that he made a mistake that led to his downfall, it is not likely. It is more likely that someone betrayed him, someone who knew that he was a police officer. The only ones in the city who knew were other officers."

Harper was thoughtful. "It's possible," he finally conceded. The priest had once been a cop. He knew that there was corruption in even the most honest of departments.

"If there was a traitor, he would no doubt be in the Task Force. That would explain its lack of success against Tremaine."

A sudden realization hit Harper. "Turner was bait. That was why you had me call the Task Force instead of Hoffman – to see if there was a traitor. No way would the inside man have let Turner start talking. So you staked Turner out as a Judas goat to draw him out. The poor s.o.b. never had a chance."

"He had a better chance than he gave Dyson Jones," Lewis replied coldly. "There might not have been an inside man. And if there was, he might not have had the opportunity to deal with Turner. As it turned out, a possible traitor has been identified and Turner met the end he deserved."

Harper shook his head. "How can you sit there and discuss the taking of human life so calmly?" he asked. "You chained a man to a bed and left him to be killed, just to flush out a suspect." Harper held up his hand. "I know, 'Vengeance is mine, says the Lord,' and you act as His agent. I've heard it before. But God is more than vengeance. He is love and mercy. Where is that in what you do?"

Lewis sighed. "Father … Richard, I have sometimes wondered that myself. Am I truly doing His work? Are my methods too harsh? There are nights I have stood in the shadows, watching as yet another man I have shot down is taken away. I ask myself if I presume too much. Are my ways His ways?

"I remember a poet from my college days," Lewis continued, "Edward Young. He wrote 'A God all mercy is a God Unjust.' I believe that. God grants His mercy to those who ask it of Him. For those who don't, there is only His justice.

"I only know," the Grey Monk told the priest, "that I do as I feel called to do, and I pray that I am doing the right thing whenever I go out into the just Lord's night."

Both men were silent for a time. Finally, Harper asked, "Will you be going out?"

"Not tonight. Let things sit for a time and settle down. Tomorrow or the day after will be time enough."

IX

Andray Davis and Andre Smith – they called themselves the A-team, after that show running on cable. They'd been together since high school. Went to jail together once, which only cemented the bond between them. Together with Lamont Turner they ran the Lafayette Ave. house for Tremaine.

After Turner got killed, the two stayed away from the house for a few days. Tremaine had other places they could work from, so the deliveries still got made on time. Finally, after driving by and seeing nothing wrong – nobody pretending to be hanging out on the corner, no delivery trucks parked at odd hours or vans with one-way windows, no new junkies lying in doorways, in other words, no sign of cop – they felt it safe to go back in and start things up again.

There had been talk of how Turner had been made, who had ratted him out and what Tremaine would do once he found him. Between the two of them, they decided that Lamont had just done or said something stupid, and got a dime dropped on him as some sort of payback. Bad luck for him, good luck for them that the cops did him before he talked.

Mrs. Watkins was at her window when the self-styled A-team returned to Lafayette St. She pressed the auto dial on her cell phone, let it ring twice and hung up. Down in a dark basement, the vibration of a similar phone told the Grey Monk that the two men were on their way.

"So, Andre, is Tremaine going to get us any more help?"

"Yeah. Didn't you see the ad in the papers Sunday? Packager wanted for drug lab. Call Tremaine at 443-" Coming into the house, the two men were talking loud enough for the Monk to hear them in the basement. The conversation continued as they went through the house and down the stairs.

"Shut up, fool. I'm serious."

"Then act smart, Dray," Smith said. "Ever since the Diceman turned out to be The Man, Tremaine's been careful who he trusts. We're on our own for a while."

"Always have been."

"Always will be." There was a slapping of palms.

From his post in the back of the basement, the Monk watched and listened. He heard their talk and saw the beams of flashlights that preceded the two down the stairs. He was standing ready to drop them should either of the two beams be directed his way. Neither was. Instead they focused on the paneling covering the hole leading to the house next door.

The Monk could have ended their lives right there. He did not need these two. Their loose talk tonight condemned Tremaine for Jones's murder. And the Monk already knew where the drug lord lived and worked. With a suspect in mind, he and Harper had started working on identifying the traitor on the police force. So why leave these two alive? Surely their actions demanded the ultimate penalty.

How easy it would be, the Monk thought, to pull the triggers of the .45s he held. His presence undetected in the shadows, his targets lit by flashlights, they would die here on the cold basement floor. The Monk could then simply walk away and leave their bodies to the other vermin of the house.

But no. If God cannot be all mercy, then neither can He be all justice. The Monk would give them their chance. He would allow them to live, if they let him.

Smith was holding both lights as Davis started to push the paneling aside. There was a click of a switch, and a battery powered worklight lit up the basement.

Startled and blinded by the sudden brightness, Davis and Smith staggered backward. Smith dropped the flashlights. Davis let go of the paneling and started to struggle for his gun

"Don't move," the Monk ordered from the darkness behind the light.

With the whispered voice echoing through the basement, it was impossible for the two men to tell from what corner it was coming. They obeyed and waited the next command.

The Monk stepped out of the shadows, making sure to keep his back to the light. A gasp from the men told him that he'd been recognized. "Slowly," he ordered, "remove your guns and place them on the floor."

Seeing the heavy automatics the Monk was carrying, Smith was quick to obey. "Do it, Dray," Smith warned when his friend was slow to comply. Davis carefully laid his gun next to Smith's.

"Kick them aside." The two guns skittered across the floor.

"Dyson Jones," the Monk whispered. "How did you know he was a police officer?"

"Tremaine, he came and said he got a call …"

"Shut up, Dray," Smith hissed. "Talking gets you killed."

"So will not talking," the Monk gestured with his guns. "Which will it be?"

"Tremaine showed up at the house," Davis said hurriedly. "I asked why, he was supposed to be laying low. He said that we had a snitch, that Diceman was a cop. I asked how he knew. He said that he had his own snitch."

"Who?"

"Don't know."

One of the guns pointed toward Smith. The voice of death asked him, "And you, do you know?"

In his mind, Smith heard the sound of cannons filling the basement. He knew it would be the last sound he heard in this life. He searched for a reply, a name, any name, someone he could give the Monk. The brief space between question and answer was all the life he had left. He remembered the dreams he once had. He thought of his life wasted on drugs and wished he'd had different choices. "Pull the trigger, man," he said in resignation, "I can't help you." He closed his eyes and waited for the end.

"Mac!" Davis said suddenly. "I heard Tremaine on the phone once. He thanked somebody he called 'Mac" and the next day we moved out from where we were. The cops raided the place the next day."

Davis looked at Smith. "Couldn't let him kill you, man."

"In the hole," the Monk whispered.

"What?" asked Smith, relieved to be alive. He wondered how long he would stay that way after Tremaine discovered Dray's betrayal.

"Go through the hole, into the next house." One of the Monk's guns disappeared inside his robes. He stooped and picked up the heavy worklight. "Push the paneling aside and go through to the next basement."

Davis put his shoulder to the wood and moved it. He followed Smith through the doorway with the Monk close behind.

"Over there by the stairway." The two moved close to the open stairs.

Staying in darkness, keeping the light on them, the Monk threw two sets of handcuffs on the floor near them.

He gave his orders. When he was done, Andre Smith was handcuffed around the stairway's bottom support post. Andray Davis's hands were through one of the open steps and shackled together.

The light went off, leaving the two in darkness. "The wait won't be long," the Monk said before them leaving them.

"Andre."

"What?"

"We going to jail, ain't we?"

"Yeah, Dray, we're going to jail."

"Be better when we get out though."

"No, it won't. Never has been."

"Never will be."

Back in the basement of the first house, the Monk picked up one of the guns dropped by the men. Then he telephoned Harper. "Did you get the address? Good, it's been confirmed. Call Hoffman and get him here. Remind him to bring a flashlight."

From Mrs. Watkins's window the Monk watched as the police arrived. First patrol units, then the Quick Response Team. Finally he saw Hoffman's unmarked sedan pull up. Then he left through her back door. He still had much to do that night.

X

The house that the Monk entered was quiet. No lights were on. With no guards inside or out, entry had been easy.

In the kitchen, The Monk stood and listened. There were no sounds of any activity. Quietly, he entered the dining room towards the second floor stairs.

His way was guided by a small votive candle burning on the dining room table. It gave off just enough light that he did not need to use his flash. It might have occurred to him that when he passed through the doorway to the living room his body would block off this light and so warn anyone waiting there, but in this darkened house he did not think this of consequence.

"We keep underestimating each other," came a voice from the darkness of the living room. There was a click and a table lamp came on. A tall, dark-skinned man was sitting on the sofa.

"I've been waiting for you," Tremaine said. "Ever since Andray, or was it Andre, called from the house where you had them shackled and waiting for ... Det. Hoffman was it?"

The Grey Monk stood silently in the doorway, disdaining to answer Tremaine. His gun was out, but down by his side. Despite his "ambush," the man on the sofa was unarmed.

"As I said," Tremaine continued, "We keep making mistakes, you and I. That first time – you thought that I was just another drug dealer and I thought that you were dead. We were both wrong. You were shot and I went to jail. This time, well, looking back, I should not have had Dyson killed. I should have strung him along and fed him false information. Or else had McKenzie take care of him quietly. But Dyson had met my lieutenants, and so was only one step away from me. But still it was a mistake."

Tremaine waved a hand at a chair, inviting the Monk to sit down. Receiving no reply he continued. "And while I did anticipate your involvement, I did not think that you would find that house where you left Smith and Davis, much less discover its secret. Who told?"

The Monk spoke for the first time. "Your involvement was obvious from the beginning, Tremaine. No one had to tell me."

Tremaine shook his head. "For shame, a holy man like you telling lies. No doubt it was that fool Turner. One of your mistakes, by the way, leaving him for the Drug Task Force like that. Easy enough for Mac to take him out." The drug dealer paused for a minute, then went on. "Let's see, what else did you do wrong? You came in here like the Wrath of God not thinking I would be waiting. I could have shot you down if I wanted. And you really should have taken their cell phones along with their guns. You weren't gone two minutes before I got the call."

"That was not necessarily a mistake," came the whispered reply

"No, I suppose not," Tremaine smiled. "Leave the cell phones, let the police trace the call made on it, especially the last call made right to this house. Sorry, but the phone that received that call is now in pieces at the bottom of my trashcan. And it won't lead here anyway."

Tremaine stood up. The Monk tensed, ready to bring his gun into play. He relaxed as the other man held his hands out from his body.

"And now comes the part where you tell me that unless I surrender, you will extract the justice I so richly deserve. Well, again I must disappoint you. I know when to cut my losses. After receiving that call, I made one of my own, to my lawyer. Smith and Davis are both facing the death penalty. I'm sure they'll give up the rest of the crew. And they have no reason not to sell me out. So I called my lawyer and he called the State's Attorney. Tomorrow I will surrender myself to the police. I will confess to various drug charges. I will identify all those who worked for me. And I will implicate a ranking member of the Drug Task Force in the murder of one of his own men – a murder of which I knew nothing about."

"You will not get away with it."

Tremaine studied the Monk for a long time, as if looking for the face hidden in the darkness of the cowl. Finally, he said, "I think I will. Oh, I'm going to jail, both for this and for violating my probation. But not for murder. Turner is dead. Davis and Smith are not the most credible witnesses. And McKenzie? A crooked cop who committed the ultimate betrayal? No. With no real proof that I pulled a trigger or gave the order I'll get the deal and send those three to death row."

Tremaine sat back down. "You can go," he told the Monk. "Leave whatever evidence you were going to plant and go."

The Monk stepped forward, his gun up. From his habit he produced a 9mm pistol. He put it on the coffee table in front of Tremaine and stepped away.

His eyes on the Monk's weapon, Tremaine slowly picked up the nine. Keeping his finger away from the trigger, he dropped the magazine out of it, then jacked the cartridge in the chamber on to the floor. Then he looked over the weapon.

"A nine. Smith's weapon. Davis likes a .380." He held it up. "I'll give this to the State's Attorney tomorrow. I'll admit that it was used to kill Dyson. I'll tell him that I took it off Smith, let's see, two days ago, when I first discovered that he was involved. It'll make me look good, like I'm cooperating. Anything else?" Tremaine smiled again, if not in triumph, at least in satisfaction of his slight victory over the Monk.

The Grey Monk moved back toward the dining room. Before he could leave, Tremaine's voice stopped him. "One last thing. Twice now, you've made mistakes and I've made mistakes. The next time …"

"There will be no 'next time,'" the Monk interrupted.

"I won't be inside forever," countered Tremaine. "And the time I do serve will be well spent. When I do get out, there will be no more mistakes."

The Monk gave no answer to this. Instead, he faded back into the darkness and left the house.

An hour before the Grey Monk had confronted Tremaine, Sgt. Brian McKenzie left his house on his way to Lafayette Ave. He was not on duty. Having been part of an officer involved shooting, he was on administrative leave until Internal Affairs cleared his involvement. He had no fears on that. For all they knew it was a clean shoot. True, he had shot Turner while the man lay in bed and then put the gun near his hand. But no one on his team had seen that. He had rushed ahead of them and was lucky enough to find Turner alone. His men came running at the sound of the gunshot. He had a bad moment when they pulled back the covers and found the dead man handcuffed to the bed. But a handcuff key solved that problem. Everyone there agreed that there was no need to bring it up. Turner had gotten what was coming to him and the cuffs would have only complicated matters, so they disappeared into someone's pocket.

No, McKenzie was not supposed to be on duty. He was definitely not supposed to be leaving his house in the middle of the night to respond to a crime scene, especially one that involved possible accomplices of the man he had killed. And he most definitely was not supposed to be armed, not while under investigation for an on-duty homicide.

But none of that mattered. He had received a call from one of his men. The Task Force had just been informed of Hoffman's raid on the Lafayette Ave. house. McKenzie had to go. He had to find out who had been taken and what had been learned. He should be okay as long as none of the brass saw him. He'd hang around the edges of the scene and try to catch Hoffman's eye. If discovered, he'd explain that he just couldn't stay away. Most cops would understand. As for the gun – hey, the streets are dangerous, only a fool goes without one.

Sgt. McKenzie got into his car. He put the key into the ignition, but before he could start the car he felt the cold steel of a gun barrel against the back of his neck. He looked into the rear view mirror and saw a hooded man in the back seat. Slowly, McKenzie put both hands on the steering wheel.

"Sgt. McKenzie," came the whisper of the Grey Monk, "I know that you betrayed Dyson Jones. You have been working for Tremaine since he left prison. You are the traitor that has been helping him spread his poison in this city. Even now his men are being arrested. They will talk, and they will speak your name."

"If you know all this," McKenzie said, trying to stay calm, "then why come to me tonight? You want something." This realization made him breathe easier. If the Monk had wanted him dead, he'd be gone already.

"However tarnished your badge, you are a police officer. Your testimony will carry more weight than the two men arrested tonight. It will put the real killer of Jones behind bars for good. Confess and testify against Tremaine. You will go to jail, but not for the length of time you deserve."

"Why should I?" McKenzie asked. "I only ever dealt with Tremaine. It's his word against mine. Whatever the others know it's nothing certain. And I don't see you testifying in court. Like you said, I'm a cop. The department doesn't need the scandal. It will turn its blind eye and let me walk."

"I am giving you a chance, Sergeant, a chance at redemption, a chance to save yourself."

"I don't need saving. You're not going to kill a cop. That would end the free pass we've been giving you."

A gloved hand slowly pulled a trigger. There was a roar and the front windshield of McKenzie's car turned red. Lights came on in nearby houses. The police were no doubt being called. The Monk left the car and watched from the shadows as they arrived. With the police on the scene, he left for his confrontation with Tremaine.

After leaving the drug dealer's house, the Grey Monk returned to where he had left McKenzie. As he expected, the outside of the sergeant's house was now lit as bright as day. From the shadows the Monk saw uniformed officers, detectives, crime lab people all working the scene. He knew what they'd find. A 9mm cartridge case on the back seat, one that would match the weapon the Monk had left with Tremaine. The Monk had not been so foolish as to kill McKenzie with one of his own guns. He thought of Tremaine surrendering himself later that morning, not knowing of McKenzie's death. He would turn in the pistol that the Monk had given him and state that he had had it in his possession for two days. The gun would be tested. A sample casing fired in it would match the one found in McKenzie's car. His own words and actions would condemn him. There was justice in that, the Monk thought.

A white van pulled up – the Medical Examiner. The Monk watched as McKenzie's body was eased out of the car, as the sergeant's body was placed on a gurney and zipped into a body bag. By this afternoon he'd be hailed as another fallen hero, one who had made the ultimate sacrifice. And there was justice in that too. In death, McKenzie would serve the police better than he had in life. Only three men would know just how far McKenzie had fallen. Tremaine would not be believed. The Monk and Harper would keep the secret.

It was time for the Monk to leave. True morning was coming and the shadows that hid him were shortening. As he watched McKenzie's body being taken away he thought of his discussion with Harper. "A God all mercy is a God Unjust." Tonight he dealt justice when mercy was refused. In the service of his Lord, he could do no more.

SEEDS OF EVIL

Nature ... has sown a seed of evil in the hearts of mortals ...which makes them dissatisfied with their own lot and envious of another's.

Desiderius Erasmus (c. 1466– 1536), Dutch humanist. Praise of Folly, ch. 22 (1509).

There were only five left – the last remaining members of the Pure Race Fellowship. All the rest were gone. Some were in prison, convicted or awaiting trial for arson, conspiracy to commit arson and various hate crimes. Others had left the movement, the actions taken by the police having cooled their ardor for the cause. The leaders of the movement were dead, supposedly shot down by police inside the PRF's headquarters. Rumor was that their deaths had actually been at the hands of the shadowy vigilante called the Grey Monk.

Those remaining were among those swept up by the police following the raid on their Essex HQ but later released for lack of evidence. These five were the ones who remained true, who did not turn and run at the first sign of trouble. Now they were together again, and were looking for payback against the system that had tried to destroy their ideals.

They met at Billi's Pour House, a tavern down in Dundalk. Billi wasn't one of them, but her sympathies lay in their direction. She kept the back booth open for their use and made sure that the pitcher of beer on their table never ran dry.

"It's the blacks who are at fault," said Morris, the self proclaimed leader of the group. "They're the ones who have to pay."

The other four nodded their heads in agreement.

"How?" asked Jimmy. At twenty, he was the youngest of the group.

"It's like this," Morris answered him, "the coloreds run the city. Everybody knows that. City Hall, the City Council, the Police and Fire Departments – they're all black at the top. And what whites we got in charge, those that aren't Jews, are afraid to use their authority. They don't want to be considered politically incorrect, or worse, racist. Let's face it, the average white man don't stand a chance, not in this city, not anymore."

Morris paused and drained his glass of beer. Holding the empty pitcher over his head as a signal for a refill, he went on. "So there ain't nobody gonna help us. And with only us five left, there ain't a lot we can do on our own. So let's get them to do it to themselves."

Morris outlined his plan. "It's simple. We start doing random drive-by shootings of blacks. Vaughn, can you get us a car?"

"Sure thing, Morris. We got a few on the lot that ain't exactly there legally. We buy them from the owners for cash, no paper work involved. The owners report the cars stolen and cash in on the insurance. We strip the cars for parts. Keep what we need, sell the rest, turn what's left over for scrap. Everybody's happy, 'cept the insurance company."

"Good, get something country-looking, a pickup if you got one. Then slap an old license plate on it, maybe with a Stars & Bars front plate."

Vaughn nodded. "That I can do."

"Better line up a few cars. We'll change every time, make it look like a conspiracy."

"Besides making us feel good, how is killing the coloreds going to help the cause."

"Good question, Pete," Morris acknowledged. "There won't be a motive, and with different cars and drivers each time, the police won't have a thing to go on. With no arrests, those blacks will be suspicious of any stranger coming into their neighborhood. Sooner or later, one of them will just up and shoot a white man. That'll bring the cops down on them. Keep things going long enough, we got a nice riot situation. And when the blacks riot, their part of the city will burn. Any questions? Yeah, Jimmy?"

"If we get a riot started, then some of our people are gonna get killed too. Probably some businesses burned out."

"So much the better. It's only when real people get hurt or killed that the cops do anything. Whites dying will make 'em crack down harder and faster." Morris paused. "This is war. Sacrifices have got to be made. Anybody got a problem with that?"

No one spoke. "Okay then. Walter, getting the guns is up to you."

"I'll drive down to Virginia tomorrow. There's a gun show outside of Arlington. Get 'em cheap with no sales records. Shotguns okay?"

"What else? Now then who goes first?"

Pete drew the short straw, or rather, the short pretzel stick, and the plan was set. Next Friday night, the new and revived Pure Race Fellowship would strike back.

It might have worked. In a city where racial tension was always a bit high, it just might have worked. However …

Pete's first problem was that he should have had a driver. Without one, he realized too late, he would have to slow down or stop completely to do the deed. He thought about going back for help. But he didn't want to admit he needed it. Okay, he thought, I'll just stop at a crowd, fire into it, and put the peddle to the metal and haul tail out of there. He decided not to get too close to make his getaway all that much easier.

Pete's second problem was that he wasn't that good a marksman. So when he finally did find a crowd of black people large enough for his purpose and fired into it, he mostly missed. Those he did hit suffered only minor flesh wounds from pellets fired from too far away.

Pete never knew how little damage he did. Someone in the crowd also had a gun – a semi-automatic pistol to be exact – and was a much better shot than Pete. There was a crack of gunfire and the breaking of glass as a 9mm bullet broke the back window of the pickup and splattered what few brains Pete had onto the inside of the front windshield.

So there were now only four of them. Except for seeing each other at Pete's funeral, they kept apart from each other for at least a week after the last mention of his death on the 10 o'clock news. By then they figured everybody had forgotten about it.

When Morris walked into the Pour House, he found Jimmy, Vaughn and Walter already sitting in their usual booth. Without asking, Bobbi brought over a pitcher to replace the one the three had already emptied.

"Cops were here," she told him as he sat down.

"When?" he asked, filling the mug she had put down next to the pitcher.

"Day or two after Pete got killed."

"What you tell them?"

"That whenever Pete came in, he drank alone and complained about how somebody ought to do something about the blacks."

"Anybody else say anything?"

Bobbi smiled. "Nobody else would talk to them. Worked that out ahead of time. Told them anybody said anything I'd bar them for life."

"Good girl!" Morris reached out to swat her behind. Bobbi dodged him with an ease acquired from ten years of waiting tables.

"Just leave a big tip. Hell, leave any kind of tip."

"I got a big tip for you," Walter yelled out as the others laughed.

"That's not what your wife says." The retort brought more laughter during which glasses were emptied and refilled. Then things got serious.

"To Pete!" They all shouted as glasses clinked together. After the mugs were drained, Vaughn commented, "Great plan, Morris," doing nothing to hide his sarcasm.

"It was a good plan."

"Tell that to Pete."

"Any of you got a better one?"

There was quiet, then Jimmy spoke up. "I do. That is, I think I do."

"Tell us, son."

At Walter's encouragement, Jimmy went on. "I been thinking. What good does it do to shoot 'em down in the street? They do that to each other. Half those bucks are drugs dealers anyway. They kill each other for sport. What we gotta do is hit 'em where it'll hurt."

"And where is that – Harlem?"

"No, Morris." Jimmy took a breath and told them his idea.

Nobody spoke. Nobody drank. They just sat there stunned. Finally, Vaughn said, "Kid, that's inspired – dirty, nasty, but inspired. That'll get them so riled up they can't help but riot."

"Do we got to do it all to them? I don't think I could, you know, not with one of them."

"Do whatever feels right at the time, Walt. Just remember to make it bloody and leave the body where it can be found. Oh yeah, and cut this into them somewhere." Jimmy drew a Star of David on a napkin.

Upset at first that someone else was taking the lead, Morris had to admit a good idea was a good idea. "I like it," he finally said, "especially that Jew thing. Make trouble for them as well."

"That's what I thought," Jimmy said smiling with a certain self-satisfaction. "Nothing like a twofer."

***

Amos Hoffman didn't have to ask where the body was. The crowd standing in a loose circle and the uniformed officers trying to hold them back told him just where to go. With a sigh, the detective got out of his car and slowly walked toward the crime scene.

A school yard this time. The last time it was behind a taco joint. The time before that a supermarket. And the first time a liquor store. All of them very public places.

He knew what he would find – the dead body of a young, black woman. She would have been abducted, brutalized in various ways, mutilated then killed with a sharp object. He knew this because after the second body was found, he had been made head of the task force designated to bring the killers to justice.

And he also knew just why he had been made head of the taskforce. Why it was him, a lowly detective and not a sergeant or higher. It was because of his association with the Grey Monk. This was the kind of case the vigilante was known for involving himself in. And it was made clear, although not in so many words, what Hoffman should do if his investigation began to falter. The detective, however, had other ideas. He wanted no parts of that spooky ghoul. Damn them but he'd solve this on his own.

Hoffman could feel the anger of the crowd as he pushed through it. Some were angry at the police for letting this go on, for not catching the killer. Others laid the blame on the group they thought responsible. Still others called damnation on both.

"It's the Jews."

"Cops are protecting them."

"Would find the killer if it was white girls getting killed."

"Some kind of cult."

"If they don't so something ..."

"We gonna do something."

Things weren't any better once Hoffman broke free and passed through the cordon into the crime scene. Some of the cops who knew him, who knew his background and culture, looked at the sheet-covered corpse, then to him and then back to the corpse again, their eyes coming to rest on the design etched out red against brown.

"Takes one to catch one," said one of the younger cops, thinking he was funny. No one laughed. Hoffman, still rattled by the mob, took a step towards him. He was stopped by friendlier hands. Had the scene not been public, the hands would have been slower, giving Hoffman time to take the swing that was his due.

"Not here, Amos," said another detective. "Not in public."

Hoffman gave the young cop a look of disgust, then glanced over to the uniform sergeant. The sergeant nodded, the nod telling Hoffman that the would-be comic would be taken care of, that for the next month or so he'd get every dirty detail that came up.

"Crime lab done, Darryl?" Hoffman asked his fellow detective.

"Pictures and sketch. They'll go over the body for trace evidence once it gets to the morgue."

Hoffman motioned for the victim to be uncovered. As the sheet was pulled away, the uniforms made a human wall around the body, blocking it from the view of the curious crowd.

Same as the rest, Hoffman thought, shaking his head. Same type of wounds, same sign cut into her.

"Cover her up." Leaving her for the Medical Examiner's team to take away, Hoffman walked through the angry crowd and back to his car.

***

Doors not meant to open from the outside are not usually well guarded. They are sometimes alarmed, but not the one the Grey Monk was approaching. It was a fire door that led into the Office of the State Medical Examiner.

This was not the first time the Monk had sought to pass through this door. The first time had been at the start of his career. He was investigating a murder, a woman killed in a van outside a downtown hospital. He wanted to know exactly how she had died. With no resources in the police department at the time, he decided to go to the source.

Staying deep in the shadows that hid him, the Monk circled the building, looking for a way inside. A ramp, wide enough for a large van, or a hearse, led from the street into the basement morgue. No, the eye of a camera watched this entrance and an alarm sounded whenever the heavy garage door opened or closed. The main doors were a possibility, and the locks looked like the kind he could pick, but they faced a public street. Too open, a passing car would spotlight him before he could get inside.

He went around the building, looking for an alternative. He found one other door, a heavy, metal fire door, the surface of which was flat – no handle, no lock, nothing that could be used to open it from the outside. He spent some time examining it, but could find no way to trick it open. He was about to give up and risk the front entrance when the side door suddenly opened. The Monk quickly sought the darkness of a corner and stood there, motionless, as two people exited. Unseen in his dark robe, he watched as they walked to their cars and drove away, their shift over for the night.

The Monk waited. An hour went by, then two. No one else left by that door. The next night the Monk stood in the same corner and watched the same two people leave. He noted that neither turned around as they walked to their cars.

On the third night the Monk was ready. Moving quickly but silently after the two left, he grabbed the edge of the door just before it closed and slipped inside.

He had taken the chance that at 3 a.m. there would be no one on the other side of the door, that he would not be entering into a brightly light, well-used office area. His gamble paid off. The Monk found himself at one end of a dim corridor. A stairwell to his left lead to the basement. It was there in the basement that the dead were housed, those whose deaths were sudden or unexplained. It was there that they were placed on stainless steel tables for examination, to give up the last of their secrets. It was there that they waited, to be claimed by loved ones or left for an unmarked grave.

That night the Monk had no interest in the dead. Passing by the basement stairs, he carefully moved down the hall, alert for the slightest sound that would tell him that he was not alone.

Light came from under one door that he passed. Listening at that door, he heard sounds of a TV and casual conversation. The field examiners, he supposed, the ones who went out and brought the deceased back to this temporary stop on their final journey. The Monk continued on his way, and hoped that the night stayed quiet, that no call would come in requiring them to leave the comfort of their office.

The Monk got to the office without incident and found the report he wanted. It detailed the death of Delores Smith – how she was beaten, abused and finally stabbed to death. The report also stated that after she died, her killer had cut off the middle finger of her right hand. Despite a thorough search of the van in which she'd been killed, the missing digit had not been found.

There was a final note. It directed the reader's attention to several other cases. The Monk found and read them. In each of these the victim suffered the amputation of his or her right middle finger. In none of the cases was the finger ever located.

The Monk had brought that killer to justice. And now he had come to the house of the dead in search of yet another. But this time there was no need to sneak in. Instead, he knocked softly and the door opened.

"Come in," welcomed Dr. Bartholomew Penn.

Dr. Penn was one of the people the Monk had seen leaving the week of his first trespass into the morgue. One night Dr. Penn worked later than usual. As he left the building, he was accosted by a young man with a gun who demanded the doctor's wallet and car keys. As the doctor complied, a shadow detached itself from a corner of the building and fell on the young hoodlum. There was a brief struggle after which the gunman lay motionless on the ground.

Dr. Penn watched as the shadow took the shape of a man in a dark robe. He read the papers, he knew who it was. "Thank you," he said.

"You're welcome," came the whispered reply.

"What about him?" Dr. Penn asked as the Monk turned to leave.

"He'll live. He has no need of your services – yet. Call the police."

"I only wish there were some way of showing my appreciation."

The Monk took a quick glance at the door through which he had snuck several times, then looked back at the doctor. "Actually, Doctor, there is."

From that night on, the Monk had entry into the morgue. And now he was there to learn more about the brutal murders of four young, black women.

"The thing that links the cases," Dr. Penn told him after the two settled in his office, "apart from the brutal nature of their deaths, is the Star of David cut into their bodies."

"Is it the same killer in all four cases?" asked the Monk from the darkened corner where he sat.

Dr. Penn shook his head. "There are too many dissimilarities. In only two of the cases was there evidence of sexual assault, and in only one of those was any genetic material left behind. A different knife was used each time, and the manner and nature of the wounds varied from victim to victim."

"Four different killers then, with a common purpose."

"Yes, whatever that is."

"Spreading fear and terror, Doctor. They will be stopped."

"You know who they are?"

"I have my suspicions. Tell me, do you remember a death last month? A white man in a pick-up truck fired into a crowd. He was shot and killed by an off-duty police officer."

"Yes, I do. I worked on him myself. Why?"

"What was his name?"

***

Clark's Lane was the dividing line in Park Heights. The area north of that street was mostly Jewish, south of it was predominately black. Over the years there was some of the usual trouble that comes when two different cultures met and clashed, but on the whole things had generally been peaceful.

But that was before the killings, before the news came out that led one group to believe that their race made them targets, and the other to feel that their religion was being mocked to give the killers a shield.

Each group had its defenders, as any group large enough to command people's loyalty will. There were men on both sides that were willing to fight, and if need be, kill, to protect home and family.

Already there had been incidents. Young men wandering too far north or south being set upon, beaten and warned not to return. Tensions were high on both sides of the line. The police doubled, then tripled patrols through the entire area, knowing that the slightest spark could erupt into a fire that would burn the city down.

A fifth girl was found, in a playground just off Clark's Lane. The same wounds, the same mutilations, the same sign marking the kill. Concerned neighbors from both sides came out. Angry words were exchanged, small fights almost started. Uniformed offices were hard pressed to control the crowd and protect the crime scene. The Medical Examiner was hurried to the scene, the police knowing that once the body was removed people would begin to leave.

Then the call came in. The body of a prominent businessman was found in his car behind a synagogue just a few blocks north. And he too had been stabbed to death, his body mutilated and the kill marked. Only this time an X was carved into his forehead.

That kind of news is hard to contain. First one group heard of it, then the other. Some saw it as a revenge killing, others as a plot to place blame elsewhere, to divert attention from the real killers. This time the police were not able to contain things.

Few people were seriously hurt in the riot that broke out. No one was killed. Property damage was limited to vandalized cars and broken shop windows. Police made dozens of arrests, letting most of those locked up go home once things calmed down.

Of course, the disturbance was the lead story on every evening news program. And every network picked it up and included the story in their broadcasts. Fear and mistrust ran through the city.

The Grey Monk did not hear of the riot until late that night. He had been busy learning all he could about the late Peter Coleman – where he had lived and worked, what credit cards he had had and how he had used them, how many times had he been arrested. The arrests were of the greatest interest – where, why and with whom.

The Monk learned of the riot from the late night news. He watched the news on a TV mounted over the bar in a tavern in Dundalk, a tavern where Coleman had used his credit card many times to obtain cash advances from an ATM that the owner had installed. The owner figured it would be useful to drinkers whose thirst exceed their supply of cash. That Bobbi was a nice looking lady, but an even smarter businesswoman.

The Monk sat on a stool at one end of the bar, just an average guy who stopped in for a beer before going home. Dressed as he was in jeans and a grey hooded jacket, no one took any notice of him. He just drank his beer, watched TV and listened to the four men in the booth behind him talk. Despite the fact that they kept their voices low, the Monk could hear most of what was said, all the while pretending interest in a football game.

"Anybody have any problems?" Morris asked after Bobbi brought a pitcher.

"I almost got caught," Walter admitted, "pulling mine off the street the way I did. After that ... well, killing's not as easy as I thought. I stabbed her and left the sign, but that's all."

"That's enough, you did your part. Anyone else?"

Jimmy spoke up. "Nope, it was easy. It wasn't like I was killing a real person. Had me some fun too. What about you, Vaughn?"

"Let's just say I did my part."

"So did I. I killed some in the war, but it wasn't like this. This was like Jimmy said, easy and fun." Morris looked at his friends. "So who did the ones today?"

"Which ones?"

"The girl and the Jew, Walter. Who did it?"

"Someone did a Jew? When'd that happen?"

Morris outlined to Jimmy and the others what he had heard on the evening news. Then he asked again, "So who was it?"

No one claimed credit.

"You, Jimmy? Walter?" Those two shook their heads. "I know I didn't. And Vaughn, I take it you didn't?"

"Wasn't me. Looks like maybe our work is done."

"Yeah," Morris nodded, "At least somebody else thinks it's a good idea. Maybe it'll catch on. If not, we can always go back to work."

Morris held up his beer. "The PRF," he said quietly.

"The PRF," said the others, clinking glasses.

They drained their mugs. And when they put their glasses down, they talked of other things. The Grey Monk paid for his beer and left. No one took any notice.

As the four men left separately, they were watched as they got into their cars and drove away. The last to leave was followed home.

Jimmy Pulaski still lived with his mom. His dad had passed away a few years ago and she felt safer with a man in the house. Anyway, that was what she told Jimmy. The truth was that she didn't think Jimmy could make it on his own, and at least this way he had a roof over his head, food to eat and clean clothes to wear.

It wasn't a bad deal for Jimmy. Room and board at no cost, and his room was in the basement. Using the back entrance, he could come and go as he pleased without bothering his mother. It was an ideal situation for a young man – all the freedom he wanted and very little responsibility.

After leaving the Pour House, Jimmy went straight home and went to bed. Thanks to the number of beers he had drunk, he fell asleep right away and slept soundly. So he didn't hear the back basement door open. And he didn't see the dark figure enter his house and come up to his bed. The first he knew of his visitor was when a gloved hand covered his mouth and pinched his nose shut. After a few seconds without air, Jimmy woke up choking and coughing.

When Jimmy caught his breath, he saw the figure standing beside him. Or rather, he saw the very large gun that was in front of his face, then looked beyond that to the dark specter holding it.

"I will give you one chance," came a sinister whisper. "One chance for you and those you call your friends. Call the police. Confess the evil you have done. Do this and live."

By now Jimmy was fully awake. It occurred to him that had whoever this was wanted to kill him, he'd be dead by now. So despite the gun, this freak was just talk.

"And what if we don't?" he asked defiantly.

The Grey Monk fired a shot into the pillow. Feathers flew as he put the gun to Jimmy's forehead. "I will kill you all."

Deafened by the shot, Jimmy didn't hear this last, but got the meaning. Before he could realize that he had soiled himself, the Grey Monk was gone.

Afraid to close his eyes, Jimmy didn't sleep the rest of that night. He knew that if he did, the ghost would come back. So after changing his clothes and bed sheets, he sat in a chair, shotgun in hand, watching the back door, waiting for morning. When it came he would call Morris, Morris would know what to do.

"Damn, I know who that guy is," Morris told Jimmy over coffee at a local donut shop. "Remember when Debbie and Joe got it?"

"Yeah," Pete said through a mouthful of jelly donut. "Cops killed them in a raid on the PRF place."

Morris shook his head. "Way I heard it from some guys that should know, it wasn't the cops. It was that Grey Monk fellow that's been in the papers, the one that's been killing the drug dealers, pimps and murderers in the city."

"But why's he after us?" Pete asked. Morris just looked at him. "Oh yeah … Oh Hell, we're dead. He's going to kill us, kill us all."

"Sit down, everybody's looking." Morris pulled Pete back into his seat. "Nobody's gonna kill anybody. Or rather, this Monk fellow ain't gonna kill us. He surprised you last night is all. That's the way he works. He sneaks around and catches you when you're not ready. When he comes for us, we'll be ready. He won't stop the four of us. I'll call Walt and Vaughn. We'll meet tonight and figure out what to do."

The two men finished their coffee and left. Pete went to work. Morris headed home. He'd call his boss and take the day off. He had things to do and plans to make. As he drove back to his house, he didn't notice the man in a grey hooded jacket behind him in a non-descript sedan.

The Monk followed Morris home and watched him pull into his driveway. Slowing only slightly to catch the house number, the Monk passed the house and parked around the corner. He took out a cell phone. Connecting with the Internet, he found a crisscross service and soon had a telephone number to go with the address. Disconnecting, he made his call.

"Yeah, what is it?" Jimmy's news had upset Morris more than he had let on. Trying to figure out just what to do, he didn't need the interruption of some fool on the telephone.

"I will give you the same chance I gave your friend," came the whispered voice. "It is the police or me."

It was the Grey Monk, Morris realized. "Look, Monk, or whoever you are – do your worse. I ain't afraid of you," he said more bravely than he felt.

"You should be. I know where you live and work. I could end your evil now. But you will have your chance."

"And if I tell you to go to Hell?"

"Only to pave the way for you and your kind. There is a house in Essex. You know which one. I was there once. I will be there tonight. It will be your chance to surrender. Otherwise, I will hunt you, one by one, and send you to the Justice you deserve."

The Monk hung up. Morris stared at the phone for a few minutes, then he pressed for a dial tone. "Walter, Morris. We're gonna need more guns."

***

The house had been vacant for some time now, ever since the killings and the police raid. People crossed the street to avoid passing in front of it. Local kids said it was haunted. The few prospective buyers that had looked it over rejected it out of hand. Realtors soon took it off their lists, not even bothering to show it.

Maybe the kids were right, maybe the evil that had been plotted there lived on, had seeped into the walls leaving an atmosphere of hatred and unease. Or maybe the deeds done within its walls were too much a reminder of how common such evil is, how easily its seeds, once planted in a man's heart, will grow.

That night, four men approached the house. Parking their car a block away, they came on foot, so as to give less notice to anyone who might be waiting for them inside. Each of them carried a rifle or shotgun wrapped in canvas, burlap or paper. Each of them also had some sort of handgun tucked into their pants.

"I still think it's a trap. He's inside right now waiting for us to come in. Then he'll blow us away."

Morris sighed. "We've been through this, Vaughn. If he wanted to kill us, me and Jimmy'd be dead right now. Probably you and Walter too. He's one of the 'good guys,' and they don't shoot unless you shoot first. Only when we shoot first he ain't gonna be able to shoot back."

Across the street, a man clad in a charcoal grey monk's habit waited in the shadows. He watched the men enter. He'd give them time to set up, then act.

For once, the Grey Monk wasn't sure about his plan. This was not how he liked to do things. But it was too late for any doubts. The plan was in motion and there was no turning back.

Inside the house, a light came on in the living room, a light seen across the street. The Monk spoke into his cell phone. "It's time."

"Power's still on," Jimmy said, switching on the light. No one else spoke. Instead they waited for the Grey Monk to appear. Five minutes, then ten went by.

"He ain't here," somebody finally said.

"He will be," asserted Morris. "Here's what we do. There's only three ways in. Jimmy, take the back door. Vaughn, take the basement. Walter and me will wait here in case he comes through the front or comes down from upstairs. Anybody sees anything move that's bigger than a cat, start shooting. The rest of us will come and help."

As the four were making plans, cars came silently down the street. Other cars drove into the alley behind the house. Men with guns got out and took up positions covering every approach. After each man signaled his readiness, word was given and more vehicles pulled up – vans this time, vans loaded with video equipment designed for live, late breaking developments. The people who got out of these vans carried cameras instead of guns, and they too positioned themselves to cover every possible angle. Like the men with the guns, they were professionals, and didn't want to miss a shot.

The first the men in the house knew of what was going on outside was when all the police cars turned on their lights at once. Darkened in anticipation of the Grey Monk's arrival, the house strobed blue, red and yellow. The four men inside looked at each other, unwilling to believe what was obviously happening.

"That son of a ... he lied to us!" Jimmy shouted.

"The Monk did say he was gonna give us a chance to surrender," Vaughn pointed out. He glanced out a window. "Looks like we got it."

"THIS IS THE POLICE,' a loudspeaker blared unnecessarily. "COME OUT ONE AT A TIME WITH YOUR HANDS ON YOUR HEADS." Spotlights hit the door to emphasis the request. "ANY ARMED RESISTANCE OR DISPLAY OF WEAPONS WILL BE MET WITH DEADLY FORCE."

No one suggested going out in a blaze of glory. Rifles and shotguns were laid aside. Handguns were removed from waistbands and placed on the floor. Slowly, Walter opened the door and they marched out in single file.

Despite the fact that he was nominally in charge of the operation, Detective Amos Hoffman stayed in the background. Securing the scene and taking the subjects into custody was the job of the Tactical Unit. He really had nothing to do until his suspects were in an interview room.

So after the men walked out of the house and were led into the patrol wagon for their ride downtown, Hoffman turned his back to the scene and looked into the surrounding shadows. Where is he, the detective wondered.

No matter. Hoffman found his own patch of darkness and waited.

A few minutes went by, then Hoffman, now facing the house, heard a footfall behind him. Just one, too loud and firm to be anything but deliberate. Resisting an impulse to turn he said simply, "Thank you."

"You're welcome," said the expected whispered voice. "All went well?"

"Suspects in custody, house secure, nobody dead," Hoffman said. "Not the usual end to one of your adventures."

"No," admitted the Monk.

"So why are you all of a sudden a good citizen?"

"This city's on a knife's edge, Detective Hoffman. This situation needed a definite resolution. If these men had died, there would be those who would doubt their guilt, who would still look to blame others. But now their crimes are exposed, and they've been arrested in a place already notorious for such evil. The city will have a chance to return to normal, and wounds that were opened a chance to heal."

Hoffman grunted. "This city will never be normal," he said, and almost added, "That's why you fit in so well." But instead he said, "So you figure these three for all six killings?"

Hoffman heard a rustle of cloth. Receiving no answer, this time he did turn around. He was alone. He shook his head. "No, not normal at all." He looked back at the house. Things were winding down. Best get back. He had a long night of questions and answers ahead.

Only three, the Monk thought as he slipped away from Hoffman. One of them managed to evade the police. The Monk knew he could have done it, but he hadn't credited any of the four with that much ingenuity. He made a quick call to someone he knew had been watching the late night news. The suspects had been shown on TV. Getting a description, the Monk knew which of them had escaped.

Three a.m. Morris had been watching his own house for at least an hour. No police. So Jimmy and the rest hadn't given him up. Good men, all three. Once he got resettled and the work started anew, he'd try and do something for them. Until then, though, he had to think of himself.

He had been lucky so far. When the four of them lined up to surrender, Morris knew he couldn't go through with it. Last in line, he picked up a gun and went upstairs, determined to make a last stand, maybe get to make a statement on TV before going down. Looking for the best place to set up a barricade, he opened the hall closet. There, standing open, was the access panel for the bathroom plumbing and part of the central cooling unit. It was a tight squeeze, and Morris didn't fit all the way in, but it was close enough. If the boys stayed quiet, and the search team wasn't too thorough, he might just get away. And if he was found, maybe he'd take down one or two of them before he dropped.

It all went his way. From his hiding place he heard the police come in. He heard them come up the stairs. One of the searchers shown a light into his closet but failed to notice that the panel was out of place. After they left, Morris stayed hidden another half hour. He had to work out cramps when he finally did come out, but he was alone.

The police didn't find his car either. Morris drove part way home, then parked and walked the rest. Finding a place to watch, he waited to see if the police would come.

It was time. With a revolver in one hand and his keys in the other, he approached his house. Through the back gate, up to the rear door, he slipped the key in the lock and turned it. Quietly, he entered his house.

Morris figured to grab some clothes and what cash he had on hand. His bankcards would be good for at least tonight. He'd hit as many ATMS as he could and take the maximum each time. There were also some 24-hour check cashing places he could go to. Cash some checks, max out his credit cards with cash advances, then leave town. Go north and west. There were some brotherhoods near the border that had had ties to the PRF. One of them would surely help him.

As Morris entered his living room the lights came on. Momentarily blinded, he could barely make out the dark figure of a man dressed in robes. As his vision came back, he realized that this was the Grey Monk.

"You were given a chance," came a cold, whispered voice. "You turned it down."

Morris remembered the revolver in his hand. He brought it up too slowly. The Monk fired twice, the first shot striking him in his shoulder causing him to drop the gun, the second hitting him in the chest, knocking him to the floor.

As Morris laid there in pain, he dimly heard the Monk say something about vengeance and the Lord. Then he saw the Monk start to leave.

"You ... can't ... leave ... me," he croaked out.

"Why not?" was the clear reply.

"I'll ... die."

"So?" And the Monk left him alone and bleeding on the living room floor.

Outside, the Monk took out his phone. "Call Hoffman, tell him there is one more." He gave the address. "Send an ambulance as well. No, his wounds are not immediately fatal. He may live to be arrested."

Again the Grey Monk waited in the shadows, watching the house until the police and medics arrived. Then he left. Dawn was coming. There was still more to do, but that was for another time. For tonight, the Lord's work had been done.

THE LIVING GODDESS

Diane Edwards was late. She had worked overtime correcting the mistakes her boss had made in the annual report and so missed her usual bus. The next one due, the only one she could take if she wanted to get home before the sitter started charging extra, was the Gardenville Express. That left her off five blocks before her regular stop. Time enough to get home, if she went through the park.

During the day the park was all right. Children played on the swings, people walked their dogs and the elderly sat on the benches and watched it all. There was no danger during the day. But it was different when the sun went down. Under the cover of darkness drug deals were made, the homeless crept in to sleep and shadows hid all sorts of predators hunting for the weak and careless.

Diane stepped off the bus and looked into the park. She could walk around it. That would take another thirty minutes. Or she could cut through and be home in ten. That would save her the twenty dollars her son's sitter would charge her for being late, twenty she could not afford, not on what that cheap bastard of a boss paid her. She thought for a minute how nice it would have been if he had offered to pay her for the overtime she had put in or at least sent her home in a cab. But all he had offered was time off at some later date that was sure never to come. Resolving to start looking for another job, Diane stepped off the sidewalk and on to the darkened path that would take her through the park and home.

Knowing the risk she was taking, Diane hurried through, keeping her arms at her side and her eyes straight ahead, thinking that if she didn't see anyone they couldn't see her. She was wrong.

Two sets of eyes had followed her from the second she got off the bus. They had watched her hesitation and recognized the moment when she made her decision to chance the park. One man went ahead of her, knowing the route she had to take and just where he would wait. He hardened in anticipation of what he would do to her when he pulled her off the path. He hoped she would scream, scream and fight. He loved it when they struggled. It made things that much sweeter.

A second man stepped in as she passed and followed behind her, staying in the shadows.

"Stupid, stupid, stupid," Diane chided herself as she quickened her pace. She knew the stories of went on in the park. Saving the twenty just wasn't worth it if she didn't make it home. Next time she'd just walk around, or wait for a later bus and to hell with it. And to hell with her boss. She would check the job ads this evening after getting the boy to sleep. With that decision made she walked even faster and prayed she would make it home.

Diane was three quarters there when she was grabbed and pulled off the path. She screamed but if anyone heard her they ignored her cries. They had their own business and it did not include getting involved or helping others.

Diane was dragged deep into the woods. Her blouse was ripped open and her bra pulled up. Rough hands squeezed and pinched her breasts. She fought, was overpowered and soon found herself on her back, a hand under her dress and pulling at her pantyhose. She then made the decision to stop resisting and maybe escape with her life. Her son needed her; she'd endure and survive for his sake.

A click saved her. A click that in those dark woods was as loud as thunder. She didn't know what it was but her assailant did. He stopped pulling at her clothes and turned toward the sound.

A voice came out of the shadows. "Release her," it said in an eerie whisper. The man on top of her hesitated. A louder sound, this time real thunder as a shot rang out and a bullet buried itself in the ground next to her. The man released his hold and Diane scrambled to her feet and looked toward her savior.

Even with her eyes adjusted to the dark she barely made him out. A shapeless grey form in some kind of robe, a hood pulled up to hide his features.

"Go home," he ordered.

Home? To safety? But she'd been attacked, shouldn't she stay for …

"… the police?" She said this last out loud.

"They will not bother you," came the whispered reply. "This will be finished tonight. Go. Now!"

Adjusting her clothes, Diane ran from the park.

From his position on the ground, the would-be assailant could clearly make out the dark grey shape that towered over him and the twin automatics it held in its hands. He made no sudden moves as the whispered voice spoke.

"Five women raped and beaten. This would have been the sixth. It ends tonight. I will call the police and we will wait. You will surrender, confess and plead guilty. You will pay for your sins."

The rapist knew who held him at gunpoint. It was the Grey Monk, a shadowy figure that preyed on crime and hunted criminals. Rumor was that he was a crook himself, or at least that the police wanted him gone as much as anyone. There were stories about the Monk; stories that as the rapist remembered them almost caused him to soil himself. Then he realized that he was not yet dead. This led him to believe that the stories weren't true. Slowly he stood.

"Call the police if you want, but there ain't no way I'm confessing. They got nothing on me. I may have done those bitches, but I watch those TV crime shows. I'm shaved and I use a rubber. I don't leave nothing they can use to ID me. So call away."

The poor damned fool did not realize that he had just thrown away his last chance at salvation.

Diane Edwards was just at her door when she realized who had saved her. It was that Grey Monk she had read about in the papers, the vigilante for whom the police were looking. Maybe the police wanted to arrest him, but to Diane he was better than a guardian angel. She wondered just what he would do to her attacker. Then two gunshots came from inside the park.

Detective Amos Hoffman was working the evening tour in the Homicide Unit. He had just checked in when his cell phone rang. He did not recognize the number but knew the voice all too well.

"The rapes in Gardenville Park are at an end, Detective." After telling Hoffman where to find the body, the Grey Monk hung up.

Hoffman swore. The damned spook had done it again, had taken the law into his own hands. One day, Hoffman vowed, the Monk would go too far. Until then …

Again the detective swore. It was useless. Most of the city and half the department was on the Grey Monk's side. Hoffman looked at his phone. No sense in tracing the call. The Monk used prepaid cells and changed them as often as Hoffman changed shorts. There was only one thing to do.

"Get a unit over to Gardenville. There's a dead rapist in the park. The Grey Monk's at it again."

***

India 1838

The Worshippers of Kali died. In a temple cave in Saugor they fought and died.

It was not supposed to happen. Time and again when confronted by British forces the Thuggees had surrendered without a struggle, unwilling or unable to take the soldiers' lives and convinced that by their discovery the goddess had abandoned them. So when the patrol led by Sergeant Edward Gallan tracked one of the last remnants of the cult to its lair it was not prepared for what happened next.

Shots rang out and two good men fell. Already exposed and committed to the approach, Sergeant Gallan gave the order to press forward, knowing it would cost more lives. By the time they reached the mouth of the cave another trooper was down and Corporal Weston had taken a ball in the knee.

Two natives with ancient rifles, young men just out of their teens. Their age did not save them when the soldiers reached the cave and took revenge for their fallen comrades. Gallan did nothing to stop his men. He'd served too long in this God-forsaken land and seen too much killing for two more deaths to bother him.

"Corporal, can you hold the cavern mouth?"

Leaning against rock to ease his damaged leg, Weston replied, "As long as I can, Sergeant," and lowered himself to sit behind the same barrier the dead Thuggees had used.

"Good man." And Gallan led his remaining men into the darkness.

Proceeding cautiously, the British troops advanced into the cave no more than fifty yards when they came to a grotto brightly lit with torches. There they met the remaining defenders. Strangling scarves and pick-axes should have been no match for disciplined soldiers with rifles and bayonets, but the Thuggees were fighting for their lives and their goddess. The slaughter began.

When it was over, Kali's disciples were all dead and Gallan's troop had been reduced to a handful. Himself and four men standing. With Weston outside that made six survivors out of twenty men. A high price for something that should not have happened.

Gallan gave the necessary order. "Make sure they're all dead, men."

"And if they're not, Sergeant?" That was Howard, the youngest of the troop. He'd been posted less than a month.

Gallan gave him a cold eye. "What part of 'Make sure they're dead' did you not understand, Howard?"

The young solider blanched and went off to carry out his orders.

"Sergeant, over here." Erickson was at the rear of the grotto. A chamber ran off it. "I guess we know what they were fighting for," he said

when Gallan came over.

The sergeant looked inside. Against the back wall was the expected statue of Kali. Smaller than the ones usually found, the idol was all black and nude except for a belt of severed hands and necklace of skulls. The goddess's four arms were outstretched, hands empty. Gold and silver coins, rubies and other precious gems covered the floor in front of her.

The sergeant looked the chamber over. "Kali's treasure. Well, it's Victoria's now."

"The Queen's, sergeant?"

"To whom else would it go, Erickson? Your monthly pay packet's not enough for you?" Bu then he thought of the terrible price they had paid to win this fortune. It should not all go to the Crown. He called his men around him.

"That chest there," he said, pointing to the side of the idol. "Fill it up. That's Her Majesty's share. Anything left, fill one bag each." He indicated small sacks that had been lying on the ground, picking one up for himself. "Howard, fill another bag for Weston and Erickson, fill two more. One will be for the families of our fallen comrades, the other for the captain, so he'll ask no questions."

The troopers worked through the day, filling a carved chest and their own bags. That it was treasure stolen from travelers who had fallen victim to and were murdered by thugs did not bother them. Gold and jewels belonged to whoever found them. When they were finished they buried their dead as best as they could to protect them from scavengers. When they returned to camp a detail would be sent to retrieve the bodies. Others were sent to destroy the idol and dynamite the temple so it could not be used again. Not that it mattered. Within two years magistrate William Sleeman would declare the Cult of Kali destroyed and the threat of the Thuggees ended forever.

***

Virginia Stone was born a freak and grew up that way. She almost didn't grow up at all.

When Amos McCroy heard the midwife's scream and rushed into the room, he was appalled at the monster his wife Doris had birthed. His first resolve was to wait until his woman healed then beat her good for consorting with the dark things that lived in the deep woods. He had warned her about that before. His second thought was to take this thing that could not have come from his seed and leave it in the woods for its real father.

McCroy said as much to the witch woman who had overseen the birth. She sighed. Wasn't no monster, she thought, but cousin marrying cousin way too many times. She'd tried to tell them but no one listened. Like stayed with like and that's the way it had always been in these parts of the hills.

But that was no reason to put this child out for the animals. There was another way, a better way for all. When she told McCoy what it was a smile came to his face.

"Least some good will come of it," he said, looking down at the girl thing now sucking at its mother's breast. No way I'm touching that again, he decided. He'd give the bitch the beating she deserved then put her out. No, better to let her stay and invite her younger sister Donna to move in with them. She'd always been the better looking of the two anyway.

Doris cared for her daughter through the winter, knowing what was to happen come spring.

April. The last of the frost was gone and the trees were budding again. Easter passed. Then the fist week of May.

The caravan came down the main road that connected the small hill town with the outside world. It traveled through town and set up camp in the open field on the other side. And then, for one night only, The Stone Brothers' Traveling Carnival and Natural Oddity Exhibition opened for business.

The next night was a time of celebration. Kids spent their allowance on rides and cheap trinkets. Grownups tried games of chance, watched the shows and gawked at the freaks. And if they could, some of the men snuck away from their wives to watch strange women wearing very little clothing dance to exotic music.

Later, after the kids were asleep and some wives were wondering just why their men were so frisky, Evan Stone stood in the shadows behind his office trailer and handed over a sum of money to McCroy. In exchange, he received a warmly wrapped bundle that cried but once then went back to sleep.

"Don't worry," he said to the man who had handed it over, "we'll take good care of her."

McCroy shrugged. He didn't care what happened, wasn't his kid and it wasn't his problem, not anymore. He would give the witch woman her cut then it was back home. Probably have to beat the wife again to shut her up, then he'd take care of the sister. Or she'll take care of me, he thought, remembering how that dancer with the hand cymbals had rolled her belly. He hurried home and thought no more of the child he had left behind.

Evan Stone had been a carny all his life. His mother was a tent dancer and when she got too old for that life she hooked up with a pitchman who didn't care what she had done before as long as she promised not to do it again, not with anyone but him that is. Evan was the oldest of three and his parents saw to it that all their sons got the best education the traveling life could provide. They were the ones who had convinced then owner and manager Jack Mullen to hire a tutor for the carny brats.

Evan took to numbers, then finances, banks and investments. When the time came for old man Mullen to retire, Evan bought him out and made his brothers partners in the show.

The traveling life is not an easy one and Evan grew up hard. He had had to do a few things of which he was not especially proud. In fact, he had had to do more than a few of those things. Buying babies was not one of them.

To Evan, anyone who would sell their own child did not deserve to have one. So over the years as his show traveled the back roads earning just enough to make it through to the next season, whenever someone offered him a child that was somehow different or deformed, he always found the money and took in the child.

He named the girl he'd bought from that creep McCroy "Virginia," after the state where he and his wife had met. Like all such children he gave her his surname. Evan decided to foster the girl with two of his dancers who, because of their close, personal relationship, were unlikely to ever have children of their own.

The Stone Brothers Carnival struck the booths, folded the tents and packed up the rides the morning after little Virginia became one of its members. After waiting a bit to see if any child was so desperate to leave its parents as to run away and join them they moved on towards the next town.

***

England, 1892

Two carriages, one stolen, one borrowed, raced through the streets of London. The one in the lead was the faster, but its horses were tiring and its pursuer was gaining ground.

"We almost have 'em, sir."

"As I've reminded you again and again, Inspector, 'almost' benefits no one. We'll succeed only when we catch those ahead ... easy now."

The Great Detective swayed and held his seat as the Inspector took a corner at speed. The carriage rocked and nearly tumbled over.

"I would say that was an almost to our benefit, sir."

"Indeed." The near wreck caused the Detective to consider the chase. It had been in progress for the last quarter hour with but one end in sight. Those ahead would stop quickly in an open area, pour from the carriage and flee on foot. By the time the Scotland Yard man halted their conveyance, the thieves would be gone. True, the treasure of the British Museum would be safe, but only until the next attempt. There must be a way.

Knowing London better than any man alive, he considered their possible routes. Yes, if they take this turn it may work.

The lead carriage made the expected move. "Speed up, Inspector. Force them to go faster. And be prepared to stop."

The inspector obeyed. "When, sir?"

"You'll know when the time comes."

The policeman urged his team on just as the driver of the lead carriage looked back. Seeing his pursuers come close, he gave the whip to his horses.

"Slow down, Inspector."

"But they'll get away."

The Great Detective smiled. "I think not. At the speed they're traveling, the next turning will do for them."

As usual he was right. The corner came up fast and the fleeing driver lost what little control he had. A wheel clipped a corner and that was sufficient. The carriage tilted and for a brief time seemingly hung suspended in the air before it came crashing down. There was a crack of wood as the harness shaft twisted and broke and frightened horses ran out of view.

"We have them. Quickly now, Inspector."

The two men, an officer of the law and a consulting detective, leapt from their carriage and hastened to the fallen one. Not for the first time since this case began did the detective wish the good doctor was still by his side. But the man had a new wife and a thriving practice and had reluctantly given up the game. Still it would have been nice to have him here, if only for the Webley revolver he always seemed to have at hand. That and his medical knowledge that had saved more than one man in their many adventures.

"This one's 'ad it, sir." The Inspector was standing by the body of the driver, whose head had violently struck the cobblestones when he tumbled from his seat. The Detective clambered onto the upended coach to check on the passengers.

"There are two in here, Inspector," he said, holding open the door and peering inside. "One is beyond help, the other ..."

Uttering a strange cry, the other reached up from inside the coach. The Detective fell back so as not to be pulled inside, allowing the one inside to emerge.

Despite his conventional dress, the man's dark skin marked him a stranger to the Isles. So did the pickaxe he held in his hand. Not a common weapon for a London crook to wield. And this man wielded it well, nearly impaling the Detective with his first swing.

It is difficult to keep one's balance while standing on the not-so-steady side of an overturned carriage, even more so when swinging a pickaxe. As the man struggled to keep his feet, it was an easy matter for the Detective to use a Baritsu throw to toss his opponent to the street. The man did not survive his fall.

"You were right, sir. They were darkies of some sorts, Hindoos by the looks of them."

"'Darkies' was not quite the term I used, Inspector, and I think you'll find these men to be Thuggees, not Hindus."

"Thugs. You're right there, and not your common British kind. But tell me, sir, how did you figure they were going to rob the museum?"

The Detective thought back. Two murders in Limehouse, both strangulations. Threads on the necks of the victims – silk from India. This and the ritual mutilation of the bodies indicated that perhaps Sleeman was premature in his announcement that the strangler cult was no more. As for the museum, its well-advertised exhibit of "Treasures of Empire" was certainly a target for all types of thieves. He was there on lookout for the Professor when two natives of India came in. Their slight bow to an idol of Kali, unnoticeable to all but one who was looking for it, confirmed his suspicions. If it had not been for the unavoidable affair of the blind waiter he would have been on time to prevent the robbery, not just recover the goods.

"It was all quite elementary, Inspector. I will explain it tonight at dinner."

"With me paying, I suppose."

"If you want all the credit, a dinner is a small price to pay."

The Inspector nodded and climbed up on to the coach. "Looks like the treasure is all still here," he said, looking down into it.

"Indeed." The Detective replied absently. He had seen it – gold, silver and jewels taken from several displays, nothing of any significant meaning other than the wealth it promised. Was that all it was after all? A common robbery? Then his attention was drawn to the chest the loot had been stored in. A wooden box from the sub-continent, the image of Kali carved on its lid and other engravings on its front, sides and back that told a story of destruction and death, resurrection and birth, carved so that one image flowed into the next in an endless cycle. He lifted the lid. The box was empty, having spilled its contents in the coach before being thrown out in the crash.

As he moved to close the lid the trained eyes of the Great Detective looked at the bottom of the chest, then at the ground and then at the difference between the two. I almost missed it, he thought, then remembered that 'almost' didn't count. He closed the lid as if the chest were nothing special.

It was rare that the Great Detective accepted a reward for his services – payment, yes, when hired by a client, but not when he acted to serve a public institution. Yet when the Curator of the British Museum offered, the Detective was quick to accept and claimed the carved wooden chest as his.

Back in his lodgings, the Detective decided that there was nowhere in England where the chest would be safe. If there were three Thuggees, there may be and probably were more. Best to get it out of the country. The good doctor was scheduled to travel to America to meet his wife's family. It would be safer overseas. Perhaps a museum there would appreciate a gift from a veteran of Her Majesty's Indian campaign.

***

Virginia Stone grew up happy. In a world where being different from the rest of society was normal, her mild deformity was not regarded as anything odd. When she was seven, Evan called a meeting of the freaks.

"What do we do with her?" he asked those assembled in the dancers' tent after one of the shows.

"She ain't one of us," said a fish-faced man. From the looks he got from everyone else he added, "I mean she is one of us and all, and she's a sweet kid, but she ain't no freak, at least not enough of one."

"Maybe she could take tickets when she got older," offered the Monkey Prince. "Be a nice bit, and she could work twice as fast as a norm."

"Now, Shiu," countered an incredibly thin woman, "you know those extra two are mostly for show, they hardly work at all."

"When gets into her teens she could dance. Be kinda nice if she grew four ti-"

The strongman's fist connected with Ronald the Geek's face. There was a thud as the latter hit the ground unconscious.

"Samson, if you broke his jaw again it'll be you biting off chicken heads come the next show."

"It be worth it, Mr. Evan. He shouldn't be saying things like that about little Ginnie."

"He should not be saying things like that at all, but he's the only geek we've got. And we all love Ginnie. But I guess the question is should we keep her?"

Evan Stone waited out the expected outburst. When it was quiet again, he continued. "Except for me, everyone now in this tent is a freak." He paused. No one took offense at the word. They knew what they were, had accepted the name and adopted it. "By nature or design you are all different. And nothing can be done to make any of you any shorter, taller, thinner, fatter or better looking. But Ginnie, do you all agree that she's not enough like you?"

"Except for a few things, she could be a norm," said the illustrated man.

There were nods of agreement. In his hoarse voice Shiu added, "We're all Hermans and Lilys. She could be Marilyn." More nods. "So what do we do, dump her off with the social workers in the next town?"

Samson's hand fell on his shoulder. "We don't dump anybody, Chimp Boy. We take care of our own."

"He's right," Evan said. "Now I've talked this over with her mothers. Ever since Ginnie came to stay with us I've been putting aside what I can. So have they and the other dancers. I'll get the pitchmen to work the rubes a little harder and in a few years we'll have enough to pay for what needs to be done. By chance or by choice we're all stuck here. But Ginnie could have a real life, a good life, and we're going to give her one."

***

New York, 1939

The Manhattan Museum of Antiquities was quiet; the only sound the echoing footsteps of the lone guard making his rounds, pausing here and there at some of his favorite exhibits. He liked the Egyptian wing with its picture writing and animal-headed gods. They were what he felt gods should be, strange and different yet somehow familiar. Nothing like what was in the India section. For some reason that place bothered him – the smiling fat man and that woman with the arms. He dreamt about her, all black and naked, wrapping all four of her arms around him. Sometimes his dreams were nightmares, and she used her arms to tear him apart. Other times, the arms were used in other, more pleasant ways. Those dreams disturbed him more than the nightmares. To dream of a god that way, even a pagan one, that had to be some sort of sin, one he could not easily confess to his priest.

So it was that the guard would hurry through that part of the museum, barely pausing to see if all was well. But why wouldn't it be? Who would bother to steal from a second rate museum tucked away in the cheaper part of Manhattan? And if someone did break in, what would he find to take? Old mummies and statues that the better places had turned down or sold off. Vases and ornaments made by less than master craftsmen. And odd furnishings like that old wooden chest with that disturbing goddess on it.

Had the guard lingered just a bit, he might have heard the creak of a skylight as it opened. He might have seen a rope drop from the ceiling and four dark-skinned men climb down. He might have confronted these men as they made their way through the rooms looking for an old wooden chest.

But then the guard would not have heard the back door being forced. Surprised by this sudden intrusion, he foolishly ran to the source of disturbance instead of sounding the alarm as he should have. That would have done him no good, as the wires to the local precinct had already been cut in two separate places.

Running out of the exhibition halls the guard watched as three men made their way through the storage area. In his last minute of consciousness, he was struck by how much they looked alike – all of them tall, blonde and in what appeared to be perfect physical shape. But then he was grabbed from behind. A hand covered his mouth and an arm around his neck applied just enough pressure. He fell silently to the floor and would awake in the morning with a headache and no memory of the night's events.

The three men made their way into the public area, looking for the India exhibit and an old wooden chest, unaware of the dark form that watched and followed.

In another part of the museum, more ropes were dropped from the open skylight. A harness was rigged, one that would lift the chest through the roof once it was retrieved by those who had gone ahead.

Under the gaze of Kali, the two groups met, the blondes coming in from the west corridor, the dark-skinned men from the east. They stared at each other, then knives were drawn by one group and pickaxes by the other. There was only one prize in the room, one that each side wanted and was prepared to kill to obtain. A silent slaughter was about to commence.

But that was not to be, not yet anyway. There was a third presence in the room, one that hid in blackness. It was by his hand that the two groups had come together that night.

It had been a week ago that two separate events had drawn his attention. One of his contacts had reported a sudden increase in staff at the German consulate. Under cover of darkness he had invaded the small piece of the Fatherland in New York and learned that the newcomers were part of a very elite group, one that was responsible for obtaining items of occult interest. He did not, however, learn anything of their intended target.

Not until the second event. A dockworker in his employ reported that four men had deserted a ship recently arrived from India. This was followed by a series of strangulation murders, the victims of whom were all wealthy Indian natives. Working quickly both as the Nightmare and as Michael Shaw, he soon learned of the possible presence of members of the Cult of Kali.

Which lead him to the Museum of Antiquities. It was there that the only serious exhibit of Indian artifacts was on display. Then began a series of movements, a game of cat and mouse as he alternately delayed and encouraged the two groups so that they would each invade the museum on the same night.

His plan worked. He stood there, laughing quietly to himself as the rival gangs stood ready to kill over – what? What in the room was so important?

"It is ours," said one of the Germans.

The reply in Hindi was short and impolite. Both sides readied to kill the other.

He thought about allowing it, about waiting in the shadows and letting the fight go on. He could then easily dispose of the victors. But that was not his way.

At the two sides advanced on each other, the room filled with a spectral laugh. It started low, barely audible, then grew until it could *not be ignored. Searching for its source, all seven finally turned to the west entrance. As they did, the Nightmare stepped from the darkness and addressed them.*

"You come as thieves and robbers, coveting power which is not yours. I give you one chance, one choice. Surrender and live, resist and die."

Their rivalry forgotten for the moment, men from two different parts of the globe united. Pickaxes and knives were raised and as one they advanced on their black-clad foe.

They had had their chance, had been given their warning. From beneath his coat the shadowy figure drew twin .45s. As the group charged him he fired mercilessly into its midst, cutting down each man before he could go more than a few steps.

Minutes later the grim avenger stood alone, the dead sprawled at his feet. Knowing that his shots would have been heard, that by now the police would have been summoned and would soon arrive, he quickly searched the room for that over which seven men had died. Had he had more time, he would have found it. Instead, the growing wail of sirens caused him to withdraw.

The police arrived soon after. An ambulance was called for the unconscious guard, a morgue wagon for the deceased. In the excitement of the investigation, no one took notice of an old wooden chest in one corner of the room.

***

A cab driver has to pick up any and all fares. That was the law and the rules of the Taxi Commission. If a cabbie was caught deliberately ignoring a passenger because of race, color or the way he was dressed he could lose his hack license. But that was only the law. Those assholes in the capitol and fools in the City Council didn't have to drive for a living, with most of the money coming from tips. And a driver should not have to pick up those people who were not likely to give over the proper fifteen or twenty percent.

That was what Romano Smith thought as he cruised his Regal Cab through the streets of the city. To hell with the Taxi Commission. He'd pick up who he wanted where he wanted. And if he passed some waving black guy in a T-shirt and low hanging jeans because up ahead he saw a suit with a briefcase, who was to say he just didn't see the man.

It was rush hour and Smith was working the Inner Harbor, mostly taking tourists to Fells Point and Little Italy for dinner. It was a good time. Neither locale was that far away and most could not tell if he put a few extra miles on the meter. Plus tourists almost always tipped big and then there were the kickbacks from certain restaurants if he could get them to their doors.

He saw the two dark men standing in front of the Gallery. They were waving but a couple of cabbies had already passed them by. Smith still had a block before he had to decide if they were worth it.

Young but well dressed, not in suits but in the casual style that people nowadays wore to dinner. And as he got closer, Smith saw that they weren't exactly black, more an Indian light brown. Making his decision, he cut across two lanes of traffic and pulled up next to them.

"Where to?" he asked as the two got into his cab. They gave him an address on Aylesbury Rd. Damn, he thought, that was all the way into the county. Worse yet, the tall one had given the address in a local accent. Great – riders who probably knew the way and a long trip with no return fare.

But they were already in his cab. So Smith pulled off toward Gay St.

He was just on the I-83 ramp when the taller one spoke up.

"We have some business with a video distributor. Exporting old movies to Bombay in exchange for Bollywood musicals."

So? Smith thought. BFD.

"We'll only be about thirty minutes more or less. Any chance you could wait? Getting a cab in Timonium this time of day is a bitch."

Smith's day was suddenly brighter. He tried not to show it. "I dunno. One I drop you off the ride's officially over, and a city cab's not allowed to pick up fares in the county. Course if I let the meter running ..."

"That will be fine." The shorter one at least sounded foreign. Maybe he was out-of-town money. "We will make it worth your time and effort. And thank you very much."

So a much happier Romano Smith drove his cab north as his fares sat in the back, talking some nonsense about eyes looking for a chest. He guessed it was a horror movie they had both seen.

Twenty minutes later Smith stopped his Regal Cab in front of the address given. He checked the numbers. This was the place, he thought, but it looked closed.

"Are you guys sure ..."

A silk scarf wrapped around his neck, cutting off his breath. He fought to free himself but the tall man behind was strong and held him fast. Smith weakened, started fading as the darkness moved in. Soon his struggles ceased.

The small man looked around as the tall man released his victim. "There's no one around," he said. There wouldn't be, not in this area this time of day. They had spent the last three days watching to make sure.

"Should we finish him here?"

"Yes. But Yash, it must be done in the old way, Her way. We'll carry him to the woods over there." From the case he carried he took a small pickaxe. "You may have the honor while I recite the holy words."

"Thank you, Uttam."

Minutes later from the woods there came the sounds of metal striking bone and flesh. They were accompanied by prayers and chants in an old, forgotten and forbidden tongue. And when all was again silent, the body of Romano Smith lay covered by dirt and leaves hastily thrown over him.

The cab drove away, Yash at the wheel. Uttam sat beside him, counting the money he had taken from the body of the driver as well as the fare receipts he had found in a bag under the front seat.

"Where to?" Yash wanted to know.

"I had thought the airport, but if that driver was correct, a city cab might attract attention. Try Penn Station. There should be someone there in need of a taxi. But drop me off at my car first and I'll meet you. Someone might remember two cab drivers. Just remember, Yash, businessmen or tourists, they have the most money."

***

"This can't be happening." Brian Moses kept telling himself that. He had hoped it was all a horrible dream, a nightmare from which he could not awake. Nightmare it was, but Brian was wide awake.

It had started at the train station. He and his family – wife, son and two daughters – had come down from Boston on a week's vacation. See the National Aquarium, the Science Center, maybe take in ballgame. So what if it wasn't the Red Sox. He'd root against whomever the home team was playing. He hoped it was the Yankees.

Brian had heard the stories about the city, knew about its high crime rate. But that was mostly in the drug areas. Tourists and visitors were supposed to be safe. It wasn't like it was New York or Miami.

They were all jammed in the backseat. A tight fit but in his broken English the cabdriver had insisted that the law prohibited front seat passengers. He had suggested that the women take another cab, but Brian wanted to keep the family together.

Being from out of town, it took a while before Brian realized that the cabbie was not taking them to their Inner Harbor hotel. Instead he seemed to be driving out of the city at a very fast rate of speed. Brian tried to get him to stop, but the driver ignored him. With his cell phone in his suitcase in the trunk, there was nothing he or his family could do until the wild trip ended. Then, Brian decided, if need be he would fight off the driver while his family ran to safety.

The driver stopped in what looked to be a vacant industrial park. Before Brian could get his family out, three more men appeared. All shared the driver's coloring. They had scarves around their necks and were holding sharp tools.

"When we get out, everybody run," Brian told his family. They did, but other men appeared and soon all were caught and held fast.

"You should have let your wife and daughters take another cab," the driver told him.

That was Brian Moses began to hope that he was in the middle of a horrible dream.

Held fast, Brian was turned to face his children. Men came up behind them, looped scarves around their necks and slowly tightened them. He closed his eyes but could not block out the sounds of his children dying.

When all was again silent. Brian opened his eyes. No sign of his children or their bodies.

"They are gone," explained a man in front of him. There was a scream and Brian recognized his wife's voice. "She will be joining your children soon. But first …" He gave Brian an unmistakable leer. "We will be taking turns all night, so this will be a mercy for you."

A scarf was wrapped around his neck and pulled tight. With his wife's cries echoing in his ears and with one final prayer that he wake up in Boston, Brian Moses passed from this world.

***

The Hamilton had started life as a theater, an elaborate showcase for the best that Vaudeville could offer. A new show every week, five shows a day, six on Saturday before going dark on Sunday. Only the finest played there – Fields, Jolson, The Marx Brothers, Mae West and Ethel Barrymore. Then dark times fell and the Hamilton was reduced to hosting burlesque revues. But even then the grand old lady attracted the top names. Gypsy Rose Lee played there, as did Blaze Star, Irma the Body and Tempest Storm. But the act performed by the notorious team of Bubbles O'Reilly and Fifi O'Rourke prompted a police raid, and the theater was shuttered for two years.

When the Hamilton reopened it was as a motion picture palace. Again her seats were packed with crowds, all eager for the latest offerings from Hollywood. But as the city's population moved to the suburbs, she lost the first run films and started running double features at a reduced price. A bad economy and a few changes of ownership later, the Hamilton became home to XXX adult movies, her faded seats now occupied only by desperate, lonely men pleasuring themselves while watching things that would have made O'Rourke and O'Reilly blush.

Videotapes and DVDs sounded the end. With no more need to travel across town and sneak into the darkness for self-gratification, even the lost and depraved stopped coming. Again the shutters went up over the windows and doors of the Hamilton.

Slowly the neighborhood changed, for the better this time and the building that was the Hamilton was again sold. Life is nothing but ironic, and it is said that even God appreciates a good joke. If so, He must have roared with laughter when the theater that had seen the fan dance of Sally Rand, heard the jokes of Sophie Tucker and witnessed what made Linda Lovelace infamous reopened as the New Kingdom Revivalist Gospel Church. Every Sunday and several times during the week the sounds of joyous praise could be heard filling the room, and the people inside left feeling good about themselves and full of love for their fellow man.

But not even good things last forever. There was a falling out as members of the congregation began to argue over God's plan for His faithful. Some held that the Savior would have them be meek and mild at all times and eschew all earthly pleasures. Others said that man was put on earth to have fun and praise the Lord. They argued that wealth and success were signs of God's favor and to deny them and the pleasure they brought was to deny the One who had provided them. The resulting schism left few regular worshippers and with little funds to pay the rent, the church closed and the building was again sold.

It did not reopen. There was talk that it would be made over into a recreation center, a grocery store or private apartments. None of these rumors came true. Slowly, the Hamilton became just another vacant building on the streets of city.

That is not to say it did not see use. There were those for whom an abandoned building was just the right meeting place. Addicts, the homeless, the forgotten all at one time would seek its shelter. But then there came those who forced the others out.

Theirs was an old cult. Its founders had once been hunted down and all but destroyed. But nothing really dies, and one by one the survivors found each other and slowly reformed. Once scattered all over the globe, they eventually gathered together on the shores of the new world, united in a single purpose, the worship of a dark and terrible deity, a goddess long thought dead.

Entering off an alley in the rear, coming in through a back door behind the screen, every week they met and turned their attention to a cheap replica of a statue that had once been at the site of a great and terrible defeat. The idol was of a woman, all black and nude except for a belt of severed hands and necklace of skulls, her four arms empty and waiting to be filled. She was Kali, creator and destroyer, giver of life and bringer of death. They were her people and she was their god, and they waited for the time when she would return in all her terrible glory.

For some of her sect, Kali's return was as distant as the Jew's Messiah or the Christian's Second Coming. It would happen one day but not in their lifetime or in their children's but sometime in the future.

But there were others, those who felt the presence of the goddess every day. For them Kali's promised coming was something they had to bring about. So they listened to the words of those in charge, obeyed their dark demands and shared in the rewards.

Every week, when the rituals had ended and most of the worshippers had left, eight men remained. They were the inner circle, the heart, hands and eyes of Kali, the true heirs of the cult that had spread terror so long ago.

Apart from and above the others, they would watch the rituals from the balcony. Then they would meet and discuss their sacred work.

"What progress has been made?" Mahesh would ask. They had all taken Indian names, rejecting their American ones. Mahesh saw himself as the Heart of Kali, the leader of the group.

Most times the others had little to offer. The group was little known, so there were no threats for Kali's Arms to defend against. The Eyes of Kali would report on what they had learned of the goddess from the media and the Internet. Most times there was little to mention except what all of them already knew.

Uttam looked out over the balcony and down at the idol. He saw himself as leader of the Arms and second only to Mahesh.

"One day we will have enough to buy this building and make her a proper temple."

"And how will we explain where the money came from?"

Uttam shrugged. "If we have enough, Mahesh, no one will care."

The Heart of Kali nodded in agreement, but added, "They will care if they connect us with those we killed. It was different in the beginning. The British didn't care how many natives were killed, as long as it was just natives. But this is not then. Should the police connect us with the deaths before She comes …"

"That time may be soon," said Rohit, one of the Eyes. "I've found the Chest of Saugor."

His companions looked at him in amazement and disbelief. Then as a man, they looked out from the balcony and down towards their goddess and her empty hands. They turned back to Rohit.

"No way!" said Gajanan, a fellow Eye.

Rohit smiled at him. "Way."

"Impossible, "Uttam sneered, "the Chest is a myth."

"Why then are the goddess's hands empty?" came Rohit's retort.

"Because it is said that when She truly returns She will fill Her own hands."

"That is a myth, Sagar, and as an Eye you should know better. I tell you I've found the Chest."

Mahesh leaned forward. "Supposedly the Chest has been located several times before. Each time attempts to retrieve it have failed. It was last seen in New York but was said to be lost when the museum burned down. Most think that those who died trying to retrieve it were chasing a dream."

"It is a dream, a dream that we all have. And where better to find dreams come true than…" Rohit held up a ragged looking videotape box "… Hollywood."

The goddess Kali had not been treated well in the movies. Films such as *Gunga Din, Help* and *Temple of Doom* were reviled among her followers. The worst was the 1951 epic *Son of Gunga Din*, a supposed sequel to the classic in which the title character returns to Tantrapur in search of treasure. Instead he finds a revived cult of Kali terrorizing the village. Of course he stops the cult and finds his "treasure" in the young woman he must rescue from being sacrificed. It was commonly held to be one of the worst movies ever made.

As the tape box was passed around Sagar asked, "Why bring this crap here? It is an insult to the goddess."

"Because," Rohit explained, "what the movie lacked in writing, acting and all else, it made up for in authenticity. The director knew he had a dog and tried to dress it up by using real Indian artifacts. Let's go into the office and I'll show you."

The office was off the Hamilton's projection room. The eight gathered there around a television and VHS player.

"This better be worthwhile, or you're taking the short way off the balcony." Yash was the largest and strongest of the Arms and very likely to make good his threat.

The movie began playing. Rohit fast-forwarding through most of it, stopping about fifty minutes into the film. The TV screen showed a gang of white actors in poorly applied blackface menacing a beautiful young actress. Rohit paused the film.

"Look in the background, to your left."

What the group saw was a carved wooden chest.

"So, it's a chest. That doesn't mean it's *the* chest."

"Just wait, Abhay, just wait." Rohit fast-forwarded another fifteen minutes then hit play.

The hero was down, struck unconscious by a man he trusted but who had joined the cult in hopes of getting the girl and treasure for himself. The camera zoomed in on the son of Din lying on the floor. Rohit paused the film just as the chest came into plain view.

It was ornately carved, the image of Kali on its lid with a story of death and destruction, birth and redemption on what could be seen on its front and sides.

There was a collective gasp.

"It could be," admitted Gajanan.

Uttam shook his head. "I'll admit that it matches the description, but even so, what good does it do us? That movie's over fifty years old. Who knows where the chest is now?"

"I did say I found it." Rohit brought out a notebook computer, plugged into a phone jack and went online to an auction site. He quickly brought up an image of the chest.

"The studio that made the film went bankrupt in the 60s. Most of its props went into private collections. The owner of the chest just died. His heirs are selling off the estate."

Sagar looked at the current bid on the chest. "We can afford it; of course we may have to take down a few more tourists."

"There's no need to buy it. We just wait until the auction over and see who wins. We track him down and ..." Rohit smiled knowingly. Mahesh, the Heart of Kali, picked up on his meaning.

"Yes. Uttam, Yash, Abhay, Jayant. It is time that we find out if you are true Arms of the Goddess. This chest will be ours and should it prove real, then it can only be a matter of time before She returns."

Uttam remained after the others left. "There may be a better way," he said to Mahesh, who had also stayed behind.

"How so?" Uttam explained. "Yes, that would be less risky. We'll do it your way."

***

from the private journal of John Declan

As hard as this job is sometimes, there are times when things just fall into your lap. Today two kids came into the office. I call them kids because to me anyone under forty's a kid. They were probably in their early twenties. They looked foreign but spoke good English. Maybe their parents or grandparents were from Pakistan or Persia or wherever. Anyway, the two seemed to have been born and raised here.

I don't usually have clients like this. Usually it's husbands and wives wanting me to prove their better halves are cheating. Sometimes they just think their loved one is cheating and want me to show otherwise. Those are the ones I wind up disappointing. Or else it's a guy who owns a business and wants to know just how his employees are stealing him blind.

These two wanted something different. They had seen something on one of those auction sites on the Internet. They had tried to buy it but got outbid. Now they wanted me to find the winner so they could buy it from him.

That was the first thing wrong about their story. People their age know more about computers than I ever will. It should have been easy for them to find the guy they wanted. Instead they pay a peeper like me to do it.

The other thing was their names. When I asked they said they were "Joe" and "Jim." I might have believed them but they didn't look like any Joe or Jim I knew and they kept forgetting which of them was which. But that didn't matter. What they wanted me to do wasn't illegal. It wasn't hard and they paid in cash, enough cash that I didn't care what they would do once I found this chest of theirs.

Like I said, it's a good day when a case like this falls into your lap. Easy money for very little work. After the kids left I booted up my own computer. Compared to some I don't know much about search engines and e-bids and stuff like that, but I've been looking for people and things for over thirty years and I know how and where to look for them.

I know that when you don't where to find something you start from where it's been. So in this case I didn't worry about the bidder. I concentrated on the seller.

He was easy. He was a dealer in antiques, collectibles and just plain junk from the movies. He had an online store and a toll-free number.

At first he gave me crap about client confidentially and how it wouldn't be ethical to give out the names of winning bidders. His ethics changed when I offered him fifty bucks. What did I care? It wasn't coming out of my pocket. Any it wasn't the only thing I was going to tack on the "expense account" I'd be giving Joe and Jim when I gave them the final bill.

Turned out the new owner of the chest was a movie nut out of New York. I got his name and address then thanked the seller very much. Then I made a note that if I ever bought anything really expensive online I'd have it shipped to a drop point under a phony name.

I made one more call. That was to the guy who bought the chest after looking his number up in the criss-cross. I made out like I was the seller checking the shipping location. Maybe he didn't notice that I had blocked his caller ID or maybe he didn't are. Either way he verified it for me.

Now comes the hard part. I have to write a report that makes it seem like I did two days work on this. At a couple of hundred a day that's easy money, not to mention my "expenses."

Wonder what those kids want with the chest and how they plan to get it. They said it was an old family heirloom, lots of sentimental value. I believe that like I believe their names are really Joe and Jim. Sabu and Mowgli more likely. As long as I'm paid, whatever they plan is no concern to me. Or maybe it is. I'll have to watch the NY papers. If they steal it there might be a reward. More easy money. Sometimes I love my job.

***

It was two in the morning, the time when night starts to become day. A dark grey form hid well within the shadows and watched the City Morgue. A crack of light appeared and became a rectangle as a back door opened and the night crew of Medical Examiner's Office ended its shift. The dark shape counted the people going out. When he knew all but one had gone, he carefully approached the door, knocked once and was admitted.

"Come in, my friend." Dr. Bartholomew Penn stepped aside and allowed his visitor to enter. He was a tall man, but that was all the doctor knew for his body was covered in a charcoal grey habit, his head and face completely hidden by a deep cowl. Dr. Penn knew one other thing, that beneath the robes were holstered a pair of .45 caliber automatics, weapons that had been used often and to deadly effect against those who would do harm to the city and its people.

As always in this situation, Dr. Penn had a feeling of excitement, a thrill of doing something forbidden. Standing before him was The Grey Monk, the vigilante who waged his own private war against crime.

Officially the Grey Monk was wanted by the police for over a score of murders he was said to have committed, each of them either a criminal shot down during the commission of a crime or one who had escaped the law only to be met by the Monk's brand of deadly justice. Unofficially, the police no longer actively searched for him, at times actually seeking his help in tracking down and putting an end to threats against the city.

Dr. Penn had met the Monk when the grey clad avenger saved him from a mugging just outside the morgue. After that, the doctor had become a source of information, giving the Monk needed results of autopsies and sometimes alerting him to crime in the making.

This was one of those times. There were many people in the city, on both sides of the law, who would give much to know where this man was right now. Yet the Monk had trusted the doctor enough to come at his request.

"You called for me, Doctor?"

The Grey Monk's voice was a whisper, yet one distinct enough that Dr. Penn heard every word. He could only imagine the effect it had on criminals when they heard it coming out of the darkness.

"Yes. Let's go into my office."

When the pair had settled themselves, the Monk as usual declining an offer of coffee or tea, Dr. Penn handed over several manila folders, case notes and results of post-mortem examinations.

"You may find these interesting. It started with cabdrivers, three of them over the past few months. They may be more; at least two others are missing. They're presumed dead, but their bodies haven't been located. All the cabs have been accounted for, found in areas far from where the bodies turned up."

"I take it, doctor, that the cause of death for each was the same."

Dr. Penn nodded. "Let's say similar. Two of the cabbies were strangled; we found traces of silk around their necks. The other died from puncture wounds to the upper torso, yet on examination I found similar fibers, as if he'd been choked before being killed."

"The two who were strangled, were there also marks on their bodies?"

"Got it in one. And all the wounds seem to be from the same kind of weapon, a pick or an ice axe, something like that. The police didn't catch on at first, since the killers are smart. They grab the cab in one jurisdiction and leave it and the body in two others. It was only after the second body was found that we were able to link things together.

"You said 'killers,' Doctor. How do you know?"

"The weapons used struck bone, leaving toolmarks, different ones in each case."

"What else, Doctor. You said it started with the cabdrivers."

"Yes." Doctor Penn hesitated. He had been working with death for over twenty years. He had seen its myriad forms, teased out its secrets from those it had taken, there was little about it that bothered or upset him. Yet recent events had shocked even him.

He handed the Monk another folder.

"This is why I called you. Your detective friend from Homicide, Amos Hoffman, told me that every time one of those cabs went missing, so would some out of town visitors. Three businessmen, a family from Boston and newlyweds from Hawaii. All on record as having arrived, some at BWI, others at Penn Station. The newlyweds and two of the businessmen even checked into their hotel. But after that ..." Doctor Penn shook his head. "Missing Persons was handling the missing travelers. The city's Homicide Unit along with Anne Arundel and Baltimore County's were investigating the dead cabbies. Up until now the two cases were not connected."

"Until now?"

Doctor Penn let out a deep breath. "The bodies of the missing family were found off Eastern Avenue, that old business park near the underpass. A crew was getting it ready for renovation, cleaning it out. They found them buried under some rubble. The causes of death – strangulation or puncture wounds."

He directed the Monk's attention to the folder he had just given him. "Father, mother and three kids, the oldest only twelve. There's evidence that the mother was gang raped before, during and maybe even after being killed."

Dr. Penn watched the Monk's cowl slowly move from side to side, then lower as if the man inside was at prayer. A moment passed, then two. The doctor thought he heard a whispered "Amen," just before the Monk asked,

"What about the children?"

"Clean kills, if there is such a thing. Good news, there's plenty of DNA evidence. Bad news, none of it matches anyone in the system. Detective Hoffman tells me that Homicide, Missing Persons and Sex Offense are all working on this. All leaves have been cancelled and a task force is being established. He says that the mayor's calling the Police Commissioner at least three times a day which means the PC's calling down to Homicide at least twice a shift. All the resources of three counties are being employed."

"Yet you have called me?"

"I think it's more in your line than theirs. There's evil here, an evil with which the law is incapable of dealing, not properly anyway."

Doctor Penn took the folder from the Monk. Carefully, almost reverently, he removed photos from it and laid them on a table between them. Crime scene photos, autopsy photos, photos of a murdered father, strangled children and a brutalized mother.

"These deaths call for a justice greater than the law allows."

***

"The Mass has ended. Go in Peace."

As Father Richard Harper finished the morning service, he looked around for his sexton. Not seeing him the priest grew concerned. The absence was not like Lewis. Even on his busiest nights, Lewis always made it back in time for the closing prayer. That he wasn't in church could only mean one thing – something had happened to him.

Where was he, worried Harper. Could he be lying in an alley somewhere, slowly bleeding to death? Or maybe whomever he had been pursuing had turned the tables and even now held the man prisoner. Or could it be that the Law had finally captured him? No, the last was not even a consideration. If that were so, by now detectives would have brought a search warrant to the doors of St. Sebastian Church and rectory and he himself would be in custody, arrested as an accessory to the supposed crimes of the Grey Monk.

How long had it been, Harper wondered, since the man who called himself Lewis had come to his door seeking aid and comfort? A year? Two? It seemed as if he had been helping the vigilante with his crusade forever. Yet less than a decade ago the priest had himself been a police detective who had been called from one life of service to another.

From cop to priest to secretly adding the self-appointed agent of God's vengeance. It had to end sometime. Was today that time?

Those were Harper's thoughts as he cleaned the altar, put his chalice away and removed his vestments. As he walked to the rectory he wondered how long he should wait for Lewis before making phone calls that might reveal the secret that had been carefully kept by the two men.

Maybe there was something in Lewis's room that would provide a clue as his plans. On his way there the priest noticed a light on in the study. There he found his prodigal sexton surrounded by open reference books, staring intently at a computer screen and pausing only to take notes.

Harper let out a sigh of relief, then offered up a silent prayer of thanksgiving that Lewis was safe.

"You missed Mass."

Lewis turned. "Sorry, Father. I hope I didn't worry you."

"No."

But Lewis had heard the priest's approach, and his sigh.

"It's a sin to lie, Father, even for a priest."

"Okay, I was worried. You usually let me know when you get back."

"My apologies, but I had good cause. I returned shortly after Mass had started and immediately began my research." He told the priest what he had learned from Dr. Penn.

"My God!"

"A god at least. The strangulations, mutilations and burials all spoke of ritual slayings. It did not take me long to discover their purpose. What do you know of the Cult of Kali?"

"Kali, she's the Hindu goddess of death, isn't she?"

Lewis smiled and shook his head. "That's a common belief, at least in this country, thanks mainly to movies, comic books and pulp fiction. And I admit that's what I believed until tonight. But Kali is held by many to be not only a destroyer but also a creator, a mother goddess and protector, usually in union with Shiva. It is only that her name can be translated as 'terrible' and her image is, shall we say, somewhat frightening."

Lewis turned to his computer and displayed a picture of the goddess. She was nude but there was nothing sensual or erotic about her. Her skin was the color of night and she held a bowl, a spear, a sword and a severed head.

"Her four arms," Lewis explained, "represent the dimensions of space and time and at the same time the cycle of creation – birth, growth, decline and death. And yes, those are human heads around her neck and arms about her waist."

"I've known mothers like that," Harper said dryly.

"Unfortunately there were those who concentrated only on her more ferocious aspect and came to worship her as death incarnate. In her name they preyed on native travelers throughout India, joining them, gaining their confidence then striking them down. Their preferred method of execution was the ruhmal, a strangling scarf. They would then dig their victims' graves with a sacred pickaxe. Any monies they took from their victims would go to further the cause."

"From what you've told me, times have changed."

"Unfortunately yes, Father. Our modern day Thugees are now using the pick as a weapon and have added rape to their sins."

"It's to bind all those involved to the crime. I saw it when I was a detective working gangs. Strangulation is an individual crime. Having everyone participate in either mutilating the bodies or brutalizing one of the victims makes accomplices of them all, and so it's less likely one will turn against the group. But, Lewis, you said that these Thuggees preyed on native travelers."

"Yes, they did. The feeling was that to attack the occupying British would be to invite disaster, that the white man would not care what the natives did to each other. And for the most part they were right. But finally some decent men came forward and began the campaign that was believed to have destroyed the cult. But evil is never fully destroyed."

"But if the Thuggees attacked only natives, why are their targets this time mostly white and black cabdrivers, tourists and businessmen?"

"All of whom, Father, can be considered 'travelers' and are all no doubt 'native' to this country, as I am sure are the killers."

"What are your plans?"

Lewis shrugged. "There is little I can do for now, except provide another pair of eyes and ears on the street and pray that in time the Lord will provide a way to put an end to this horror."

***

News article – the Baltimore Sentinel

Acting on a report of a foul odor, police found the body of John Declan in his downtown office. The rooms were reported to have been ransacked and his death is being treated as suspicious.

Declan was a twenty year veteran of the police department who retired under what some officials called "a cloud of suspicion" following an in-custody death of a murder suspect. Following his retirement, Declan became a private investigator most noted for his involvement with the Lauren Guthrie kidnapping. While some believed him to be a principal in the girl's abduction, most credited him with bringing the case to a successful conclusion.

While a police spokesman declined comment, a source at the Medical Examiner's Office stated that Declan's death apparently occurred over the weekend and that the cause of death may have been strangulation.

***

Harper had just finished reading his Office and was working on his weekend sermon when his phone rang. It was Detective Hoffman.

"Got time to talk."

"Sure, Amos. To tell you the truth I was expecting your call. How soon can you get here?"

"I'm knocking on your door now."

"Cell phones are wonderful things, aren't they?" Amos Hoffman said after he and Harper were settled in the priest's study.

"There was a time, Amos, when you couldn't stand them."

The detective smiled. "That was then, Rich. But these days everybody's got one. And you take one off an arrestee or find one on a body and suddenly you know all his contacts, everybody he called or who called him. How can I not love something that makes my job easier? And I get such interesting calls on mine, like from that friend of yours."

"Amos, if you mean The Grey Monk, he's no friend …"

Hoffman waved a hand at the priest. "Save it, Rich. I know he keeps in touch with you, and I don't care. Not right now anyway. Just like I don't care that he's got a snitch down at the M.E.'s. Speaking of which, did he get my message?"

Harper nodded. "If you mean about the murders, yes. He believes they're cult slayings, the work of …."

"Yeah, the Cult of Kali. We're not stupid, Rich. We've got computers and people who can read and all that."

"Then why …"

"Call him in? It wasn't my idea. You know how I feel about that damn spook. He's dangerous, a wild card that will one day go too far and get innocent people hurt, including you and me."

"He's done some good, Amos."

"He's judge, jury and executioner. And one day …." Shaking his head, Hoffman let whatever comment he was going to make trail off.

"I was ordered to bring him in on this. 'All available resources' was the code the bosses used, so if things break bad they can deny it. If we find the killers first you'll probably hear it on the news. If he finds them …" Hoffman paused, took a breath and resumed, "have him call us when he can."

"Amos, are you saying what I think you are?"

"All I'm saying, Rich, is that after seeing what these monsters did to that woman and her family, nobody cares too much what happens to them. We just need one left alive to tell us where the other bodies are. As for the rest, I was told that's between the Monk and God."

***

Uttam selected five of the most promising followers, those who could someday be Her arms, and gave them their instructions. Taking separate cars, three drove north to New Jersey and took the train into Manhattan. One caught a Chinatown bus at the Dundalk Travel Plaza and the others went by Amtrak. They met up, seemingly by accident, at a subshop off 47th St and Lexington and walked down to the U.N. Plaza.

"You know what to do." It was less a question than a statement. Uttam had briefed them thoroughly before leaving the city. At their nods he said, "And remember, should there be any resistance, avoid killing if you can. This time we are the travelers, not those in the house."

"What about that guy in the office. We did him and he wasn't going nowhere."

Uttam looked at his challenger. "He was a traitor, Tapan. He took our money and would have sold us out. Death is the penalty for betrayal." As he said this the thought crossed his mind that Tapan might be a man to watch, and to watch out for.

Another asked, "What about any women?" That one had not been involved in the attack on the Boston family but had heard of it and wanted his turn.

Uttam thought a minute then shrugged. "If the opportunity arises, have fun. But do so quietly and remember our purpose."

They parted, each to his own hotel. The next day they met again in Central Park.

"It's a private home so there's no doorman to worry about. I've been watching since morning and it appears that everyone has left but the housekeeper."

"Is she pretty?"

Uttam ignored the question. "Tapan, you play deliveryman. Rush the door as soon as it opens. Devang, once Tapan's inside, follow him and give the signal when it's safe. We will follow one by one."

"And if anyone sees us?"

"If they bother to take notice, they'll see only the color of our skin. To them we'll be servants or workers, no one of consequence."

It went as planned. Tapan forced his way in, Devang followed and soon the rest were inside.

Uttam was the last to enter. As he did he heard the muffled cries of the housekeeper and the creaking of an old sofa. Let them all take their turn, he thought, it will distract the police and have them looking in the wrong direction. He began his search for the chest.

This time there was no Great Detective to interfere with the plan, no Dark Avenger to strike them down. The Chest of Saugor was found in a second floor den that had been made over into a museum of the cinema. They filled the chest with other valuables and collectibles and smashed most of what was left before leaving the traumatized housekeeper sobbing on the living room floor.

They returned in the same manners as they came, Uttam driving the chest back himself.

A special service was held once the chest was in the temple. Emptied of the loot removed from the private museum, it sat alone before the figure of Kali. No prayers were said, her worshippers just sitting before her in thanksgiving that they were a part of this historic moment.

"We should open it."

"No, Sagar, the time is not yet. We need something more worthy than that." Mahesh indicated the poorly made replica that was before them.

"It was opened," came a whisper from the back, "I saw them taking stuff out of it."

Sitting closest to the chest, the Heart, Arms and Eyes of Kali looked at each other. Was there truly one who had not heard the story of the Chest of Saugor? Who did not know why most of the Goddess's few remaining servants laid down their lives in its defense? Were there others? If so, they must be told so that they could best appreciate the moment.

"Rohit."

"Yes, Mahesh?"

"If it wasn't for you the Chest would be just other box in some rich man's collection. Tell these fool why it is important, why so many of Her servants have died trying to reclaim it."

Rohit told those assembled the secret of the Chest of Saugor. And they were amazed and felt even more honored to be present.

***

"You wanted to see me, Evan?"

Virginia Stone stood in the doorway of Evan Stone's office trailer.

"Yes, Ginnie, come in and take a load off."

Evan waited until the girl was seated. This day had been long in coming and he had been rehearsing this moment ever since the decision was made. Now that the time was here, he found it difficult to begin.

"Ginnie, you're going to be a young lady soon and ..."

"Evan, I know all about 'the birds and the bees.'"

Evan's face reddened. "I'm sure you do. I'd be surprised if you didn't. I'm sure your mothers did a more than adequate job explaining things. But that's not why I called you in here. As I said, you're going to be young lady soon, and a very pretty one at that, I'm sure."

It was Virginia's turn to blush. Then she waved her arms. "Except for these."

The carnival master smiled. "Even with them. But that's what I wanted to talk to you about."

And Evan told Virginia about the meeting that had been held years back and what had been decided.

"We finally have the money, and there's doctors willing to do the surgery. In no time at all ..." And tears came to the old man's eyes at the thought of losing this girl to the real world.

Virginia's eyes welled up too, at the thought of leaving, of having a chance at being normal and of what her family had done to give her that chance. She sprung out of her chair and hugged Evan as hard as she could, wrapping all four of her arms around him.

***

The Grey Monk prowled the night. He knew that the police were staking out the train station, travel center and the airport. They had undercover officers driving taxis and picking up anyone who looked like he might be of East Indian origin or ancestry. And they were working with immigration investigating those who had recently arrived from that part of the world.

That left the streets to the Monk. None of his usual contacts or agents were of any help. No one knew of any gangs whose members fit the supposed profiles of the cultists. So each night he went out, attending cultural events, seeing movies, going to anything with a connection to India, its beliefs or its people. He became a regular at certain restaurants. He would sit in the back and scan the crowd for possible suspects – young men who by their voices, gestures and attitudes seem more radical or secretive. And each night he would make his selection then leave ahead of his target. Donning his grey habit, he would wait in the shadows and follow the chosen young man, praying that this would be the one who would lead him to the cult. Each night his prayers went unanswered.

"No luck last night?" Harper asked over breakfast following the Monk's latest outing. Lewis shook his head.

"This city's Indian population is not that large. Someone must know something but if they do no one is talking."

"At least not in front of an outsider like yourself."

"There is that. Still, one of the ones I've followed should have led me someone other than home."

The two men ate silently. They finished and as Lewis was clearing the dishes, Harper spoke up. "Maybe there's something in the works. When I was with the Department, gang activity was low and crime down just before something big was about to occur. It was the bad guy's way of lulling or suspicions. It didn't take us long to figure out that when things were looking good they were about to break bad."

"It could be, Father. But if the cult is planning something, the question is what."

With that question unanswered, they made ready for morning Mass. As Harper donned his vestments, Lewis prepared the altar. As he did so, he noticed Amos Hoffman sitting in a back pew.

Lewis went into the sacristy. "Detective Hoffman is here. It could be that the police have a lead in the case."

Harper smiled. "Or maybe he's finally figured out that being church sexton is only your part-time job."

"I don't think so, he's not smiling."

Leaving the church right before Communion, Hoffman was waiting in the rectory's visitors' lounge when Mass was over. As Lewis found work to do elsewhere, Harper led the detective into the study.

"A break in the case, Amos, or have you decided to convert?"

"If I thought it would help I'd consider it. But you're right; there's been ... a development."

"If I remember my cop-talk, that means something unexpected has happened but no one's sure if the news is good or bad."

Hoffman nodded. "That's about it. We got a case-to-case DNA match from that family that was slaughtered. Yesterday the CODIS database hit a new entry out of New York, a home invasion & rape. The victim was left alive and described her attackers as four or five, and I quote, 'Indians, Pakistanis, Arabs or one of that crowd down there.' The NYPD crime lab was able to isolate four DNA profiles, two of which hit what we've got."

"So that means that either the cult has moved on ..."

"In which case, it becomes somebody else's problem."

"Or the cult is expanding."

"And is now a bigger problem for everybody. You know what that means, don't you, Rich? Joint taskforces, the Feds getting involved and bringing in Homeland Security and the FBI. And if you remember, they don't like your creepy friend."

"I can understand why. He did make them look a bit foolish."

"And for that I almost forgave him. Anyway, I have to report in." As he left Hoffman handed the priest a sheet of paper. "For what good it will do, here's a list of what was stolen. Mostly movie junk and stuff. Guy who owned the place was some kind of collector."

Getting the list from Harper, Lewis closeted himself with his reference books and computer for the rest of the day, not emerging until late evening.

"Not going out tonight?"

"No, Father, that approach does not seem to be working. Another is needed but I have an idea."

"Did you learn anything from your research?"

"Something significant, I think. I just don't know its meaning. There were quite a few items stolen from the New York home. As Detective Hoffman said, all movie memorabilia and the like. Props, signed lobby cards, original scripts, clothing worn by this actor or that. Only one had any relation to India or Kali, an old chest that had been used in sequel to Gunga Din."

"I've heard of that. Supposed to be pretty bad."

Lewis shrugged. "The quality of the movie is not at question. The provenance of the chest is. It was obtained from a Manhattan museum that closed during the Second World War. Prior to the war, a, uhm, predecessor of mine broke up an attempted robbery during which both Nazi soldiers and what were described as 'Calcutta thugs' were killed."

"Interesting."

"Even more so, Father, when one considers that the chest was donated by an ex-British army surgeon noted for his stories about a master detective, one who foiled a similar robbery at the British museum and who claimed the chest as his reward."

"And how did the British Museum come by the chest?"

"That is explained in *In Her Majesty's Service,* which is a memoir by a Sergeant Edward Gallan, who fought in India and participated in the campaign that was believed to have wiped out the Thuggee cult. The chest held treasure looted from a temple of Kali and later presented to the queen, most of it anyway. Here is his description of the idol as he remembered it."

Lewis handed the priest a page printed from an Internet site devoted to preserving public domain works of fiction and nonfiction that would otherwise be forgotten.

"That's not right, is it?"

Lewis shook his head. "No, it's not. But assuming that the sergeant was correct, that leads one to a certain conclusion. It explains why the Thuggees fought so fiercely and why death seems to follow this chest wherever it goes. But knowing only tells us why. It does nothing for the who and the where."

"You said you had an idea along those lines?"

"It is not a good one, Father, but the best I can do for now. And I will need your help."

***

It was called the "Star of Bombay." It was not the biggest restaurant in the city that featured Indian cuisine, nor was it the best. It was not located in Fells Point, the Inner Harbor or the new Theater District. It was in a strip mall along Harford Road in the northeast part of the city. And while it had a few older patrons, its clientele was now mostly young people whose parent or grandparents had emigrated from the sub-continent, many of whom were raised in the old ways and customs.

"It is possible that one or more member of the cult eat here on a regular basis," Lewis explained. He and Harper were in a non-descript late model sedan parked on the lot outside the restaurant.

"And you're hoping that these one or more people are here tonight and that one of them was in New York or down in that industrial park."

"Not hoping, Father, praying. As I'm sure you are. Thursday seems to be the busiest night, so if we are to get any results, now would be the time." Lewis paused then added, "I would not ask this of you, Father, but I have eaten there a few times and might be remembered. Yours will be a strange face."

Harper nodded, left the car and went into the Star of Bombay. Lewis remained behind, watching and waiting.

Midway through his meal, Harper looked at his watch. Almost time he thought. He patted the small package in his pocket. "All noise and smoke," Lewis had assured him, adding, "should it go off." He hoped, or rather, prayed that that would not happen. He also prayed that things would go as planned and not lead to a general panic. He again checked the time. He got up and went into the men's room. When he came out, he no longer had the package. It was instead, hidden behind the trashcan in the bathroom. Not wanting to look at his watch a third time, he sat back down.

Lewis should be making the call soon. It is fortunate, Harper thought, that these days a threat against a minority owned establishment was taken very seriously. Just then two worried looking men came into the dining area.

"Ladies and gentlemen," one of them announced, "I regret that I must ask you all to leave immediately. While there is no danger, there is a … problem in our kitchen and we are closing just as a safety precaution. Please leave now in an orderly manner."

There was a moment of confusion and then the patrons obeyed, some with looks of concerned and others glad to have just received a free meal. Harper was neither the first nor last to leave but when he did, he made sure to take his coffee cup and table utensils with him.

Seeing the crowd emerge from the restaurant. Lewis made his second call of the night.

"Unknown caller" was the display on Amos Hoffman's caller ID. "Yeah, right," the detective said to himself. He knew who it was. He had several time considered getting an unlisted number but realized that it probably would not do any good. The spook would find him. That dammed spook would always find him.

Wondering if God hated him or was just having a little joke, Hoffman answered the phone.

"Yeah?"

"Detective Hoffman. Tonight a bomb threat was made against the Star of Bombay restaurant."

"And how do you know this? No, I forgot, your kind always knows. What of it?"

"An unexploded package will be found. And while your crime lab may not find any evidence on the device there will be plenty of drinking glasses, plates and such from which they might obtain fingerprints and DNA."

Hoffman was about to ask, "And so?" then he made the connection. The Grey Monk had just provided him with an opportunity to collect comparison samples that the police could not have otherwise obtained, not legally anyway. It would take a while but it would be interesting to run the results against what was in the database. Very interesting.

***

"Mahesh."

"Yes, Uttam."

"Some of the followers are becoming … impatient."

"Impatient, how?"

"After what Rohit told them, they wonder why the chest has not been opened, why we delay in summoning Her."

"And I'm sure you have done nothing to fan this impatience."

"Mahesh, I assure you that …"

"Never mind."

The two were alone in the temple that was once the Hamilton Theater. The Heart of Kali stood and walked to the stage and stood facing her image.

"Look at that. A cheap plaster statue, a poor imitation of how She used to be portrayed. The idol in *Son of Gunga Din* looked better than this. But it was all the cult could afford when it was started, but now …" He turned and faced Uttam.

"If you were a goddess, would you return to that? We need something … better, more worthy of for Her to inhabit."

"Like what?"

"I wish I knew."

"I do."

Gajanan had come in from behind the screen. He bowed to Kali's image then joined Mahesh and Uttam.

"You've found a replacement, Gajanan? A stone or bronze sculpture, maybe?"

"Better than that, Mahesh, better than that." The Eye handed Mahesh a copy of that day's Sentinel.

"Yes, I know, Tapan got his name in the paper. He should have known better."

"No, Mahesh, check out the local section, page four. Any other time it would have probably been a big human feature story, but with all the killings and the election for mayor and all that, it got pushed back and buried."

It was a small article about a young girl born with polymelia, or extra limbs. It told of how she grew up in a traveling carnival and how her fellow carnies raised the money for the operation that would make her normal. There was a photograph of the girl with her arms around the owner of the carnival and the two women who had adopted her.

Uttam and Mahesh stared at the picture, not believing their eyes. "The Goddess provides," Mahesh finally said. "Well done," he told Gajanan. "Gather the others, the Arms and Eyes. There are plans to be made."

***

"There's an article in the morning paper that might interest you," Harper told Lewis when woke the next day. "It mentions the bomb scare at the restaurant. Talks about how tragedy was avoided by the fact that the explosive device failed to go off and the need for more tolerance or minorities in the city. Surprisingly it praises the police for their diligence and hard work in so thoroughly investigating the scene."

Lewis took the paper from the priest's hands and looked at the accompanying photograph of the restaurant's manager in his office.

"I wonder what the writer would say if she knew the reason for all that diligence and hard work, and who was behind it?"

Lewis did not reply to Harper's musing. He was still busy studying the picture. Finally he handed the paper back to the priest.

"Do you see what I see, Father?'

"The manager, Tapan something or other. I can't say the last name."

"Look at what's on the bookcase behind him. It's not in clear focus, and the quality of the picture is poor, but what does it look like?"

To Harper, the object Lewis pointed out looked like a small multi-armed figurine. He said as much.

"It looks as if I may have wasted my time following the restaurant's patrons. I'll have to go back to make sure, and then the Grey Monk might have to pay a visit to this Tapan and see what he knows about the Cult of Kali."

***

Faith Memorial Hospital was not the largest in the city. Located in the upper northeast, it was not as well known as some of its sister facilities to the east, northwest and downtown. It had no major cancer treatment wings, no world famous burn unit and no cutting edge transplant teams. It did have a dedicated staff of talented men and women dedicated to the care and well being of the patients who came to them for help. And like most of the other hospitals in a city whose majority of citizens did not have health insurance or a primary care physician, it also had an emergency room that was filled to capacity almost every night.

Driving a borrowed car, Uttam pulled into the visitors' parking outside the ER. "Remember, Rohit, you are sick. Your name is Arjoon and you are visiting from New Jersey. Your wife has been called and is on her way with your papers and insurance cards. You have a headache, backache, chest pains and occasionally feel like you're about to faint."

"Am I pregnant too?"

The glare that Uttam gave him said that this was a serious matter, that it was no time for jokes. "No, but it would help if you were somewhat disoriented. Every once in while ask where you are. That might dissuade them from giving you serious pain medication."

"And how long should I be sick?"

Uttam thought for a minute. "Thirty minutes after you're first seen, an hour at the most. We just need to establish that we're legitimate visitors. After that just gather your clothes and walk out. This place is usually so busy that no one will notice. And if they do probably won't stop you."

They went in, Uttam and Yash on either side of Rohit.

"Tell me why I'm doing this and not one of the Arms?"

"Because it does not require strength and Abhay and Jayant are waiting in the van on the parking lot. It may take all of us to get the girl to the temple."

The three walked in, registered and sat down to wait. Since Rohit did not appear to be dying or in great pain and his complaints were so general that the triage nurse had heard the same symptoms several times that night, their wait was a long one. Two hours went by before the name he was using was called.

Uttam and Yash watched as he disappeared into the back.

"What if they suspect him?" Yash asked in a low voice.

"They probably will, if he's still here when security locks the place down. If so, there's not much to be done about it. He won't betray us. He knows that our goal is more important than any one of us."

"And if we're caught?"

Uttam shrugged. "Then that is Her will, and it is not yet Her time. The others will keep the chest safe until it is."

The pair approached the security guard.

"Excuse us," Uttam said smiling, "our friend was just taken in the back. Do you know how long he'll be?"

"Quite a while," the guard said, wondering as he did every night how many more times he'd be asked that question. He knew what was coming next so he added, "If you're hungry there's a self-serve cafeteria down the hall in the main hospital. Just machines but they're kept full. Only don't eat too much or you'll wind up back here." Having made his usual joke he smiled his usual smile, pointed the two in the right direction and checked his watch. Only three hours left in the shift.

The pair walked down the hall in silence. To be safe they stopped in the cafeteria and bought food from the machines, Uttam a bag of chips and Yash some cookies. Each got a soda. When they were done Yash said, "We should get back and see how he's doing."

Uttam nodded his agreement and the two left. But instead of going back to the ER they instead turned into the main hospital.

That time of night, there was no one to challenge them as they waited for and got on the elevator.

"How do we know she's on the fourth floor?" Yash asked.

"One of the followers has a sister who works here. The girl and her visitors are all anyone talks about. Everyone's finding an excuse to come up and see the freaks."

What Uttam and Yash were about to do would once have impossible. Even at night a hospital wing should have been filled with nurses and orderlies tending to the needs of the patients. Hard times and budget cuts have changed that. One or two nurses now cover an entire section and the few orderlies working move from floor to floor as needed. When the elevator stopped, Uttam and Yash got off on a mostly empty ward.

The nurse at the floor station watched as the two apparently lost men approached her. "Can I help you?"

"Yes, Ma'am, down at ER they said our friend was being brought up here and ..."

"No one's due to come up here," the nurse interrupted. She called up new admissions on her computer, looked down at the screen. "If you tell me his name I can ..." Something made her look up and when she did, she saw that both men had knives.

"Be very quiet," said the shorter man. "One word, one sound, one scream and you're dead. Anyone else on the floor?" Remembering the warning, the nurse shook her head. "If you're lying, anyone we see is dead and so are you. Now, anyone else here?" Again the nurse shook her head. "Good, take us to the circus girl."

The page unit around the nurse's neck had a panic button. Intended for use if a patient began to code out, it also served as a security alert, sending a silent alarm throughout the hospital. She started to use it to summon help, but thought that if confronted and trapped, the two men with her would fight back and that she and some of the patients could be hurt or killed. She decided to wait until they left with the girl or tried to harm her.

Led into Virginia Stone's room, Uttam and Yash each felt the thrill of religious awe when they saw the girl lying on the bed, all four arms out of the covers. This was She, Goddess to be in the flesh and they were the first of the faithful to behold her. After a moment's silence Uttam turned to the nurse.

"Sedate her."

The nurse hesitated. "I, I can't."

"You can and will. We're taking her out of here. If she wakes up, she may be hurt." He gestured meaningfully with his knife.

Without a word the nurse walked to a secure closet, unlocked it, took out a prepared syringe and injected the sleeping girl. "That will keep her out for an hour at least."

"Good. Yash, my friend, you may have the honor, but first, do what you must."

Yash moved quickly for a man his size. Before his partner finished speaking he was behind the nurse and looping a silk scarf around her neck, cutting off her wind before she could scream. He held her so until her struggling stopped, then gave the scarf and extra twist and pull just to be sure.

As Uttam checked the halls to make sure no one was about, Yash lifted the sleeping child with all the reverence due a deity. Then the pair left with their charge the same way they came in, the few people who saw them thinking nothing of a man carrying a blanket wrapped girl. This was after all a hospital and they appeared to be taking her to the ER.

Ten minutes after the cult's van pulled off the hospital lot the second nurse assigned to fourth floor returned from lunch. Not seeing his coworker at her station he assumed that she was with a patient. When there was no answer to his page he went looking for her. Five minutes later and much too late the alarm went out and the hospital was locked down. By then the soon to be living goddess was on her way to be worshipped at the Hamilton Theater.

***

The Star of Bombay remained closed. Clean up from the bomb scare and police investigation was still in progress. Several of the employees had suggested that the next time they should let the bomb go off, that it would probably make less of a mess than the police had. Did they really have to put that black powder everywhere? And why take all of the customers' glasses?

The crew had worked from morning into evening with the goal of opening in two days. It had grown dark. One by one as they finished their tasks they said their goodbyes and left through the back. As they did, none of them noted a shadowy form lurking in the darkness.

The Grey Monk was waiting for the last employee to leave. He knew how many there were. He had been standing and counting as they entered and had stood watch as they came and went throughout the day. Soon only the manager would remain, the man identified in the newspaper as Tapan. There were questions to be asked of him; questions to which the Monk was determined to gain answers.

The last two workers left, a young couple who took brief advantage of the alley's darkness to express their affection toward each other. There was a rustle of clothing and just as the Monk was thinking of how to scare them off without betraying his presence the girl said, "Now not, wait until later."

"But what if you're parents are home?"

"Then it will be much later, won't it?" and she lead her Romeo off by the hand.

Finally, thought the Monk and prepared to enter the restaurant. Just then his cell phone vibrated once beneath his robes.

The Monk waited and soon felt the phone again. Twice was Harper's signal that the call was urgent.

"What is it?" the Monk whispered into the receiver, hoping that Tapan would not chose that minute to leave. Then the priest told him of the abduction from the hospital.

If only we had known, the Monk said to himself. How could we have missed it, he asked. But he knew that there was only One who knew all and that now was not the time for recriminations. It had not taken the police long to make the connection between the missing girl and the cult they were hunting. It was obvious as to why she had been taken. The only questions were by whom and to where.

The Grey Monk looked at the back door of the restaurant and knew that those answers could very well lie behind it. To himself he said a brief prayer asking forgiveness for what he was about to do, then silently entered the Star of Bombay.

Tapan was in his office, looking over his books. Maybe, he thought, his employees were right. The bomb should have gone off. At least then his insurance would have covered the losses. Instead he was looking at two nights closed, no money coming in, all his workers still to be paid. And how many customers would come back now that a very real threat had been made? Mahesh had been right; he should not have given the interview.

Thinking of Mahesh reminded Tapan of more important matters. He looked at the small idol above his desk, closed his account book and switched off his computer. He'd leave those worries for tomorrow. Tonight he had to be at the temple.

Tapan turned and let out a cry of terror. A grey form was standing in the office doorway. Dark and shapeless, to Tapan it was a demon from his nightmares. He wondered briefly if it was real but the large pistol in the thing's hand told him that this was no dream.

"Step out," came a whispered command and the Grey Monk moved aside to allow Tapan to leave the office. As he did the manager wondered if he should make a break for the door.

As if reading his thoughts the Grey Monk said, "If you try to escape I will shoot, and you will never run again. Sit." Tapan found a chair. "Where is the girl?"

Tapan did not answer, he could not. He knew nothing of a girl. He looked deep into the darkness of the Grey Monk's cowl and hoped that the vigilante would see the truth in his eyes.

Whatever the Grey Monk saw, his next question was, "Where is your temple?"

This Tapan knew but he would not betray his friends, could not betray Kali. He shook his head in refusal.

"I do not have time to waste," came the menacing whisper. "Consider this. There are in this kitchen knives, cleavers and tenderizing hammers, all of which I am prepared to use tonight. And should they fail, there is hot oil and grease. Your screams will not be heard, and the police should they come will not care. They will know who you are and what you have done and they will leave you to me. Just as your god has left you to me. Kali has abandoned you, she no longer protects you. Why should you suffer to protect her?"

Again Tapan shook his head, although with much less conviction than the time before. Noting this, the Monk picked up a carving knife from a workstation.

"As you wish," he said and slowly approached his captive.

Tapan sat there watching as the knife in the Grey Monk's left hand came closer toward him. It was closer still and seemed to heading toward his right ear. It was true then, Kali had abandoned him. Tapan had no way of knowing that the man before him had learned early on that the mere threat of pain and torture was almost always sufficient. And when it was not, there were better ways.

The knife came closer, its edge touched Tapan's ear where it joined to his skull. He felt his bladder go, then his bowels. He shouted out an address. Then the pistol in the Monk's right hand struck him and all went black.

***

Mahesh was waiting when the Arms arrived at the Hamilton and brought Ginnie into the theater. She was still unconscious but starting to stir.

"Take her in the back and strip her," he ordered.

This stunned all of them. Yash, who still bore the girl in his arms, was the first to protest. "No, we're not, we can't be going to …" he was thinking of the industrial park and New York City.

Mahesh gave them all a look of disgust. "Get your minds out of the gutter. Look at her; she's wearing teddy bear pajamas. In the back room you will find a necklace and girdle such as She wears. There is also black clothing, see that she is dressed in it. There is dye for what parts of her skin still show. She is to be our goddess and must appear as such."

"And the chest, is that back there?"

"It is. When the girl is ready and the faithful have gathered it will be brought out and opened. Then the time of Kali will be at hand."

As she slowly awakened, Ginnie Stone at first thought she was back at the carnival, roughhousing with the Mason twins. But they wouldn't be trying to take off her clothes, not for a few years yet, anyway. Then she remembered that she was in the hospital, or supposed to be. As she came out of her drug-induced sleep, she saw that this was not the case. She was in a small room with four men. One of them was beginning to unbutton her top.

She screamed and lashed out but her struggles did her little good as they made her ready for her ascension to godhood.

**

For a minute the Monk considered calling the police and telling them where to find the cult and the girl. But only for a minute. He knew their procedures. The building would be surrounded and secured. A demand for release and surrender would follow as the Quick Response Team planned an entry. A warrant would be obtained. Only after the legal hurdles had been vaulted would a rescue attempt be made.

All this would not matter to those inside. They were devotees about to bring their god to Earth. They would believe, with absolute certainty, that Kali would protect them and thus care little for human demands. By the time the police acted, it might be too late.

On his way to the theater the Monk called Harper and gave him the address.

"Wait an hour, then call Hoffman. Tell him all."

"Are you sure of your timing?"

"It will all be over by then, Father, one way or the other."

"And if you're still inside when the police arrive?"

"If it's God's Will, Father, I'll be gone. If not, it is still His Will."

***

The faithful had gathered and were seated as Mahesh walked out on stage. "My brothers and sisters," he began, "you are blessed to be here on this historic night. Tonight the Goddess will be restored to Her proper place. Tonight She returns to us. Tonight this," he gestured to the statute behind him, "becomes so much plaster and paint. The Goddess of the Empty Hands will be no more."

At Mahesh's signal, The Eyes of Kali brought out the Chest of Saugor and lifted the lid. Rohit reached in and removed the false bottom that had for so many years concealed the scared objects those in the temple cave had died to protect. Out came a jeweled skull, a silver bowl, a sword of gold and spear carved from ivory.

"These were the treasures of Kali," Mahesh proclaimed, "and they belong in her hands. But this," and again he looked back at her idol, "this is not Kali." The Heart gave another signal. "Behold – the Living Goddess!"

The Arms led Ginnie on stage. Tired from fighting the men, she had ceased her struggles and now did what they demanded.

They had her dressed in dark, form fitting clothing. Her exposed face, arms and hands were covered in black make-up. She appeared to be nude, the illusion supported by a belt of life-like hands at her waist and a necklace of tiny skulls around her neck, both covering what was not meant to be seen by mortal eyes.

The fifty or so people in the audience gave out a collective gasp when they saw their goddess come to life. They gave out another when they realized this was not a trick or special effects, that the being in front of them had the attributes of Kali.

"Equip her," Mahesh commanded, "and once her avatar's hands are filled, once the Treasures of Saugor are again in her possession, Kali herself will descend and her rule on Earth will begin."

He began a chant. "Kali, Kali, Kali, Kali …" that was soon picked up by the faithful. And to the sounds of the name repeated over and over Rohit passed the sacred objects he had taken from the chest to Gajanan and Sagar, who in turn handed them, one each, to the Arms.

As the crowd continued to chant "Kali, Kali, Kali, Kali …" Jayant put the Spear of Life in Ginnie's upper right hand. Abhay then pressed the Bowl of Plenty into her lower right hand, holding it there to keep the girl's weak arm from dropping it. Likewise Yash held the Skull of Fate in her lower left hand. Uttam completed the circle by placing the Sword of Destruction in Ginnie's remaining hand.

Her avatar's hands now filled, Kali's worshippers chanted her name even louder – "Kali, Kali, Kali, Kali …" – and waited for her to appear before them in power. And they waited and waited and waited …

***

Despite the lateness of the hour the street on which the Hamilton Theater was located was well lit and busy with both vehicle and pedestrian traffic. There would be no entry for the Grey Monk from the front. The alley in the rear of the building was dark and empty, but the lock on the back door was a strong one and the Monk did have the time to spare on it. Besides, one never knew what was on the other side of a locked door. He did not want an alarm raised too soon. That left the roof as his first option.

A fire escape at the end of the block took the Monk to the top of the buildings. Counting houses, he walked to where the theater would be. There he found the prayed for skylight. Looking down into it, he discovered it opened into an office.

Blocking out the traffic noise, the Monk put his ear against the glass to listen for any sounds below. Hearing only a rhythmic chant of "Kali, Kali, Kali, Kali …" he took a small pry bar from beneath his robes and put it against the window frame. He pulled up and the frame and lock popped loose. Slowly opening the window, he looked down. Seeing no one, he carefully lowered himself into the office.

***

Ten minutes had gone by, then fifteen. Kali still had not revealed herself. The chanting was slower and not as many people were joining in. Some in the audience were visibly restless and many were beginning to doubt that goddess would appear at all.

"What's wrong?" Rohit asked Mahesh.

"I don't know. According to lore and prophecies, the restoration of her treasures was sure to bring Kali back. And the girl is perfect. It seemed like the right time. It is the right time. We are doing something wrong."

"Maybe," suggested Sagar, "It is because the body in which She is to manifest already has a soul occupying it. The vessel might need to be emptied before it can be filled."

"Dare we?" asked Rohit.

"Have we a choice?" And with that Mahesh took out his ruhmal and stepped behind the girl.

***

The chanting was louder now. There was a door from the office into a darkened space that had been the projection room. The Monk went in and peered out into the theater.

There he saw the missing girl, held by two men with others surrounding her. She was the image of the Kali he had seen on websites and in books. She did not appear to be in any danger. Maybe, he thought, this can be done without violence. He'd unlock the front door and wait, then when they arrived invite the police in with a few gunshots into the ceiling. Then it was out and off the roof.

But no. The chanting was slowing. The men on stage were talking and one was moving behind the girl. There was no time for the police.

***

Mahesh stepped behind the girl and looped his strangling scarf around her neck.

"What are you doing?"

"What I must, Yash, what I must."

The Heart of Kali spoke the truth. Even if the girl's death failed to bring Kali forward, it would still be necessary. Alive she was a witness against them.

Feeling the ruhmal tighten around her neck, Ginnie began to struggle anew. Up until now she had not been resisting, recognizing that what was going on was a kind of show, one her carny nature could appreciate. Had those who had taken her from the hospital bothered to tell her their plans she might have even played along.

But now things were more serious. The crowd was losing its enthusiasm and it wasn't a game anymore. The scarf around her neck was tighter, it was becoming hard to breathe. She fought but the men on either side kept their hold on her and she felt the coming darkness.

Sensing something new happening, the faithful again began repeating the name of Kali. The chanting grew, then over it came a new sound, that of two well-placed gunshots. As both Jayant and Uttam fell mortally wounded Yash and Abhay released their hold on Ginnie. But Mahesh held her firm with one hand tight on the scarf around her neck. With the other he pointed to the back of the theater.

"There, there is the reason Kali is not among us. It is an asura, a demon sent to destroy her and us."

The crowd turned. Framed in the doorway was a shapeless figure clothed in grey. In his hands were two large pistols, the weapons he had used to drop the men on stage. In the minds of the crowd it very well could have been a demon.

"Release the girl!" the Grey Monk commanded over the noise of the crowd.

"Destroy him!" ordered Mahesh from the stage.

The crowd surged forward, but not as many as the Heart of Kali would have liked. Some who had recognized the previous sounds as gunfire wisely remained in their seats. Likewise there were those who had no wish to fight anyone, man or demon. And some had stopped believing and only wished to leave. But enough rushed the Grey Monk that he knew that to reach the girl he would have to fight his way through. Putting his trust in God, the Grey Monk charged the crowd.

The followers of Kali died.

It should not have been. The Grey Monk had no wish to take their lives. When he could he clubbed them with his guns or inflicted what he prayed were non-fatal wounds. But at times the mob threatened to overwhelm him and in those moments he shot to kill.

As cultist after cultist went down, all but the most devout fell away and the Monk made quick work of these. Soon there was no one between him and the stage.

Again the Grey Monk commanded, "Release the girl."

Mahesh shook his head. "I don't think so. Drop your weapons, or I strangle the life out of this child." He gestured with his head. Yash and Abhay moved to leave the stage to confront the Monk.

But his gesture caused Mahesh to loose his hold on Ginnie ever so slightly. The girl, raised in the rough and tumble world of the carnival, was quick to take advantage. She kicked out behind then stamped down hard. With unexpected pains in his shin and instep Mahesh lost his grip on his ruhmal. Ginnie dropped and rolled. The Grey Monk fired one of his remaining shots and the Heart of Kali stopped beating.

Other than those moaning in the aisle or cowering in their seats, only five foes were left the Monk. The Eyes took a look at the bloodstained agent of God's Vengeance and fled through an emergency door, leaving only the two remaining Arms, each approaching the Monk from a different direction.

Beneath his cowl the Monk gave a grim smile. The two came nearer. "No closer," he ordered.

Abhay hesitated. He did not know how many shots the big guns he faced held or if there was one left for him. He weighed his odds and did not feel lucky. He turned and followed the Eyes.

Yash shook his head. It was over, he knew that. The Inner Circle was broken, the Goddess had proven false. If his life was to end he would at least destroy the one responsible.

Yash rushed forward. The Monk's last remaining bullet shattered his knee and he went down.

"There is but one reason you were spared, and that is because the police wanted it so. They will be here soon. You will tell them everything, or we will meet again."

When Kali's last remaining Arm looked up at the dark figure towering over him, he found a new god in which to believe, one of wrath and vengeance and he vowed to do whatever was commanded of him.

The Grey Monk led Ginnie out another emergency door and into the welcoming night. In their dark colors they moved invisibly in the dark alley until they were close to the street. Sirens announced the fast approaching police.

"Go around to the front," he told the girl. "You may frighten a few people but you will be safe. Wait for the police. Tell them all that has happened."

Leaving the girl, the Grey Monk faded away.

***

The crime lab team assigned to process the scene at the Hamilton Theater swore, collectively and individually they swore. They cursed the name of the detective who had called them there. They cursed the cult that had started it all. Most of all they cursed the Grey Monk. Even for him the body count was excessive.

Carol Thompson, the leader of the team, was up on stage with Amos Hoffman. "What should we do with this stuff?" She indicated the objects held not so long ago by Ginnie Stone.

Hoffman looked around. "Throw them in that chest over there. Seal it shut and send it to Evidence Control Unit. We'll need it all for court."

"I guess when this is all over some museum will get it all."

"This won't be over for a long time, Carol. And for all I care, that stuff can sit in the ECU warehouse forever. But somehow I don't think it will."

***

The story of the Cult of Kali filled the tabloids for the next week. There were daily revelations of murders, orgies and human sacrifice, some of them true, most made up. Virginia Stone became a celebrity and The Stone Brothers' Traveling Carnival and Natural Oddity Exhibition began playing more lucrative venues. The role of the Grey Monk was played up in the local media while the out of town press tended to doubt the existence of what it called "an urban legend."

"It seems that Miss Virginia Stone has decided to postpone her operation," Harper said as he reading the Sentinel.

"How do you know that?"

The priest folded the paper to the entertainment section and handed it to Lewis. There a full-page ad proclaimed:

KALI RETURNS!
COME SEE THE LIVING GODDESS!
ONCE THE CAPTIVE OF A CRAZED CULT SHE NOW TRAVELS THE
COUNTRY BESTOWING HER BLESSINGS.
EXCLUSIVELY WITH THE STONE BROTHERS' TRAVELING CARNIVAL
THIS WEEK ONLY AT THE CIVIC ARENA
(FREE KALI SKULL NECKLACES FOR CHILDREN TWELVE AND UNDER)

"The surviving cult members should be pleased," Lewis commented, "their prophecy has come true, only not in the way they would have liked. Kali has returned and will be adored by thousands. At least until the next sensation comes along."

THE ONLY JUSTICE

Richard Harper looked at what was left of his meal – his last meal. What had it been? He couldn't remember now. All he knew was that his time was growing short. Each sweep of the second hand brought the end closer and closer. Thirty minutes left, now twenty, now ten. Harper heard footsteps coming down the corridor. He knew who it was – the warden, two guards, a priest. He didn't need the priest. He'd done nothing wrong, had committed no sin.

He'd been in here how long? He thought back. He couldn't remember. He'd been tried, convicted, sentenced. That much he knew. The rest was a blur.

The footsteps came closer. Four men came into view. No, there were five.

"Are you ready, my son?" Harper looked up at the minister. Not a parish priest, but instead a monk, one clad in a dark grey habit. Harper nodded, then stood.

"Last chance, Rich." The fifth man spoke. "Give us what we need and I can still call the Governor. Don't hang for someone else."

Harper tried to speak. There was something he knew, something he wanted to say, but the words stuck and wouldn't come out.

"I … I can't. Sorry, Amos."

Detective Amos Hoffman shook his head, then gave the go ahead to the warden.

The cell door opened. Harper stepped out, immediately flanked by the two guards. With the monk leading the way and Hoffman and the warden following, Harper walked his last mile.

"Dead man walking," the monk intoned, as if it were part of a liturgy. Somewhere in the distance, a bell rang slowly.

Suddenly, Harper was outside, climbing the thirteen steps of the scaffold. The hangman, his face covered by a dark grey hood, fitted the noose around his neck. Cinching it tight, the hangman asked, "Have you made your peace with God?"

Harper permitted himself one last smile. "We've never quarreled," and stepped on to the trapdoor.

The hangman pulled a lever, the trapdoor opened, Father Richard Harper fell and felt the rope tighten. He screamed.

And woke up.

Harper looked around to assure himself. He was in his bedroom in the rectory of St. Sebastian's Catholic Church. All was well. It wasn't really, but at least he wasn't a condemned prisoner on death row.

Harper looked up to see Lewis standing in the doorway. With the light coming from the hallway behind him, all Harper could see of his sexton was his silhouette.

"Another one?" Lewis asked. Harper nodded.

"What was it this time – firing squad, electric chair, stoning?"

"Hanging."

"Better than the guillotine."

Small comfort, Harper thought, but Lewis was right. The guillotine last night had been the worst – laying there face up, watching the blade come down. He shuddered.

"Are you all right?"

"I'm fine, Lewis. Thanks. Now that it's over, I'll sleep through the rest of the night."

"Then I'll leave you to your rest. We'll talk in the morning." The sexton left him alone.

No, Harper thought as he drifted back to sleep, we won't. I can't.

Nothing was said at breakfast. It wasn't until Lewis was putting the dishes away that he said, "If attending executions bothers you that much, stop hearing their confessions."

"I don't have a choice, we're assigned on a rotating basis. Besides, it's never bothered me before."

"No, it hasn't," Lewis said quietly, and left the room.

He came back with file folders, which he put down on the table. Sitting across from the priest, he began. "The man who was executed last week, John Davis, stood accused of killing twelve people in armed robberies. He'd hold up businesses, get the money, then kill the cashier for no apparent reason. With his arrest, all twelve crimes were marked closed. He was tried and convicted of three such crimes five years ago and sentenced to death. The sentence was carried out last week."

Lewis paused. With no comment from Harper, he continued, "Davis confessed to you." He looked at Harper. The priest's face remained impassive. "Davis confessed to you, but not to all of the crimes of which he stood accused. There were two, maybe three, murders that he denied committing."

Harper's eyes widened in surprise, confirming Lewis's deduction.

"You're trapped," the sexton said. "You know for a fact that there's another killer out there, but because of the Seal of Confession, you can't tell anyone."

Harper finally spoke, "So now what? You're going to investigate, find the killer and bring him to justice?"

"It's what I do. As you said, you've been to executions before and it never bothered you this much. When you started with the nightmares, I surmised another cause. I had one of my police sources get me the file." Picking up one of the folders, he slid it towards Harper.

"Davis's prints were found on three of the crime scenes. They were what lead to his arrest when he was picked up for DUI. Of the other nine scenes, bullets from two of the victims are a 'probable' match with those from the first three. Close enough to infer his guilt, but not definite enough to convict. None of the remaining bullets were suitable for comparison.

"That leaves us seven scenes," Lewis continued, "two of which were outside the general area where the rest occurred. These two are, perhaps not coincidentally, higher market types of shops – an antique shop and a jewelry store. The others were groceries, liquor and bookstores."

"You suspect a copycat?" Harper asked, choosing his words carefully.

"Worse than that." Lewis passed two more folders over to Harper.

"When I first became the Grey Monk, I stopped a serial killer known to the police as 'The Bird,' so called because of his practice of cutting off his victim's right middle finger. He was officially credited with sixteen murders. Before he died, he confessed to me that he had killed only fourteen."

"And you went after the killer of the other two?"

Lewis shook his head. "I meant to, but before I could, I ran afoul of Tremaine. By the time I healed and settled that matter, I am afraid that I let other cases take precedence."

"And this other folder?"

"A more recent case. What remained of the Pure Race Fellowship tried to foment civil unrest by brutally killing young black women. They were charged with, and admitted to, six murders. In fact, they committed only four. I believe that if we were to research other serial killings over the years, we will find other such copycat crimes."

"So you think there's someone out there," Harper said, "waiting for a pattern of deaths to occur, and then committing his own murders." Lewis nodded. "Why?"

"It could be for the thrill, both the excitement of committing a crime and of having another blamed for it, but I doubt it. Look at the victims. In each questionable case, the victim was a person of substance. In each of these deaths, someone could have benefited."

Harper shook his head. "This is too farfetched. Murder for hire, using serial crimes as a cover. And you base this on what? A few murders that don't exactly fit a perceived pattern? The word of a confessed murderer who may have being playing mind games? The nightmares of a parish priest who doesn't have enough sense not to get involved with vigilante justice? You're going to need more than that."

"I know," Lewis said. "I've already made the arrangements."

***

It was 2 a.m. Detective Amos Hoffman had ended his tour of duty at midnight. He'd been home for an hour. He'd already had two beers and was thinking about having another while he waited for the phone to ring.

He had just about made up his mind when the call came in. He picked up the receiver. "Outside," was all his caller said.

Hoffman had been expecting the call. He picked up a folder and went out, the knowledge of what he'd learned that night weighing heavily on him.

Hoffman's house was across from a park. The detective stood at the tree line and peered into the darkness. Despite his vigilance, despite knowing that he was coming, Hoffman didn't see or hear the Grey Monk until the vigilante made himself known. One minute Hoffman was alone, the next …

"Detective Hoffman."

The policeman turned. The Monk was there beside him. "Damn you," Hoffman swore, thrusting the folder at the grey robed figure. "Damn you," he said again with more emphasis as it was taken from him and safely stored within the grey habit.

The Monk ignored the curses. "How many more?"

"Three, maybe four more, not counting the ones you told me about."

"Those convicted were not innocents, Detective. They deserved their fates."

"Yeah, but now you tell me there's someone out there, using the department, using me, to get away with murder. And there's not a damn thing I can do about it."

The dark figure nodded in agreement. "No, there is not. Were you to bring this to light, the police would look like dupes. The guilt of those imprisoned or condemned would be cast into doubt. Killers would be given new trials, and some set free. Worse, my quarry would be warned. This one is clever. He disguises himself not as a sheep, but wears instead the cloak of the wolf, leaving the blame to others. Once this is exposed, he will find another way. Or else move and begin again. No, Detective Hoffman, leave this in the dark with me."

"I have no choice," Hoffman said, then added, "the information he used to disguise his crimes, most of it was not public knowledge."

"I know – the missing fingers, the graffiti left by the alley slayer, the warning notes …"

"You knew about …"

"Yes, I knew, rather, I suspected. I called you to confirm my suspicions, and to warn you of what is to come. Before this is over, blood will be spilled. Someone should know why."

The Monk vanished into the darkness, leaving Hoffman with a greater burden. He knew the Grey Monk too well. There was a bloodbath coming, one he'd have to clean up after. But the Monk was right. There was no way that the brass would investigate those cases. Officially they were closed – the public safe, the killers caught and executed. Too much trouble, too many problems to reopen them now. They'd consider the consequences of a thorough investigation and decide that sometimes it was better to let crimes go unsolved.

This time, Hoffman thought bitterly, the only justice would be vengeance. "Damn you," he said to the darkness. Then he turned and went inside.

***

"So how did you find out, if not from Hoffman?" Father Harper asked later as Lewis looked over the files.

"As you know, I have my sources. And it is clear that my quarry has his."

"Maybe they're both the same?"

Lewis thought about this. "Two people can drink from the same well. But then again, there may be two different wells, each supplying the same water."

***

Gladys Neveski had a gambling problem. A year ago she was near bankruptcy from too many lotto tickets, too much Bingo and far too many trips to Atlantic City.

No car – unable to keep up the payments, the finance company had repossessed. No home – the eviction notice had come that morning. And soon, no job. Gladys worked for the police department as a clerk in the Records Division. With the time missed from "sick day" trips to the casino and creditors garnishing her wages and still demanding more, she had received her final warning to straighten up or be terminated.

That night, she had sat alone in her bedroom, wondering which method of suicide would be the least painful. She had just decided on pills when she realized that she wasn't alone.

How he got in she didn't know. But as she looked at the man in the charcoal grey monk's robe standing in front of her, she knew one way or the other, her problems were over.

If he kills me, he kills me, she thought, already prepared to die. But the air of menace about this man didn't seem directed at her.

"Ms. Neveski," the whispered voice cut through her like the cold wind of a winter night, "that way lies damnation." The cowled figure pointed to the fatal mixture of vodka and prescription painkiller she had prepared. "Why do you seek the tortures of Hell?"

Gladys shrugged. "It can't be any worse than what I'm going through now."

"The fires of Hell no worse than human life?" the Monk asked, shaking his head at this absurdity. "Any creature there would gladly trade places with the most pitiful person here on Earth. Those in Hell are damned beyond Hope. You can still be saved. Would you like your life back?" Without waiting for an answer, the man went on. "By tomorrow, your debts can be cleared, the next day, your job secure. Next week will see your lease renewed and your car returned. If you are willing."

"That easy, huh? And what do I have to do for you, or is it to you?"

"I am the Grey Monk." Gladys knew of the Monk. She read about him in the papers and in some of the reports she filed. "In your job, you have access to sensitive information, information that I sometimes need, information you can provide me. I am willing to help you, as long as you will help me."

Suddenly Gladys was, not afraid exactly, but apprehensive, nervous. She felt as if all her money was on the next roll of the dice, and her point was four.

"What you want, that's not legal."

"Neither is writing a check on an empty account." The Monk made a sound. Was it a laugh? "And neither is killing a criminal who has placed himself above the law. I worry more about what is just than about what is legal."

"And I suppose you'll want me to give up gambling."

"On the contrary. Before, you risked only your savings, your home, your career. I'm asking you to hazard much more, for you to chance it all – your reputation, your freedom, maybe your life if it is learned that you work for me. You gamble for the thrill, because life as it is holds no meaning without risk. I offer that risk, along with a chance to do good. Take it, and you will need nothing else. Or take that," the Monk pointed to the deadly cocktail on the table, "and again you'll need nothing else."

Since becoming one of the Monk's agents, Gladys found she didn't need the cards, or dice, or ponies as much as she had. Soon she stopped gaming altogether, her desired thrills coming each time she risked scanning reports and sending the information to that week's email address. Each time she did, it was the longshot coming in.

That was a year ago, and she hadn't seen the Grey Monk since. He was instead a message on her computer, a note suddenly appearing at work, at times a voice on the phone. But now here he was, standing in her bedroom much like the first time.

"I need your help." The same icy whisper.

"Of course, but why …"

"The files were computerized when?"

"Five years ago."

The Monk handed Gladys a list.

"The last four cases then. Can you learn who accessed them? Not recently, but sometime after the investigations began. It may not be the investigating detective."

Gladys looked at the list. "It may take some time. I'll need an excuse to go into the database history."

"If questioned, say that the request came from Detective Hoffman. But try not to be questioned. Send the answer as soon as you can, in the usual manner."

The reply came three days later.

"Anything?" Father Harper asked seeing Lewis going over the printouts.

"Only that it is remarkable how easy it was for my source to obtain supposedly confidential information. Otherwise, there are no common factors."

"Of course not," Harper replied, picking up the papers and looking over them. "When you crack a database, do you log on as the Grey Monk? Was this stuff emailed to vengeanceismine@agentofgod.com? You're going to need personnel records, see who was working each time a file was accessed, then cross compare the lists." Something caught Harper's eye. "No, wait, look here, at the top of the printout. That's a station code. Whoever pulled up these files may have used different identifiers and passwords each time, but did so from the same terminal."

"Which means," Lewis said, "that it's someone who, using the same computer, has access to everyone's screen name and passwords."

Gladys was emailed. A reply came back the next day with the leave records of the people who worked in the department's Management Information Section. Only two of them had worked there for five years or more. And only one of was working each time the records had been accessed.

***

Roberta Maples always worked the evening shift, getting off at ten p.m. Each day she worked, she parked in the same spot, walked the same path to Police Headquarters. She took her lunch at the same time each day, eating it at the same cafeteria table. Each night at 9:45, she logged off her computer, packed her things and left. When she went home, she drove there via the same route. This had been her routine for the last six years.

Boring? To some, but Roberta liked it boring. Well, not boring, but predictable. Roberta liked knowing what was going to happen. And she did every thing she could to avoid surprises.

Which is why she received an alert when someone accessed her leave record. She had set things up that way, to give her some warning that she might be under investigation. She didn't know why or who – the inquiry appeared to have come direct from the Records Division, so it wasn't a detective, they had their own system – but someone was checking up on her. So before leaving work that night, she made a call on her cell phone. Roberta didn't like surprises, but she didn't mind arranging them for others.

When Roberta left for that night, she was followed by an old, nondescript sedan. Like the many nights before this one, she drove straight home, seemingly oblivious that this time she had a shadow.

As Roberta Maples pulled into her driveway, the Grey Monk slowed his car and looked for a place to park. Not on this street, he thought, too public, too well lit, too many neighbors to wonder to whom the strange car belonged. Better a side street with access to the alley. He pulled off the road. A car behind him switched off its headlights and made the same turn.

There was a squeal of tires as the one car pulled up beside the other. Then muffled gunfire, as the clip of a silenced 9mm was emptied into the Grey Monk's car, the gun's quiet pops lost in the sounds of breaking glass, lead hitting metal and brass falling on the street. Then, briefly, silence. Another squeal as the shooter's car peeled away from the scene, leaving only a bullet-ridden car and a grey clad shape lying on the grass beside it.

Inside the house, the phone rang.

"You were right, Roberta. Someone was following you."

"And?"

"He won't be following you anymore."

"What if he was a cop?"

"In that old heap. No, some kind of private do-gooder, maybe a PI, maybe some player looking to cut in. Anyway, he's done."

Roberta hung up the phone. And tomorrow, she thought, I'll take care of the loose end at work.

Roberta thought about tomorrow as she took her shower. By then, the car and body will have been discovered. The police will be done and gone by the time I leave for work. What a shame, I'll tell them if they come to the house. And this used to be such a nice quiet neighborhood, too.

Her shower over, and dressed only in a short robe, Roberta stepped into her bedroom. It was dark. Odd, she thought, I know I left a light on. She flipped the wall switch and screamed. There before her, his robe torn, dirty and in place bloodstained, was the Grey Monk.

He whispered an order, "Quiet!" and she obeyed. The gun in his hand told her to make no sudden moves.

"In the car, it was you. But you, you're … "

"Dead? Killed in ambush by your employer. Others have thought so as well, but only One has ever returned from the dead. Fortunately, I'm under His protection."

"W-what do you want?"

"The name of the man who kills for hire, the man who disguises his murders as the work of others, the man to whom you sell the information that lets him do this."

"I-I don't know his name."

The gun rose in front of her. "Do not lie to me," the icy voice warned. "The dead demand vengeance. If you do not atone by confession and repentance, then vengeance it will be. Tomorrow, the next day, the day after – someone will find your lifeless body here on the floor."

"And if I help you?"

"I promise you your life, nothing more. You will lose everything else."

Roberta gave up a name, David Goodkin, and an address not far from where they were.

"How do you know that I won't call and warn him?"

"I expect you to," the Monk replied. "In the hope that he will succeed where he once failed. If he does, you are free. If not, then you had best not be here when I return. The choice to gamble with your life is yours."

With his gun, the Monk motioned her into the bathroom. The door closed, he again turned out the lights, and left through the same window by which he'd entered.

Outside, the Monk watched as a patrol car pulled up to his damaged car. Luck then, that Goodkin's house was in the opposite direction, and within walking distance.

The Goodkin house was brightly lit, a light shining from every window. The front porch light was on, as was the backyard flood lamp. There was apparently no safe approach. So she had called. No matter. He would get in. Did not Matthew 7 say, "Knock, and it will be opened to you?" The Monk planned to go to the back door and knock.

If Goodkin had planned another ambush, the lights worked against him. If he approached a window, he'd be clearly silhouetted. The Monk walked slowly towards the back of the house, watching for the smallest eclipse of the light and listening to the darkness behind him.

He almost missed it. Not a shadow in the brightness but a sound in the night. A small rustle of cloth, the slight scuffle of a shoe. He turned. A glint of metal, the gun reflecting light from the house warned him. He bent low just in time, the bullet passing harmlessly over him. His assailant didn't get another chance. The Monk fired once, and a body fell to the ground.

Without stopping to see if the man was alive, dying or dead, the Monk lifted him and carried him toward the house, hoping the back door would be unlocked. There wasn't much time. Gunfire in this area did not go unreported. And this close to where his car had been found, the police may have heard the shots themselves and would soon be here to investigate.

The door was unlocked. The Monk got himself and Goodkin inside just as a patrol car drove down the street and the police helicopter lit up the backyards. With all of its lights on, the Goodkin's house stood out among its neighbors. But to turn them off would invite suspicion. The Monk stood away from the windows and waited.

"How did you know I was out there?" Goodkin asked from the sofa where the Monk had laid him. His voice was weak, his breathing labored.

"I am too much a creature of the dark to be deceived by it." The noise from the helicopter was fading. His face away from Goodkin, the Monk lowered his cowl and risked a look out a window, just another curious citizen. The patrol car had gone.

His cowl back in place, the Monk turned to the wounded man. "Your wound is serious. You will be dead soon if you are not taken to a hospital."

"Then, call the medics, please."

"You are a hired killer. When you can, you use the cover of other murderers to hide your crimes. Correct?"

"Yes, but I need help." Goodkin's voice was fainter. "For God's sake …"

"Yes, for His sake," the Monk interrupted. "Who were your clients? Who paid you to kill? You must have a list somewhere, insurance against a day like this."

"No … list … never knew … she told me who to kill … and how… all her idea … upstairs in folder."

"Who told you?" the Monk asked, then realized that, like men are apt to do, he had seriously underestimated a woman. "Roberta Maples," he said. The man on the sofa nodded.

The Monk went upstairs, found the folder. He started to leave, turning off lights as he did.

"Wait," came the weak voice from the sofa, "you said you would take me to a hospital."

"I said you needed to go to a hospital. I did not say that I would take you." And the Monk left the man alone in the dark to await judgment.

***

Her bags almost packed, Roberta Maples was just gathering the last of her things when the phone rang. "Hello." There was no answer. "Hello," she said again. "David, is that you?"

"No, it is not." His car towed away, the police gone for now, the Monk had come in the same window he had before. He put away his cell phone and took out his gun.

"David's dead, isn't he?"

"By now he is."

"Thank God. The things he made me do for him."

The Monk grabbed Roberta by the blouse and threw her on the bed. "Do not lie to me, and do not use His name unless it is to beg forgiveness. People seeking murder done would contact you. You then searched police files to find a way to disguise the deed. Goodkin was your tool, the weapon you used to commit the crime."

Roberta pulled herself off the bed. Stepping away from the Monk, conscious of the gun trained on her, her manner changed. She dropped her act as the weak-willed woman who had only been doing a man's bidding. Now when she spoke, she was strong, confident. This man, like most men, wanted something from her. And he would pay her price to get it.

"And why should I tell you anything? That list is my only bargaining chip with the cops. My client list for a reduced sentence. Or rather, David's list. Fool's dead, he might as well take the blame off me. So go ahead, call the cops."

"There will be no police. I will have the list."

"Or what, you'll kill me. That won't get you the list."

The Monk lowered his gun away from Roberta's face, pointing it at her stomach. "I said nothing about death. If I fired now, the bullet would shatter your spine, damage other major organs. You'd live, but would suffer the rest of your life – a life confined to a wheelchair, no control over your body's functions, needing others to provide what pitiful care prison offers. For you would go there, wheelchair or not. And in such a state as to be prey to everyone else."

Roberta watched as the hooded man before her slowly clicked back the hammer of the gun. He will do it, she realized. Not so confident now, not so strong, still she bargained.

"If I tell you, no getting gutshot?"

"No."

"No prison?"

"No prison."

"You'll let me go?"

"I will let Justice find you."

"Hand me my purse."

From the bag Roberta took a tablet computer, one no bigger than a paperback book. "It's all on here," she said, bringing up the file.

The Monk looked at the screen, while still keeping his gun trained on Roberta. It was all there – names, places, amounts paid and people killed. The tablet disappeared within his robes.

Again the Monk raised his gun, trained it on Roberta.

"Wait," she protested, "you said you'd let me go."

"I said that I would not cripple you, that Justice would find you." He fired, striking her in the chest, killing her instantly. "Now it has."

***

The Monk was tired. The minor wounds he had bound earlier were starting to bleed again, the painkiller he had taken starting to wear off. He had walked several blocks away from Roberta Maples's house and was now at the limit of his endurance. His will could carry him no further. He was safe now in the shadows, but dawn was coming. He took out his phone.

"Father, this is Lewis, I could use a ride."

Back in the rectory, after his wounds were treated and cleaned by a doctor who knew not to ask too many questions, Lewis was put to bed by Father Harper. He slept through the day, waking up in the evening. When he awoke, he found the priest watching the news.

"You had a busy night," Harper commented. "Two deaths, and a car that the police believe is somehow tied into them. Can it be traced?"

Lewis shook his head, "It was bought for cash at the police auction of abandoned cars, and registered in the name of Grant Maxwell."

Harper laughed. "So who's buying the next one?"

"Vincent Harrison. Father, I need to confess."

"Now?"

"As soon as possible."

The matter was taken care of, the penance given arduous but, Lewis agreed, fair. Afterwards Harper asked, "So how did you get out of the car in time?"

"I probably wouldn't have if Goodkin hadn't cut his lights. That made me notice him. When he slowed down and I saw that his passenger window was open, I leapt out my far side just as he fired. With my car between him and me, I was unable to return fire. I laid there as if dead hoping he'd stop further up or come over to check on his work. Instead he drove away. Fortunately the bullets that struck were simply graze wounds and didn't slow me down too much."

"Well, at least it's over."

"No, it's not. There's still the list of Maples's clients. They used her as she used Goodkin, as a weapon. They are as guilty as she was."

"And what do you plan to do about that?"

"Tomorrow Detective Hoffman will receive a copy of the list. Then I will wait to see how and if the police handle the matter. If they don't act, I will."

"More blood."

Lewis nodded. "The dead must be avenged, murderers must not profit. If there are those on the list who have truly repented and have somehow atoned for the sins they committed, they are safe from me. Otherwise, the Grey Monk will mete out the only justice they are likely to face in this lifetime."

Involuntarily, Father Harper made the sign of the cross, blessing himself against he knew not what.

IF THY HAND OFFEND

And if thy hand offend thee, cut it off: it is better for thee to enter into life maimed, than having two hands to go into hell, into the fire that never shall be quenched – Mark 9, 43.

In an urban canyon created by old warehouses, forgotten men gathered. Abandoned by their families and rejected by society, they came together each night for warmth, companionship and protection. Huddled around a fire burning in a fifty gallon drum, they shared what they had. Those who could passed around what they had scavenged during the day. Some told stories, remembrances of better times. Others dropped in scrap wood to feed the flame.

By turns they stood watch, two at a time. Bricks and clubs in hand, they guarded the entrance to their haven, ready to fight off any lone intruder or to give the alarm should a youth gang or worse, the police, appear.

From time to time a stranger would come into their midst, drawn by the light and the need for company. If, as sometimes happened, he was of confused mind or besotted with cheap wine, he would be cared for, fed if there was any to spare, and gently led to a nearby shelter. Otherwise he would be watched, allowed to join but not quite trusted, not until he proved to be one of them. If he could not fit in, if he would not contribute, if he were loud, violent or in other ways drew unwelcome attention, he was sent away as forcibly as needed.

Such a stranger was with them that night. He seemed all right. Like them, he carried all he owned with him, in an old duffel bag. His clothes were no better or worse than theirs – threadbare jeans a bit too tight, a faded flannel shirt somewhat too big, a hooded jacket that did little to keep out the night's chill. The first night he approached them quietly, answering the guards' challenge with "Please, I just want to get warm." After some hesitation, a space was made for him around the fire. Things being the way they were, they turned down his offer to share the half bottle of T-Bird he produced. It was open, and he wasn't yet trusted. The next night he offered a full bottle, the seal still good. Carl took it, broke it open, gave it back to the stranger indicating that he should take the first drink. The new man did, then passed it back. Carl took his taste, and the bottle went around.

The evening got darker, the fire burning low. The last of wood was added. The group broke for sleep. Lying in groups of two or three for warmth, they sought the corners and hugged the walls, sharing blankets. The new man slept alone, his place along the wall the closest to the street.

"Tray," Carl said, "you and Charley stay up." Carl's glance went toward the stranger. "Keep your eyes on things. Wake me and Augie at two. We'll take it til dawn. These days, you can't be too careful."

Charley nodded. "Two bells then." None of them had a watch, but the chimes of St. Sebastian's could be heard through the night ringing the hours.

Morning came. Augie felt himself being shaken. He woke slowly. "Two already?" he asked.

"Past that," Carl answered. "Almost dawn. Wake the others. We got to leave before the citizens show up for work."

"Charley and Tray, they didn't wake us."

"They're gone," Carl said, looking at a smear of blood on the wall. "Got took in the night like the others we heard of."

"The new guy?"

"He's gone too."

Both men shook their heads at this cost of trusting strangers.

***

Two weeks before, Dr. Bartholomew Penn was alone in his office at the Medical Examiner's working the late shift. He had just finished reading an article on death by methanol ingestion when his cell phone chirped. Looking at caller ID number he saw that was no need to answer. Instead, he got up to admit his visitor.

When Dr. Penn opened the back door all he saw was darkness. Then the darkness shifted and resolved itself into a man wearing a charcoal grey monk's robe. The hood of the robe was up, hiding the man's face.

"Good evening," Penn said as his guest entered.

"Good morning, Doctor," the Gray Monk corrected in his usual whispered tone. Then, seeing Penn looking around the outside, the Monk added. "Don't worry, I was not followed."

"No, you wouldn't be, would you," Penn said, closing the door. Still doesn't hurt to make sure, he added to himself. "There's tea in the office, make yourself comfortable."

When he returned to his office after locking up, Penn found the Monk standing by one of the two chairs. He had ignored the tea. Penn poured himself a cup and sat behind his desk.

"Your message said that you wanted to see me?"

"Not so much wanted as needed," Penn told the vigilante. "Things are going on that the police are keeping very quiet, and perhaps not working on as hard as they might."

"Such as?"

Dr. Penn handed the Monk a file folder. "Here's the first three. The fourth is downstairs on ice. Want to take a look?"

A few minutes later, the Monk and Dr. Penn were standing near the smallest of the three freezers in where the deceased who were brought into the Medical Examiner's Office were stored. In one of the freezers was kept those bodies on whom autopsies had been completed. In another were bodies awaiting autopsy. Unfortunately for the Monk, they were in the workroom just outside the third freezer, the one in which was kept those bodies that had not been discovered before decomposition had set in. When Penn rolled out a gurney and unzipped the body bag, the stench of decay hit the Monk like a fist to the face.

"Put this on," Penn said, offering the Monk a carbon filter mask. "It'll cut down on the smell."

The Monk took the mask and turned away. His back to the pathologist, he dropped his cowl and quickly put on the mask. Raising his hood again, he turned back to the doctor.

"I warn you," Penn's voice was slightly muffled by his own mask, "he looks worse than he smells." Penn pulled back the folds of the body bag to reveal the torso, for that's what it was – no hands, feet or head – just a trunk of what used to be a man with only stumps where the limbs used to be.

Penn gave the Monk time to take in the sight of the deceased, then he said, "There have been three others like him, two male, one female. This one was found last night, but from the looks of him he was killed first. The others were all a bit more fresh when found."

"Any identification?" the Monk asked. Somehow his voice was clear even through the mask.

Penn snorted. "On what basis? There are no toe or footprints, no finger or palm prints, no teeth for dental records and no head for a photo to pass around."

"What about DNA?"

The doctor shook his head. "Not in the database. No, my friend, John Doe he is, John Doe he'll stay, and it will be as John Doe that what's left of him will be buried."

"What do you know about him?"

Now that the Monk had seen the body, Penn zipped the bag shut and returned the gurney to the deep freeze. "Let's go back to my office. The investigators are out making a pick up, but they may be back any minute. Unlike you, I can't disappear into the shadows, and I'd rather not have to explain why I'm down here playing with dead bodies at two a.m."

Back in the doctor's office, Penn sat and explained wile the Monk browsed through the case folders.

"Our Mr. Doe is, or was, a middle-aged male, severely underweight and malnourished. He had a variety of medical problems that would have killed him one day soon – liver disease, incipient kidney failure, chronic bronchitis and pneumonia. As pickled in alcohol as his organs were, I'm surprised that his body was able to decompose. And there's evidence of occasional drug use. His skin shows all the signs to constant exposure to the elements."

"A vagrant, then?"

Penn nodded. "Vagrant, yes. Or else a wino, an alky, a smokey or a bum. The correct term these days is homeless person."

"It says here, doctor," the Monk said, reading the case reports, "that there was no insect infestation present. Isn't that unusual?"

"Yes, it is. No fleas, body lice or any other small parasites that our outdoor citizens generally pick up. Not only that but, barring the ground-in dirt that no amount of soap, water and scrubbing will take away, all the bodies were unusually clean."

"Hospital clean, doctor?"

"You've read that far. Yes, hospital, even surgically clean. Which makes sense when you consider that their limbs and head were removed with surgical precision. The one who did this has had medical training."

The Monk finished reading the reports in silence. When he was done he asked, "What are the police doing?"

Penn shrugged. "If they're doing anything at all, they're doing it very quietly. Beyond thanking me for my reports and cautioning me against talking to the press, they haven't said a thing to me. There might be a task force out there somewhere. But given that in life these poor men had no power, no influence and nothing but the rags on their backs, and given that no one in homicide or missing persons will return my calls, I'm not so sure the deaths of four of society's discards even rate a task force. That's why I called you."

***

"Well, there is a task force," Father Richard Harper informed his sexton Lewis.

"You called Detective Hoffman?" Harper nodded. "Is he assigned to it?"

"No, not this time. He's busy trying to find Tommy Moran. It seems that our city's favorite gang leader and convicted murderer skipped jail with some outside help and a few bribed guards. Rumor has it that he's still somewhere in the city. Hoffman's on the team trying to find him before he flees the country."

"What did he say when you asked about the torso killings?"

Harper smiled, "The usual. He knew I was calling for you. I quote. 'Tell that damned grey spook to keep his cowl out of our way.' Unquote. You'll note that he didn't say that you weren't to work on it."

Lewis nodded. "By now he knows it's useless to ask the Grey Monk not to investigate. Plus the police need this case closed quickly."

"You're right," Harper agreed. "They can't keep the media out of it forever. When the story does break, there'll be camera crews at every shelter, doorway and steam grate in the city. 'The plight of the homeless' will be the topic of every special report."

"And the one behind this will become wary of the added scrutiny and quietly leave for another hunting ground. I'd best be going."

"You're sure this is the only way?" Harper asked.

"The only way I know, Father. For good reason, these people distrust the police, and are naturally fearful of strangers. My normal persona would only cause them to flee. I must go among them, become one of them. Only then will I learn what they know – who is being taken, when and from where."

"Maybe you'll get lucky and someone will try to snatch you."

"Luck for me, bad luck for whoever tries." Lewis put two heavy .45's under his shirt. He then rolled up his monk's robe and put it at the bottom of his duffel bag. "I'll be leaving now."

"Go with God, Lewis." Harper made the Sign of the Cross in the air

"Always, Father." Lewis said, accepting the blessing.

***

It was a rough two weeks. Wearing clothes from the charity box, Lewis had gone from one homeless group to another looking for acceptance. He began at the shelters, hearing the stories, confirming the rumors. But he knew he wouldn't find what he was looking for in those places. They were safe, secure. He needed to go out into the night, among the men who, for reasons of their own, preferred the open air to the closeness of the indoors. They were the ones being hunted, that was where he would find the hunters.

The first two groups he approached chased him away. They, too, had heard the stories and were fearful of strangers. The third accepted him, taking his offering of cheap wine and stale bread much too readily. Right away he sensed something wrong, something not quite right about the group. Lewis looked past the outwards signs. Their clothing was soiled and torn, but the tears were too even and the dirt seemed rubbed in. Likewise their faces and hands. Dirty yes, even filthy, but on the surface only. There was not the ground-in dirt that came from years of missed baths. And the hair - unwashed, but not matted.

Maybe some in this group were like he pretended to be – new to the streets, still dazed and lost by the circumstances that had brought him low, still learning the rules of survival. Maybe some, but surely not all. Were these the ones? Was this group formed so as to lure people such as he seemed to be? Lewis waited, and pretended to sleep, putting his trust in his God and the guns hidden under his too-large shirt.

Behind his closed eyes he listened. Soon there was the beeping of a cell phone, then the hissed curse – "Turn that damned thing to vibrate."

On alert, Lewis heard the whispered conversation. "Nothing yet ... two or three ... no, none of them seems a threat ... yes, sir, we'll maintain until 0600."

Lewis laughed to himself, and prepared for a good night of sleep, his first since hitting the streets. There was no danger here, not with so many police around. He wondered what they'd think if they knew just who they were protecting that evening. The next morning he moved on.

In with a new group now, provisionally accepted, Lewis settled against the wall for another night's vigil. "Tray," he heard the one called Carl say, "you and Charley stay up. Keep your eyes on things." He felt rather than saw all eyes on him. He knew he was suspect. This was a wary band. They too had gotten the word to beware on the streets. "Wake me and Augie at two. We'll take it til dawn. These days, you can't be too careful."

An hour went by, then two. Fighting sleep, Lewis watched through half-closed eyelids. Charley and Tray fought to stay awake as well. They walked back and forth, waving their arms for warmth, talking low so as not to wake the others.

A dark van drove by. Lewis noted it only as yet another vehicle that occasionally drove past the site. Sometime later it, or one just like it, drove past again, this time slower. Lewis readied himself. He stood, gathering his blanket around him.

"Whata you doing," Charley asked, gripping his brick tightly.

"Gotta go," Lewis said, feigning the grogginess that comes from waking.

"Go where?"

Lewis squeezed his legs together and held his hands in front of himself. "You know, I gotta *go*." Dancing in place, he waited for permission.

Charley caught on. "Oh," he said, and nodded his okay. Lewis took his duffel and made for the alley used for that purpose.

Lewis didn't pause to relieve himself. Instead, he passed through the alley to the street on the other side. There he got into a non-descript older model sedan.

Lewis drove around the block, past the opening where the men slept. He parked a block away, on the opposite side. When he got out, he was no longer the man who called himself Lewis.

Taking a charcoal grey robe from his duffel, Lewis had slipped it on, after first transferring the .45s that were under his shirt to specially designed pockets in the robe. Emerging from the car, he was now the Grey Monk, whose task that night was to discover who was preying on the homeless of his city, and why.

Street lamps were few in that part of the city, and the dim light they cast was easily avoided as the Monk made his way back. Staying in the darkness, and with the cowl of his habit pulled up, he was invisible to anyone who may have been watching. He got back to the canyon just as the van pulled up a third time.

This time four men got out, their movements quick and sure. Like the Monk, they were dressed in dark colors, their heads covered by hoods, their hands protected by gloves. The Monk watched as they rushed Charley and Tray.

Tray went down easy. Charley tried to fight back. For his efforts he was thrown against the wall, his head striking its concrete surface. He slumped unconscious. All this was done without a sound, without the others waking.

The Monk left as the assailants were loading Charley and Tray into the van. Had he sensed a killing situation, the Monk would have intervened.

But this was clearly an abduction. The Monk needed to know where the men were being taken. And so he waited in his car until the van drove away. When it turned down a side street he made a u-turn and followed at a distance.

The van pulled on to Hudson St., then Conkling. Turning left, it took the O'Donnell St, bridge to the highway. With more cars on the road, the Monk was able to move in closer.

Fifteen minutes, then twenty went by. They were in the county, past Dundalk and into Essex. They drove until the houses became fewer and further apart. The Monk dropped back until the van's taillights could barely be seen. He said a prayer that he would not lose sight of their dim red glow. He had let two men be taken that night, and he would see them freed before the morning came.

They were in a mostly wooded area now. Finally the van turned off on to a dirt road, one that led down to the water. The Monk drove past, found a clearing off the road and backed his car into it. Should he have to leave quickly he could pull straight out.

On foot he moved through the trees. He found the dirt road, barely visible in the darkness. Keeping to the woods, he followed it down to the water's edge. There he found a workman's shack and a boathouse out on the end of a rotting pier.

The boathouse was dark, but the lights were on inside the shack. The van was parked in front. This was where the homeless men had been taken. This was where the Monk might find the answers he was looking for, where he might find a solution to the horrific murders that had plagued his city.

The Monk started to leave the woods, to move closer to the shack. He wanted to see what was happening inside, to hear what was being said. Before he could, he heard the sound of a car approaching. He stepped back into the darkness just as an SUV pulled up.

One man got out, carrying a brief case. By the light from the window the Monk could see that he was dressed well – his expensive top coat over the designer slacks said that this was a man in charge, come to see what the four in the van had found. Once he was inside, the Monk moved closer.

Staying in the shadows, the Monk went around to the rear of the shack. There he found a window with a piece of its pane broken out. Trusting that the darkness of his robes would keep him unseen, he looked in from the side. Listening closely, he could hear what was being said through the small opening.

"Is this the best you could do?" It was the man who had arrived last. His voice was accented, most likely British.

"We take 'em as we find 'em, Mr. Starkly. Not many bums up in Guilford."

"No, Albert, there wouldn't be," Starkly replied. "The rich wouldn't allow it. No matter."

The Monk could see Tray. The man was gagged and tied to a chair. Charley was not in the Monk' line of sight, but was probably similarly bound

Starkly looked Tray over carefully. "This one will do."

"What about the other one?" the Monk heard Albert ask.

"We only need one tonight," came the reply.

"So we should …"

"Yes. Weight and dump the body in the river. Afterwards deliver the other one to the lab."

The time for watching was over. Before the men inside could act, the Monk was at the front. Guns in hand and trusting to God, he kicked the door open.

A small room, two innocents he had to protect, five foes, a certain one of which he needed alive. All this went through the Monk's mind as he charged through the doorway.

The Monk's attack took those inside by surprise. Before any of them could react, head shots from twin .45s took two of them down, their brains painting the walls behind them red and white. A third had time to draw his own weapon, but blasts from the Monk's automatics drove him backwards through the rear window.

Starkly tried to flee when the Monk turned to deal with the fourth man. The Monk clubbed him down with a gun-weighted hand just as a bullet whizzed by him, burying itself in the wood of the door.

The fourth man, Albert, had taken refuge behind the bound Charley. The Monk shifted as two more shots came his way. Fired in haste and panic, neither struck home. The Monk returned fire, arming high over Albert's head so as not to strike Charley. He missed of course, but his shot caused the gunman to duck low, giving the Monk time to find and flip the light switch.

The room was now in darkness. The Monk was standing silently in a corner, his breathing still and controlled. Labored breaths from the two prisoners masked that of the gunman.

One second went by, then two. A minute passed. The two opponents waited. The Monk was patient. After a second minute, he began to move slowly, silently.

The light suddenly came on. Albert blinked at the sudden glare, then swept his 9 mm around the room. Empty, there was no one there but himself, the prisoners and the unconscious Starkly. Had the strange, dark man given up, fled the scene? No, it was more likely that he was outside the door, lying in ambush, waiting for Albert to try and leave.

"Ahem."

The sound came from behind him. Turning, he saw the dark clad man standing outside the window. Knowing it was useless, he brought up his nine in one last desperate act. .45s blazed and ended his life before he could even form the thought to pull the trigger.

Entering the room, the Monk freed Tray and Charley. "You may of course, leave," he told them. "But you are miles away from your familiar haunts. You'd best wait for the police. They will question you extensively for most of the day, especially when they learn I am involved. You will eventually be released. It is a better fate than what these men had planned for you."

Using the cell phone he found in Starkly's briefcase, the Monk then called a familiar number.

"Hoffman here."

"Detective Hoffman, this is …"

"I recognize the whisper. How many dead this time and where are they?"

Ignoring the question, the Monk gave Hoffman directions to the shack. "You will also want to check the river. A dive team will no doubt find several bodies there. There are also two witnesses, victims of an abduction. Please take care of them for me. Kindly see to it that they are given hot meals, clean clothes and if possible, rewarded for their cooperation." The Monk broke the connection and returned the phone to the case.

When the police arrived, they found Charley and Tray waiting for them. And if the pockets of the four dead gunmen were turned out, and if the Charley and Tray seemed to have more cash than is usual for people in their situation, no one said anything about it, everyone considering it just compensation for their ordeal. Of the Grey Monk, Starkly or his briefcase there was no sign.

***

The pain woke him up. There was a throbbing in the back of his head worse than any migraine he'd had when a boy. Slowly he opened his eyes.

Geoffrey Starkly discovered that he was chained to a bed. The chain was long enough for him to reach a chemical toilet in one corner of the small room which was his prison. It would also allow him to reach a table on which were bottles of water and a loaf of bread.

After surveying his surroundings, Starkly tried to remember how he had gotten there. The last he recalled, he was in the shack. Albert and his crew had just brought in two more indigents. He'd chosen one and had given orders about the other when – there was a dark shape, then gunfire. He tried to flee and – and that's why his head hurt.

Starkly looked over at the table and hoped that his captor had thought to provide him with a bottle of aspirin. Bad luck, there was none. I am probably concussed, he thought. I shall need medical attention when, no, if I get out of here.

And where was here, he wondered. Then the throbbing in his head sent out more pain signals and he decided that for now it did not matter.

Then the door opened and the same dark shape that had struck him down entered the room. In the light it resolved itself into a man wearing a dark grey monk's robe, the hood up hiding its features.

Starkly put on a brave front. "Whoever you are, I am not answering any of your queries." The figure in front of him remained silent. "Who are you, and where am I?" Starkly half rose off the bed. "I am a British citizen. I demand to speak to my consulate." Shouting, he rose to his feet much too fast. A wave of nausea and dizziness hit him and he fell backwards on the bed.

The figure finally spoke, its voice a cold, emotionless whisper. "I am the Grey Monk, Mr. Starkly. Your papers and cell phone have told me most of what I need to know about you and Dr. Owens."

This was not good. If this Monk person knew of Owens, then he knew enough to break it all open. But then, why am I here, Starkly asked himself. Why not dead or in the hands of the police?

As if in answer, the figure spoke again. "The other four are dead," the Monk said, "and the men they abducted released. You and Owens are currently engaged in illegal medical experiments, experiments on human beings. The cleanliness of the bodies that were found and the precision with which the extremities were removed told me that much. The homeless were selected because they were least likely to be missed, and their bodies mutilated to hinder identification. Your phone's memory has given me several numbers for Owens. From them I can obtain addresses. I'm sure that I will find him, and his laboratory, at one of them."

So he doesn't know Owens, Starkly realized. That just might help me. "You know all this, why do you need me?"

"I don't know that I do," came the whispered reply. "You have rations for maybe a week, if you're careful. Starvation is a mean way to die, and this is a poor place in which to breathe your last."

"You would leave me here?" The Monk remained silent. "You would, wouldn't you?" Starkly looked at still figure before him. He looked over at the water and bread on the table. Poor fare, and not much of it. It would be gone in two days, maybe three. When left alone he could scream for help. But would this Monk leave him someplace where anyone would respond to such pleas?

Starkly considered his fate. He was not a brave man. He talked, and told all he knew, what he and Owens were doing, and why. He only lacked knowledge of the who. When he finished, even the Grey Monk, who thought he had seen the worse of what one human could do to other, was shocked.

Shaken, the Monk left with Starkly chained to the bed. Outside the room, he made a call that would ensure the man's delivery to the police once twenty-four hours had passed. By then the Monk would have achieved his goal, or failed in his mission.

Starkly had said that Dr. Owens would most likely be found in the laboratory. The lab was located in an old downtown medical arts building, once home to the best physicians the city had to offer, now vacant and forgotten with their exodus to more accessible and far safer medical centers in the surrounding suburbs.

Getting in was no problem. The building had been constructed with multiple entryways, none of which were well locked or guarded. The Monk chose a side door, on a street with few lights and heavy with shadows. In darkness he approached. He checked for alarms, found none and was inside within minutes.

Returning his lockpicks to his robes, the Monk found himself in a side corridor off the main lobby. Walking carefully, his rubber-soled shoes making no sounds, he sought the stairs.

From where he was, the stairway was across the lobby, in the center of which was a uniformed guard sitting behind a desk. From this desk, the guard could, by turning in his chair, keep an eye on all the first floor passageways. He could, that is, had he been awake. The snores coming from the man behind the desk said otherwise, and were, in fact, loud enough to cover the slight creak the stairwell door made when the Monk opened it.

Three flights up. .45 in hand, the Monk climbed the stairs cautiously, alert not only for a more vigilant guard but also for any extra security Dr. Owens might have employed.

He reached the lab without incident. Trying the door, he found it unlocked. He went inside and closed the door behind him.

There was a woman sitting at a desk that may have been once been used by a receptionist. She was of middle age, somewhere between late forties and early sixties. Her once brown hair was mostly gray, and she could have been any of the women who attended morning Mass at St. Sebastian's. She was, instead, Dr. Beverly Owens.

She did not seem a threat. There were no weapons visible. Still, the Monk kept his gun on her as he moved forward. Dr. Owens watched his approach.

"You're the Grey Monk, aren't you?" she asked calmly. The Monk nodded. "I've read about you in the papers. It's over isn't it?"

"Yes," came the whispered reply.

"I knew it was. It was on the news, what happened out at the shack." She indicated the radio. "I was listening to a talk show, waiting for Starkly to bring my subject when the report came in. I was expecting the police."

"They will come, eventually. For now, where are the others?"

"There are no others, just Starkly and … oh, you mean the subjects. They're in the examination rooms, but I'm afraid you more than a little too late. Once I heard the report, I took care of things." She held up a syringe. "Yes, you're much too late."

The Monk looked at Owens, then back towards the exam rooms. He moved towards them, but stopped, not wanting to leave the doctor alone.

"Go," she said, seeing his hesitation, "go and see for yourself. I'm not going anywhere." There was a strange smile on her face.

There were six rooms. Each was occupied by a single body – five men and a woman. None were alive. Glancing back, the Monk saw that Owens had not moved. He took his time examining each victim.

Remembering what Starkly had told him, the Monk looked at their feet and hands. He saw the suture marks that joined them to legs and arms. Even to the Monk's untrained eye it was obvious that none still had the appendages they were born with. What was worse was what the Monk found in the freezer in the last room.

Owens's voice came from the outer room. "I thought at first my problem would be in tissue rejection. The drugs they make these days, they took care of that. No, the problem was in the suturing. Never could get that right, and my mother a seamstress. Went through dozens, you may have found some of the bodies by now. These last were the best I could do. Not good enough, not yet. He was going to give me more time, but time ran out."

The Monk was now standing by her side. "Who, where?" he demanded.

Owens shook her head. "I'm a murderer a dozen times over, but I'm still a doctor. I will not betray my patient." She nodded towards the phone. "You can call the police now, or shall I?"

There was no normal persuasion that would make Owens talk. The Monk knew this, knew that stronger methods would be necessary, and had prepared. Eventually, she talked.

***

North of the city, almost in Pennsylvania. It was almost morning by the time the Monk arrived. He would have to act fast. Soon it would be dawn and he'd lose the advantage darkness gave him.

He took the last exit before the state line. A mile or so later, he turned on to a side road, and then another. He was close. Leaving his car, a pack over his shoulder, he continued on foot through the woods.

He was visible now, a dark blur against the brightening day. The trees hid him somewhat, but a watchman looking his way would catch his movements. Fortunately, it was not a populated area, with more trees and land than houses.

Finally, the Monk came to his destination, a small two-story house in the middle of a large, unkept lawn that had once been all grass, but now was mostly winter weeds and patches of dirt. The driveway leading through the lawn from the road was cracked and pitted with holes and the house itself gave every sign of having been neglected for far too long. No doubt the neighbors were glad of the trees that hid this place from their view, the Monk thought as he looked around.

The Monk, too, was glad for the cover the trees provided. He could not now help being seen, but the fewer who spied him the better.

There were men on guard, two in the front of the house, their attention directed down the driveway. They moved slowly, probably the night shift watching the road more for their relief than for any intruders. There would also be men out back, the Monk supposed. They too, he prayed, would be tired, slow to react and expecting an attack even less than those in front.

Moving cautiously, the Monk moved through the trees until he was close to the back of the house. He moved slowly, wanting to delay the moment when he would be discovered.

Finally, the man out back looked in his direction. Shouting an alarm, he reached into his coat. The Monk's guns were at the ready, and as soon as he saw the faintest glint of sunlight on metal he fired and brought the man down.

Only one guard out back, but his cries and the gunfire would bring those from the front. The Monk flattened himself against the back wall, and when the first man came around the corner, he stopped with his back to the dark clad vigilante. He had only half turned around when the Monk's close range shot ended his life.

A loud pop, and the brick exploded to Monk's right. The Monk crouched down as another bullet stuck where his head had been.

"Wait," the Monk shouted, his voice trembling with fear, "I give up." He threw his gun away from the house.

"Stay where you are, don't get up." came the order. The Monk had thrown back his hood, and he knew he looked like any other man wearing a long winter coat.

The man approached him carefully, one eye on the big automatic lying in the grass, making sure it was not within his prisoner's reach. "Stand up," he ordered. Instead, the Monk dropped to his right, the .45 in his left hand roaring, taking the gunman by surprise. A third body joined the other two in death.

Five shots. In an open area such as this they would have echoed and been heard by many, but the remoteness would make it hard to pinpointed their location. After making sure that none of the bodies were visible from the road, the Monk entered the house through the back door.

Had there been any more guards, they would surely have come out when the shooting started. Either that, or they were better trained than the ones the Monk had just left lying on the cold ground. Prepared for the worse, the Monk moved silently into the kitchen.

Standing just inside the doorway, the Monk surveyed the house. Three rooms – an oversized kitchen, opening on one side into the dining room and on the other the living room. The stairway bisected the first floor, with the door leading to the basement facing him and the steps to the upstairs on the opposite side.

The kitchen was empty, as was the dining room. The Monk turned to the living room. There he found a man in bathrobe and pajamas sitting calm on the sofa. The man's face was bruised, his eyes blackened, as if he'd been worked over by an expert. And in way he had. From what Owens had told him, the Monk knew that the man on the sofa had just had extensive facial surgery.

"So, Dr. Owens gave me up," the man said through still swollen lips.

"She had little choice, Moran," whispered the Monk.

The gang leader shook his head. "Can't trust anyone these days. The ones outside?"

"Dead or dying."

"Can't get good help either. I suppose she told you everything?"

"Yes, an interesting plan. Plastic surgery to alter your features, then once she was sufficiently skilled, Dr. Owens would transplant new hands onto your arms, thus forever changing your finger and palm prints. You have many lives to answer for, Thomas Moran – the lives of all the men and women mutilated and killed in her quest to acquire that skill."

Moran shrugged. "I hired her to do a job. Let her do the answering."

"She has."

The simple and emotionless way the Monk said this chilled Moran. He was sure that he did not want to know just how Owens had paid, and he was equally sure that he would soon find out.

"So what now?" he asked, though the tone of his voice was no longer as confident as it had been. "Do you turn me in or just kill me?"

"You will turn yourself in, Moran, but only after you have written out the names of all those involved in your escape and in helping to finance the horror that you and Owens have committed. I am sure that, if successful, some of them would have availed themselves of this means of becoming someone else."

Moran shook his head. "Sorry, can't help you there. Call the cops or let me call the cops. Kill me if you like. Nothing you do can be as bad as what will happen if I rat out my partners."

"No?" The Monk reached into the pack around his shoulder. He drew out a small red plastic bag and threw it in the table in front of Moran. "You think not? Then open the bag."

Moran hesitated, then picked up the bag. Reaching in, he recoiled from what he touched. The bag hit the table, and out came a woman's hand, blood crusted around the severed wrist.

"As I said, Dr. Owens had little choice. 'If thy hand offend, cut it off.'

Dr. Owens did not appreciate this at first. Then she decided it was better to enter into prison maimed than with no hands at all."

Moran was close to shock. "You didn't … you couldn't … the police …"

"I do not answer to the police, but to a Higher Authority, One who demands vengeance – an eye for an eye, and a hand for a hand." Moran watched in horror as the Monk removed a bone saw, its blade stained red, from beneath his robes. "Think, Moran, how do you want to enter the next part of your life?"

Moran looked at the knife, then at the hand on the table. It was a bluff, it had to be. The hand wasn't real, he told himself, but he knew otherwise. There was a ring, a ring that he had never seen Beverly Owens without, and that ring was on the fourth finger of the hand before him.

Moran talked. He began naming names and when given pen and paper he wrote them down. While he did this, the Monk called Father Harper.

"Everything okay?" the priest asked him.

"Things went as expected. Call Hoffman, give him these directions." The Monk told Harper how to find the house. "Tell him to bring the State Police. It seems that I will be wanted by them now too."

When Moran finished writing, the Monk cuffed him to the kitchen stove. The list of accomplices he left in plain view, weighted down by Dr. Owens's ring. The hand he took with him.

***

That night, Lewis recounted his activities for Father Harper. "Tell me you didn't, please God tell me you didn't," the priest said when told how Owens and Moran were made to talk.

"I assure you, Father, it was necessary."

"And they believed you?"

"The evidence was before their eyes, why would they not?"

Harper shook his head. "Owens at least should have noticed that the hand was frozen."

"The office was dark, and at that point I believe that Dr. Owens was just slightly mad. So when I took the hand from the freezer in the examination room, and coated it with the stored blood I also found there, she was convinced that I had cut it off Starkly to make him talk. Moran too, only for him I used a woman's hand, warmed it in the car on the ride north, and used Owens's ring to further persuade him."

"And if they had not believed you?" Harper asked.

"They did not dare not believe. They saw their own evil deeds reflected back on them, and accepted that I was every bit the monster they were."

"At least it's over."

Lewis thought of Owens, Starkly and Moran, all three now behind bars. He thought of the men he had killed, and prayed for their souls and his own. Finally, he thought of the others he had encountered these past weeks – forgotten men whose only comforts were cheap wine and a scrap wood fire. "For some of us, Father, for some of us."

I Will Repay

Payday, the reward for two weeks of hard work, forty hours plus overtime. The day doesn't come often enough, and when it does the check always seems smaller than it should be.

Kevin Little looked at his paycheck after his boss had walked away. $555.10 for over 100 hours of work. Time was he'd keep that much in cash in his back pocket just for walking around money. Any given night he'd take in that ten times that much pushing product, keeping a third for himself, with no taxes or other deductions to whittle it down. He looked again at the paper in his hand – gross pay eight hundred with the OT, then the feds and state took their cut, then FICA took its share for Social Security and Medicare, leaving him with little less than half a gee to live on.

Still, Kevin thought, this way was better. If he were still in the life he wouldn't be paying Social Security but chances were he wouldn't make it to retirement either.

Back then it was dangerous. Kevin found that out the hard way. He'd been shot at, robbed, roughed up, and that was before he was held prisoner in a storage area by a costumed madman. And then the cops, the trial, and spending a year in another kind of storage. Of course back then he had also money, a nice crib and all the girlies he wanted.

But he didn't have Janey. He met her about six months after getting out. At the time he was pushing burgers at some clown joint. She was the afternoon manager. They got along good but she wouldn't date the help. So Kevin quit, moved a few doors down and went to work selling and renting DVDs and video games. A week later Janey said yes and they went out. A month later she let him move into her place.

Kevin put his check away and started sorting the returned movies. He looked them over, seeing if anything watchable had come back. Kevin's boss was a good guy, he let his employees scan out a movie or two for free as long at the films weren't top ten and they were brought back the next day. And it had become a payday ritual with him and Janey – He'd find a movie they both could watch, she'd bring home dinner in a bag and they spent what was left of the evening with just each other.

It was a good life, Kevin thought, not for the first time. The old one – well, it had been exciting, at times even fun. He'd gotten off on the whole outlaw thing. But now, now he had Janey and a home. Soon maybe, they'd make it legal. He could take some management training and there'd be enough money coming to think about some little Littles running around the place. Kevin was happy, and that beat the Hell out of anything he felt back when he was a player.

Kevin was still feeling good when his relief arrived and he clocked out. No OT on paycheck night, Janey would kill him. He left with two movies, an old-time black & white comedy and a recent romantic flick staring some English guy and a singer making her first movie.

Up the stairs and out the door, Kevin crossed the parking lot to his car. It wasn't as nice a ride as he'd had back then but it was bought honest. He was just about to the car when someone stepped out of the shadows.

Kevin caught the movement out of the corner of his eye. He knew right away who it was, what was happening. Watch, cash, keys – Kevin was ready to give them up. He wouldn't fight, wouldn't call out, wouldn't give the jacker any reason. Thank God Janey wasn't with him, hadn't met him after work like she sometimes did.

Kevin already had his wallet out as he man approached. The first he knew that this wasn't the usual stick-up was when the man kept coming, came in too close and slid a sharp blade between his ribs and into his heart. The man stepped back, ran away, leaving Kevin to collapse. And as Kevin Little lay dying on the parking lot, as his heart beat its last, his thoughts were on Janey, and how happy he'd been. "I tried," he said, hoping somehow he'd be heard, "I tried."

***

"Kevin Little died," Father Richard Harper said the next night over dinner.

"Yes, I read that in the morning paper," Lewis, his sexton, replied. "Some sort of street robbery gone bad."

"Will you be going out tonight?"

Lewis nodded. "Going out, yes. As the Grey Monk, no. I've volunteered to work at the shelter two nights a week. Tonight is one of those nights."

"I thought maybe …"

"Father, Kevin Little, or Little Kev as I knew him, was a drug dealer. Under duress …"

"Extreme duress," Father Harper reminded him.

"Under duress," Lewis continued, "Little Kev gave up information that led to his supplier. There is no special reason I should seek his murderer over the countless others out there."

"I thought you were the agent of a vengeful God?"

"Most nights, I am. But tonight I am the servant of the Good Shepard, and will feed the hungry, shelter the homeless and clothe the naked. Either way, I am doing His work."

***

They called themselves the "A Team." Andray Davis and Andre Smith were the baddest pair on the cellblock, or so they saw themselves. To the guards they were just goofs, tolerated as long as they didn't cause too much trouble. The other prisoners saw them as comedy relief, two guys who talked the talk but tripped and fell when they walked the walk. How else would they have gotten caught handcuffed together in their own drug lab? They were listened to and humored because there was little else to do inside, and at least these guys made people laugh.

No one expected the riot. There had been no word of trouble, no hint of discontent, no great event to set it off. It started with one con cutting in front of another in the cafeteria line. A breach of protocol, a mark of disrespect, something that could not go unchallenged, but something that could wait until the guards weren't looking. Instead, a fight broke out, just the two men at first, but soon two more became involved, then another two, and when the guards failed to quickly reestablish control, it seemed like license had been given. Hatreds flared, and old debts repaid. And just as the guards restored order in the cafeteria, a similar outbreak occurred in the common room, where an argument over the television erupted into general violence.

It was an hour before the place was calm and the prisoners locked down. Property damage had been minimal – a few tables in the cafeteria and the TV in the common room. The toll in human life was greater. Three men were down – one fatally and two wounded. The dead man was Andray Davis, "knifed in the back by person unknown," or so the report would read. By seeming coincidence, one of those hospitalized was Andre Smith. His injuries were the more serious of the two, knife wounds like his partner, and he died without regaining consciousness. The third man suffered only a broken leg, the result of a larger man falling on top of him. A minor price, considering how much he'd been paid to organize the disturbance.

***

"You saw …"

"No, Father," Lewis interrupted, "I have not read the paper, but I did see last night's news report about the prison disturbance."

"Someone's moving against Tremaine."

"So it would seem. Perhaps Kevin Little's death was not what it seemed. First him and now two more of Tremaine's former crew. I am sure that the coincidence will not escape the police."

"So you're not taking any action?" asked the priest.

Lewis shrugged. "It could be just what I said, a coincidence, or the deaths could be the start of a new drug war. With Tremaine still locked up, and yes, I checked this morning, someone could be planning a major move against him, and beginning by eliminating his potential allies. I'll question my sources and see if there is any word of a new player in his dirty game."

Harper was silent. He stared straight ahead, not at Lewis, not at anything. Finally, he said, "This worries me."

"What would you have me do, Father? The trail of Little's killer is cold. I have no entry, no trusted contacts inside the penitentiary. All I can do for now is wait and watch, then act when there's something to go on."

Elsewhere, another watched and waited. News of the three deaths had reached him quickly. In fact, he had received word before the media reports had come out. And so he watched television and read the papers and listened to his own sources. And heard and read and saw that nothing was happening, nothing was being done by either the police or … anyone else. And this was good. So he waited. Waited while large sums of money changed hands – transfers from one offshore account to another, cash donations to campaign funds, quick exchanges of full brief cases for empty ones. Soon he thought, soon.

***

Something nice and simple, Detective Amos Hoffman prayed to no one particular deity. Nothing with gang killings, racists, cult members or anything else that might conjure that damn spook. Lately it seemed that every case he was involved in somehow attracted the Monk's unwanted interest. Even when he caught easy duty like an escaped prisoner there came a phone call and next thing he was up north with three dead and a crazy man yelling out a confession, pleading to be saved from the Grey Monk. So please, Hoffman thought on his way to a possible homicide, nothing weird this time.

The scene this time was on Lafayette Ave. A residential neighborhood that had once been the center of a major drug area. Now it was relatively peaceful, with no more drug activity than anywhere else in the city.

Looks like I got my wish, Hoffman thought as he surveyed the house. Door kicked open, victim dead on the floor, defensive wounds from a knife on her hands. A B&E gone bad, the burglar coming in, confronting the victim. She screams. He panics, cuts and runs without taking anything. He'd have the district give him a list of the local druggies and break-in men. Or maybe the Crime Lab would come up with some prints. Either that or …

"Carver, what did you say the victim's name was again?" Hoffman asked the primary officer.

"Watkins, Dorothy, no Dorothea Watkins."

"Well, find out if Miss Watkins had any grandsons, nephews or people who helped out around the house. If she did we'll bring them in and find out where they were tonight."

"Looks like a burglary to me," offered Carver.

"Me, too, but that doesn't mean a nephew didn't break in, or that she hadn't just turned down a grandson for money and he killed her and made it look like a B&E."

"Yes, sir, I'll see what family we can find."

The Crime Lab started taking photos on the first floor. To get out of the tech's way, Hoffman went upstairs to look around.

It was a nice house, he noted – furnished well, clean as far as someone of her years could manage. The back bedrooms he saw were used mostly as storage, boxes and crates storing the history of Miss Watkins's life. He didn't envy the person who had to go through it all. But nothing disturbed in there. Nor was there any disturbance in the bathroom, everything there as neat as it was downstairs.

That left the front bedroom – all okay in here too, Hoffman thought as he looked the room over. Bed turned down, nightgown on top of the sheets, slippers on the floor below. No drawers pulled out, nothing turned over.

As he looked the room over, Hoffman saw a chair in front of a window, he knew what it was for.

Every neighborhood had one, Hoffman thought, the old lady or man who sat most of the day watching the world from their window, seeing everything that went on. Hoffman had solved a few murders thanks to people like Miss Watkins.

Hoffman sat down. Maybe that was it. Did you see something Miss Watkins, he asked her ghost, and did somebody catch you watching? What could she have seen, he wondered as he looked out over the neighborhood.

Nice view, from here you can see all almost down to the end of the block, and down the alley behind Carey St. It was then that Hoffman realized just what he was seeing.

Carey St. That alley was where State Police Office Dyson had been gunned down. Looking through the darkness Hoffman could almost see the house where the ambush had been sprung. Lafayette Ave. This was the block, the house was right across the street, where they had found the drug lab, and the two goofballs trapped inside.

Dorothea Watkins would have seen it all, the comings and goings, the murder, the police activity. But she wasn't the one who had tipped off the police. No, it wasn't her, it was – Damn him!

Hoffman took a minute to clam down, then patiently started searching the bedroom. He found what he was looking for in the night table drawer – a cell phone, possibly the only piece of high-tech equipment in the house. There was only one number on its speed dial, a number that had once appeared on Hoffman's caller ID, a number he knew he wouldn't be able to trace.

The next morning, Lewis had finished cleaning the church and had just entered the rectory when he heard the shouting. "Damn it, Rich, I want him and I want him now! I don't care if this is a church and you are a priest, I'll tear this place apart until I find something here that will lead me to him."

"I've told you before, Amos," Father Harper replied, all too conscious of the grey robes and twin .45s hanging behind a panel in the sacristy's vestment cabinet, "that I can't call the Grey Monk. He calls me when he needs something. Now I'm sure that if he had any connection to this Watson woman ..."

"Watkins," Hoffman corrected.

"Watkins then. If the Monk had any connection to this Miss Watkins he'll want to talk to you. He'll either call me or contact you direct. But I doubt if there's anything ..."

"Don't hand me that bull - " Hoffman caught himself, apparently he did care that he was in a church. "Look, Rich, it's one thing for that spook to run around in a dress fighting crime. I don't like it and never will. But the department puts up with it and it's his own life he's risking. One day it'll end bloody. But if he had Miss Watkins working for him and she saw something or did something that got her killed, then he's as much responsible for her death as the guy with the knife. You tell him that when you do talk to him, and tell him I want to know anything she told him."

Hoffman stormed out without saying good-bye, walking past Lewis without acknowledging the sexton's presence.

"You heard?" Harper asked as Lewis walked into the room.

"Yes." Both men were silent for a while then Lewis continued. "It was her choice. She brought herself to my attention. After her help with the Dyson case I continued to warn her of the possible consequences. She always dismissed me saying …"

Lewis was interrupted by a disturbance outside. There were three very recognizable pops, loud even through the wall of the rectory, followed by the squeal of tires as a car sped away.

Hoffman was still seething when he left the rectory. Yelling at Harper had done him no good. It was the Monk he wanted. Against his will he'd been drawn into the vigilante's world of vengeance. All those deaths, all that blood on the Monk's hands. Until now it hadn't been innocent blood, but that of criminals – murderers and rapists, men committing evil deeds who had put themselves beyond the Law's reach. And that made seem it all right. But now, now an old woman was dead, dead because of the Monk. Before this is over, Mr. Monk, Hoffman was thinking as he crossed the street to his car, there will be an accounting.

Hoffman had his car door open and was about to drop into the front seat when the dark colored SUV pulled up at the opposite corner. Before it had even stopped, gunfire came from the driver's window.

Hoffman heard the pops, knew them for what they were. He heard the breaking of window glass, felt the impact of bullets striking him, saw the car speed away all in the instant before he blacked out.

Lewis and Harper ran out of the rectory to see the still form of Amos Hoffman lying in the street beside his car. Blood was pooling rapidly around the detective's body. Lewis ran back inside to call 911 while Harper began first aid.

An hour later. Hoffman had been rushed to the shock trauma unit, his life now depending on a surgeon's skill and the efficacy of the prayers that Harper and others were sending his way. The street out side St. Sebastian's was as brightly light as day as the crime scene was photographed and searched for evidence. Inside the rectory, Harper was being questioned, again, by Detective Darryl Larkins.

"Tell me once more, Father, why Amos was here."

"As I've said, Detective Larkins, for reasons of his own, the Grey Monk has chosen Amos and me as contact people. Your command is aware of this, and has, at times, taken advantage of this relationship. Amos was here tonight because the murder of a woman on the westside is somehow connected with the Grey Monk. He wanted me to call him in. I told him, yet again, that the Monk calls me, I don't call him. That's all I know."

"What about him?" Larkins asked, referring to Lewis waiting in the next room.

Father Harper shrugged. "He's my sexton. I doubt if Amos has ever said more than hello and goodbye to him, if that much."

"Yeah, that's what, Lewis is it, told me himself. Well, if you think of anything else …"

"I know the number."

After Larkins left, Father Harper and Lewis stood awhile at the window, watching the crime scene people at work. As the tape came down and the spotlights went off, Harper said, "This is personal."

"I agree, Father. The deaths of Kevin Little, Andray Davis and Andre Smith could have been coincidental, or a move against Tremaine. But now with the murder of Mrs. Watkins and the attack on Detective Hoffman, it's clear that this is a move by Tremaine. I've twice caused his arrest, and now he seeks revenge by striking at those who helped me."

"So we know who his next target is likely to be."

"Yes, we'd best prepare."

***

The shooting of Amos Hoffman was headline news. All the papers carried banner headlines proclaiming the attack and featured stories on his career, his current investigation and his present fight for life. The TV news shows broadcast interviews with his commanding officers, fellow cops and those family members that had gathered at his bedside.

From his cell, Tremaine watched and read it all and decided that it was good. They were paying now, all those who had wronged him. Kevin, the A-team – they should have known not to cross him, should have known what always happens to punks who rat him out.

And the old woman – it had taken him awhile to figure out just how the Grey Monk had known about his lab. Dyson hadn't known. The cop hadn't gotten that far into the organization before Tremaine found about him and had him killed. Tremaine had suspected another traitor until he remembered the neighborhood busybody. Always at the window, always watching. She had to be the one. Well, she won't be at the window anymore.

The detective was just too bad. The man was doing his job, Tremaine could respect that. But he should have stuck to doing his job, and not gotten cozy with the Grey Monk.

There was just one more to go, one more act before the big finale. Tremaine planned to be there at the end, wanted to pull down that cowl, look the man right in the face and tell him "I know you. I did this to you," before ending things. Let him know who it was who took his friends, his informants, his contacts away. Let him die knowing that as Tremaine found them the Monk's other helpers would be joining him in Hell.

He'd called his lawyer this morning, told him to start the wheels turning. Time to get some value for all that money I've been putting out. Tomorrow a phone call would be made from the state capitol. The court of special appeals would take up his case. And no matter what arguments the state's attorney made to the contrary, seized evidence would be ruled inadmissible, witness statements deemed unreliable and bail would be granted pending a review of his conviction. At week's end, Tremaine would be back on the street.

***

Brian Dimas had been going to morning Mass for the last two weeks, long before he shot the cop right outside the church. Given the few people who attend each day, he was noticed right away. Noticed, that's all. No one suspected him of any ill intentions, no one questioned why he was there. That's the nice thing about churchgoers, there are so few of them these days that a newcomer is always welcomed.

He made it a habit to stay after service was over, sitting awhile then kneeling, as if in private prayer. And he did find the quiet helpful. As he sat and watched the sexton straighten up, he thought. He thought about how he was going to kill the old lady on Lafayette, about how best to ambush the cop, and about how he was going to spend the money Tremaine was paying him to kill four people.

This one, Dimas thought, watching the sexton go about his daily chores, this one would be easy. He's used to my being here. I'll just walk up to him, slide the blade home then walk out undisturbed. A phone call to Tremaine and it's two weeks where the sun is warm, the drinks are free and the women are willing.

The call had come last night. Tremaine was getting out and he wanted it done today. No problem. The man looked over at the sexton. He wondered what the man had done that Tremaine wanted him dead. Looked at him funny, maybe. No matter. If Tremaine said kill him, he dies.

"Excuse me."

Lewis turned toward the lowered voice. It was the new guy, the latest addition to the morning congregation. "Can I help you?"

The man walked toward him, his right arm stiff at his side. "Yes, what time are your Sunday Masses?" He came closer. Before Lewis could answer, the man's right arm shot out, a knife suddenly in his hand. He lunged, Lewis blocked, not quite in time. The blade slipped in. As the two men struggled the sexton felt the sting of his wound and warm blood running down his side.

Lewis pushed his assailant away. The man came at him again. Again, Lewis blocked, his left arm sweeping aside the knife, his right coming forward in a jab. The man fell, losing his weapon.

To Hell with this, Dimas thought. He'd tried to do this quiet. He stood, drew his gun, aimed it at Lewis. The church rang with unholy noise – once, twice. Then all was quiet.

A few hours later, across town, a newly released Tremaine answered his cell. "Yes," he said, after checking the caller ID.

"It's done," came the voice on the other end.

"Has our friend left town for good?"

There was a pause as the man on the other end deciphered Tremaine's question. Finally, "He's on the way out. Watch the noon news."

At home Tremaine turned on the television. "Breaking news out of the southeast," the anchor announced. "A bizarre attack at St. Sebastian's Church. This morning after Mass the sexton of St. Sebastian's Catholic Church was attacked. He was rushed to Shock Trauma where his condition is unknown. Details on the assault are sketchy, but police sources indicted that a firearm may have been used. Police have no information on the assailant or the motive for the assault."

This was followed by an interview with a very shaken Father Richard Harper, the pastor of St. Sebastian's.

"We are, of course, praying for Lewis to make a speedy recovery," the priest said. "I know that the doctors are doing everything they can, but from what I've been told, it's all in God's hands now."

The anchor came back. "This shooting takes place just a few days after a police detective was gunned down just outside this same church. For more on this, we join …" Tremaine turned the set off. No sense putting things off, he thought. Tomorrow, they'll have a story better than this one.

It had been years since Father Harper had had this many people at a weekday Mass. More than twice that of the usual crowd. Of course, in today's congregation were police officers, reporters and people drawn to the spectacle of events, the curious who are attracted to scenes of crimes and other such tragedies.

Shame we don't take up collections on weekdays, Harper thought as he gave the final blessing. He doubted if many of the newcomers would have contributed.

After Mass, Harper returned to the rectory, his thoughts on Lewis and how the patient was doing. At least Dr. Sayers had agreed to treat him. He had just entered the kitchen, intent on breakfast, when he heard a voice come from behind him.

"The back door was open, so I let myself in."

Father Harper turned and saw a tall dark-skinned man standing in the doorway from the utility room. He was holding a semi-automatic pistol, loosely pointing it at the priest. "A shame really, all those police out front and none watching the rear. But then, you don't have much use for the police, do you?"

Despite the gun trained on him, Father Harper felt calm, and perfectly safe. Had his assailant meant to kill him, he would have fired by now. "I'm sorry," the priest said, "have we met?"

The man laughed. "That is good, Father, that is good. 'Have we met?' We've danced this dance twice before, although I'm leading this time." He held up the gun, emphasizing that he was in control.

Sudden realization appeared on Harper's face. "You must be Tremaine, I've heard about you."

Tremaine shook his head. "I've told you before, Father, that a holy man like yourself should not be telling lies. Let's drop the pretense, shall we?"

Harper looked resigned. "Very well, no more lies. Let's go into the living room where we can discuss things before you use that."

Another laugh came from Tremaine. "The living room, where you no doubt have a gun stashed behind the sofa cushions. Sit down. I can say what I have to in here."

Harper sat down. Tremaine, still standing, continued. "As you said, no more lies. I really should have known from the start – The Grey Monk, mystery crime fighter in holy garb. I should have realized you were a priest, especially after the first time when you escaped my trap. We lost your trail right around here. My mistake, and ultimately yours. You cost me, Mr. Monk, or do you prefer Father Harper when you're out of uniform? No matter. You cost me – money, position, freedom. You took things I value away from me. So while in prison, I had friends on the outside do some research. That led me to the Watkins woman, and to Hoffman, and to you. Little and the A-team I knew about. They were overdue and now seemed liked a good time."

Tremaine now pointed the gun directly at Harper. "I wanted to see your face when I did this. Goodbye, Monk."

"I think not," came an icy whisper from behind Tremaine.

Tremaine knew that voice, had it heard it in his dreams on many a long cold night, had heard it in the waking world twice before this. It was the voice of the Grey Monk, a voice that he thought belonged to the man in front of him.

He hesitated. He could still kill the man in front of him, but to what avail? He'd be dead a second later. Better to take the chance.

"I don't suppose," he asked without turning around, "it would do me any good to drop my gun?"

"No," The quiet answer was not unexpected.

Tremaine turned, dodged to the left. Desperately, he sought to aim his gun on the dark specter behind him. A soft whisper, no louder than the Monk's voice, came from the barrel of the Monk's silenced weapon. The gun whispered twice more. Tremaine staggered, fell.

"Are you okay, Father?" the Monk asked, ignoring the still form in front of him.

"I am now," Harper replied, removing his shirt, stripping off the body armor beneath it. "Been awhile since I wore this. Glad it wasn't needed."

"You were never in any danger. As we expected, Tremaine came in through the unguarded back way. I watched from my car and followed. I was behind him at all times, ready to act when necessary."

"You didn't cross the parking lot like that, did you?"

Lewis removed his robes. "No, I put it on after I got inside."

"Glad to hear it. By the way, you look good for someone who's been 'in God's hands' for the last day."

Lewis smiled. "Aren't we all in His hands every day? I am always amazed by the gullibility of the media. My wound was minor, yet they believed that I was near death."

"That's what happens when their news source is a parish priest." Harper looked at the body on the floor. "What are you going to do with him?"

"Take him out tonight. His body won't be found. Let those who posted his bail forfeit their money when he fails to appear for court."

"And our patient?"

"I'll deal with him tonight as well."

***

Who would have thought the guy had a gun, Brian Dimas thought, not for the first time. It was supposed to be a quick kill. Instead, it went bad all too fast. First the man fought back. Then when Dimas pulled his piece, he saw a bigger one pointing right at him. He didn't remember much after that. There was the noise, and pain in his shoulder and side. He passed out, woke up groggy. A voice, a cold voice, told him what would happen if he didn't obey. He believed it, made the call. Slept again.

When he woke he was here, wherever that was. His wounds had been bandaged. He felt weak, but knew he would live. There was food to eat and a toilet when needed. If only the door to his room wasn't locked. If only he wasn't too weak to try to force it. If only ... if only that guy didn't have a gun.

Dimas laid back on the bed. There was little to do save read, but the only book that had been left was the Bible. He stayed on the bed, not thinking, just waiting.

A noise. He heard someone in the floor below him. Footsteps on the stairs. A key turned in the lock of his room. The door opened.

In the doorway stood a dark grey form. Dimas knew who this was, knew he was the prisoner of the Grey Monk. With a sudden insight, he then knew why the guy in the church had a gun.

"It was you," he said unwisely, "you're the guy in the church. You're the Grey Monk. I mean, he's the Monk. I mean ..."

"I know what you mean," came the same voice he'd heard before, "and that is unfortunate."

Dimas realized his mistake. "You're going to kill me, aren't you?"

The shadowy form drew his pistol. "Can you give me a reason not to?"

"You're the good guy," Dimas said hopefully.

Some sort of sound came from the Grey Monk. A laugh? "Some might think otherwise. You have knowledge that could compromise me. Yet I am an agent of the Lord, pursuing His justice. I doubt if it would be just to end your life for that reason."

Dimas felt a spark of hope. He tried fan it brighter. "You can't turn me in either. I could trade what I know for a lighter sentence."

"Agreed, Mr. Dimas. Yet there is always the chance that the police will find you on their own."

The gun pointing at Dimas seemed to grow larger. He shook his head. "There's no chance of that. Whatever else I am, I'm a professional. I know better than to leave evidence behind. The knives that killed Little and the old lady, the gun that dropped the cop, all gone. Same for the SUV. I stole that, then dumped it off at a chop shop. It's in five different states by now. And I always wear gloves on the job."

The Monk was silent, considering what Dimas had said.

"So you are beyond the Law, without a chance of facing arrest and trial for your crimes?"

Dimas smiled in relief. He was going to get away with this. "You got it."

"Then you are mine."

There was nothing left for Dimas but the sound of a gun.

***

Amos Hoffman woke up. Something had disturbed his rest. Probably another nurse, Hoffman thought, come to do something unspeakable to this poor battered body of mine. He looked around his hospital room. Still dark. Then a part of the darkness moved, becoming solid.

"Detective Hoffman," came a familiar voice. The Grey Monk stepped further into the dim light so Hoffman could make out his form.

"How did you ... no, I don't want to know." Hoffman sighed. Even here I can't get any peace. "Visiting hours aren't until one p.m. What do you want?"

"The man who shot you, the one who killed Dorothea Watkins and Kevin Little, is dead. He's paid the price. So too the one who arranged it."

"Somehow I'm not surprised." There was an air of resignation in Hoffman's voice. He thought of Little, a man whose new life had been cut short. He thought of Miss Watkins, a sad end for a woman who still had some good years left in her. "To be honest, I'm not that sorry to hear it." There was a pause, the Monk just standing there, looking at Hoffman. "Was there anything else?" the detective finally asked.

"No," came the whisper in the dark. The Grey Monk started to fade back into the shadows.

"The men you killed – their deaths, your coming here, it doesn't absolve you, you know," Hoffman said to the darkness, "not for me, not for Dorothea Watkins. The price you mentioned – we all pay it. I'm paying now, and some day so will you."

There was no answer from the shadows. Not that Hoffman had expected one. He started to drift back to sleep thinking that maybe it had all been a dream.

"I am aware of the cost, Detective," Hoffman heard just at the edge of sleep. "I have been for far too long. And it is one I willingly pay in the service of my Lord."

A few minutes later, a fire door opened in the rear of the hospital. A man dressed in white, just another orderly, not noticed by anyone, stepped out, apparently on his way home. And as he wrapped his grey coat around him, he was swallowed by the night.

JOHN L. FRENCH has worked for over thirty years as a crime scene investigator and has seen more than his share of murders, shootings and serious assaults. As a break from the realities of his job, he writes science fiction, pulp, horror, fantasy, and, of course, crime fiction.

In 1992 John began writing stories based on his training and experiences on the streets of Baltimore. His first story "Past Sins" was published in Hardboiled Magazine and was cited as one of the best Hardboiled stories of 1993. More crime fiction followed, appearing in Alfred Hitchcock's Mystery Magazine, the Fading Shadows magazines and in collections by Barnes and Noble. Association with writers like James Chambers and the late, great C.J. Henderson led him to try horror fiction and to a still growing fascination with zombies and other undead things. His first horror story "The Right Solution" appeared in Marietta Publishing's Lin Carter's Anton Zarnak. Other horror stories followed in anthologies such as The Dead Walk and Dark Furies, both published by Die Monster Die books. It was in DARK FURIES that his character Bianca Jones made her literary debut in "21 Doors," a story based on an old Baltimore legend and a creepy game his daughter used to play with her friends.

John's first book was THE DEVIL OF HARBOR CITY, a novel done in the old pulp style. Past Sins and Here There Be Monsters. John was also consulting editor for Chelsea House's Criminal Investigation series. His other books include THE ASSASSINS' BALL (Written with Patrick Thomas), Paradise Denied, Blood Is the Life and The Nightmare Strikes. John is the editor of TO HELL IN A FAST CAR, MERMAIDS 13, C. J. Henderson's Challenge of the Unknown, and (with Greg Schauer) With Great Power …

One of these days John may get a website and a Facebook page. Until then you can email him at jfrenchfam@aol.com.

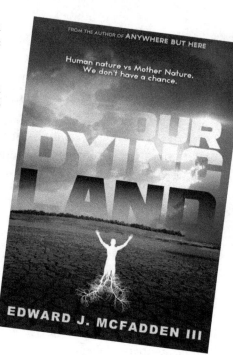
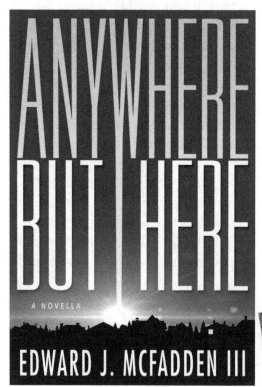
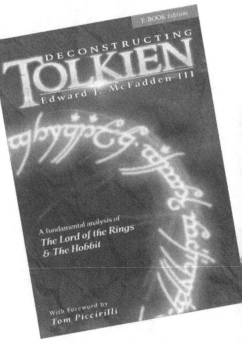

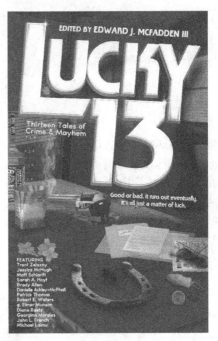

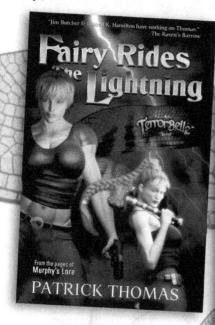

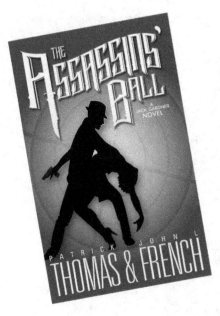

THE ASSASSINS' BALL

When there's a murder at a convention of killers... everyone's a suspect.

Coming soon from
PATRICK THOMAS & JOHN L. FRENCH

IT'S A CRIME TO MISS OUT ON THESE OTHER GREAT BOOKS FROM
JOHN L. FRENCH

John L. French is a crime scene supervisor with the Baltimore Police Department Crime Laboratory. In 1992 he began writing crime fiction, basing his stories on his experiences on the streets of what some have called one of the most dangerous cities in the country. His books include THE DEVIL OF HARBOR CITY, SOULS ON FIRE, PAST SINS, BULLETS AND BRIMSTONE and HERE THERE BE MONSTERS. He is the editor of BAD COP, NO DONUT which features tales of police behaving badly.

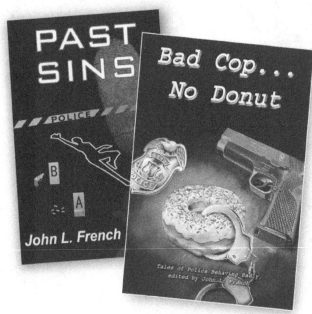

PADWOLF
PUBLISHING

More GREAT Science Fiction!

THE STARSCAPE PROJECT

As his quest begins, an artificial intelligence life form enters the galaxy and launches a series of covert attacks against the Empire. The Teconeans assume that the Federation is responsible, and galactic peace is about to unravel. As Stryker chases his nemesis into Teconean space, he finds himself thrown into the middle of the battle. Knowing that Earth will be the aliens' next target, Stryker must decide whether to let them destroy the Empire, or to join forces with his Teconean enemies against the invaders. The key to the mysterious aliens lies buried on the moon of Kennedy Prime, and it's up to Stryker to solve the puzzle before war begins. The fate of the galaxy is at stake.

ZONE OF THE TENTH DGREE

1912, an alien ship crash lands in the Atlantic ean, setting up a secret colony that remains detected for centuries, allowing them to anipulate some of the most important events in man history -- from the sinking of the Titanic to e Bermuda triangle to global warming. Now, e technology of the 26th century has scovered the aliens' distress beacon, and it's a ce against time as the Navy tries to stop a rrorist armed with a nuclear weapon from estroying the colony and triggering an all-out ar as the mother-ship approaches

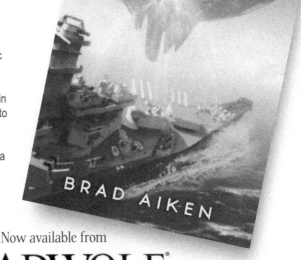

Now available from

PADWOLF
PUBLISHING

visit padwolf.com